David I

A Life on the Ocean Wave

The man lying in the bed struggled to speak and wondered why he was being asked this question. His mouth was dry and lips cracked. He looked down at his left arm and noticed the intravenous drip and the sudden realisation came to him. He had left a letter on his bedside draw some months earlier and told his wife in his final days he wanted her to open the letter and ask him the one question which would hopefully make them all think of what they have and will make them look at their lives and understand why he had dedicated his life to his chosen career. The career that would be divulged in this final letter along with details of the will and offshore bank account housing a life time of earnings which would hopefully make his family's life easier.

The man lying in his death bed is John Savage a 60 year old ex Royal Marine Commando and member of the Special Forces. Thirty years had been given to Queen and country with tours all around the world, from the streets of Northern Ireland to the Arctic wasteland of Northern most Norway, to the deserts of Iraq, Afghanistan and Mogadishu to name but a few.

John had joined the Royal Marines at the age of sixteen with written permission from his mother Rebecca. She was a strong woman who gave him much moral support and always believed in him no matter what crazy idea he had and every time he fell she would be there to pick up the pieces afterwards.

Rebecca was a single mother who had John at the age of twenty to a man who John never got to know, a man

Rebecca never spoke about and always told John that he wasn't important enough to stay around so wasn't important enough to discuss. She would rather John went without a father than know this guy. So John respected his mother wishes and at the age of sixteen with joining papers in his hand, said that he would never ask about his father again but wanted to follow his own dreams of becoming an elite fighting soldier and join the Royal Marines. He wanted to be the best and as far as he was concerned this was it, no-one else came close and if anyone tried talking to him about different regiments he snapped at them as if this want, this need had been programmed into him at birth.

John was born in the North East of England in a typical council estate, lines of almost identical semi-detached houses most with a family of husband, wife and three kids but not this house, in this house a single mother and her son resided, Miss Rebecca Savage and her son John.

Born in 1963 John, a fairly quiet child preferred his own company to that of the crowd. He was a short skinny boy who was very average in his classes and never really stood out in anything other than physical education (PE). Even then he didn't like to take part in the team sports like the other boys; he didn't like football and was too soft for rugby and other sports like cricket and tennis had no appeal to him.

It was a winter's day when the PE teacher, a brut of a man named Mr Pearce decided it was perfect weather for a cross country run. It was cold and wet with a touch of ground frost that was sure to make the going tougher than any other run they had taken part in at school. Much to the surprise of Mr Pearce and to John himself the weather didn't seem to bother John nor did the cold or the frost or the fact the boys fell over every five minutes in the cold wet mud. John came alive on this run and accelerated around the route hot on the heels of Mr Pearce. He jumped over obstacles, slid through the mud like a pig wallowing and enjoying every minute of it. John stamped through the crystal surface of the ice covered water and ran hard and fast, breathing heavily as if his life depended on it.

The run was two miles long and only lasted twenty minutes, well it was actually over in sixteen minutes for John and Mr Pearce who at the end of the run slapped the skinny boy on the back and congratulated him as if he was his own son and he was brimming with pride. John had never known emotion like this; to be given some kind of acknowledgement for his achievements was unheard of.

Mr Pearce suddenly turned to him and said "where the hell did that come from son?"

"Sir" John said looking confused "I don't understand?"

Mr Pearce glanced at him with a slightly bewildered look on his face, a new found respect had been gained and this was very out of character for this hardnosed teacher

"You did well out there today John, you should be proud of yourself. I don't understand why you don't get more involved in the other team sports. You'd be great on the wing."

John didn't really know what being on the wing meant and almost laughed out loud but thought better than to laugh at Mr Pearce when receiving such praise.

"I don't like team sports" John said sheepishly. "I'd much rather have myself to depend on".

Mr Pearce looked at the boy and asked "Not a team player eh?"

"I am sir in the things I enjoy. I just don't like these types of sports. But teamwork is one of the............" He faded out before saying something that would open him up to laughter and possible abuse from those around him.

"Teamwork is one of the what?" asked Mr Pearce curiously.

John spoke quietly now as to avoid others over hearing. "It's one of the commando values."

"The commandos" cried Mr Pearce cracking a smile but realising the boy was deadly serious.

All of a sudden John felt a surge of anger like never before. He had experienced anger and frustration at the boys and sometimes the girls who had bullied him most of his life but this was the first time he had spoken about who and what he wanted to be and to be mocked was just too much.

"Yes a commando!" he said with a raised voice. "I'll make it you'll see and I will leave this shit hole of a place and return wearing the Green Beret." John was furious and realised what he had done. It all happened in a split second. Mr Pearce grabbed John by his right arm lifting him off the ground viciously and dragged him across the yard to the PE teacher's office.

John did not speak; he simply clammed up and started to cry. All that could be heard was pathetic little sniffles and exaggerated breaths of a child struggling to breathe properly. Mr Pearce slammed the office door behind him and sat John down hard into the seat.

"What the hell got into you boy!" screamed the teacher. "You're a good kid who never steps out of line like that; I can't believe the way you spoke to me. What the hell got into you?" he demanded.

The boy sat thinking for a second before answering, after all his quick tongue hadn't paid off so far. "You laughed at me sir" the boy spoke while breaking down into tears again.

"I know I'm soft sir and a pathetic loser who nobody likes or cares about, but this is all I think about day and night. I want to prove to everyone I'm not a loser and I'm tougher than they think. I want to be an elite fighting soldier with the Royal Marines Commandos and I will make it sir I swear to you I will make it if it kills me."

John had never spoken out in this way before and the teacher was stuck for words for the first time in the four years John had been at the comprehensive school. Absolutely silent!

"John" the teacher's voice now softened. "I'm sorry I smirked, it wasn't directed at you or what you were saying. I was surprised as you've never mentioned it before or tried to take part in the fitness side of schooling so you can understand my shock, I'm sorry. It was unfair but I have to tell you John what you just said to me worries me a little."

"What did I say sir?" John was confused.

The teacher squatted down so his face was the same level as the boy as he looked him in the eyes.

"You said everyone thought you're a loser and nobody cares about you" he paused now waiting for a response but nothing came; John sat quietly waiting for the teachers next sentence.

"I'm a little worried about your statement John."

"I'm sorry but that's how I feel. I pray to God every night to come and take me painlessly in my sleep so I don't have to face the same crap every single day" the boy broke down again sobbing uncontrollably. "Sometimes I just want to curl up and die!"

The words struck hard into Mr Pearce's head and heart and he snapped at the boy "That's enough of that talk. I won't have it do you hear me?" He paused for a second before calmly continuing. "I'm sorry John but you don't mean it and I'm afraid I'm going to have to take you to the head master and call your mother into the school."

"NO!" screamed John "please don't call my mam she'll be angry with me and she has enough to worry about."

"Well what about your dad?" asked the teacher unaware of the situation at home.

"He's dead!" snapped the boy angrily. "It's just me and my mam."

"I'm sorry John, I wasn't aware. Go get showered and into your clean clothes and we'll go speak to the head master. Mr Dobson will decide whether or not to call your mother."

John proceeded to the showers. He felt scared and alone and wasn't sure what would come of his visit to the most feared man in the school, Mr Dobson. By now the rest of the class had finished and moved onto their next class with tongues already wagging. Had Mr Pearce caned the boy for his insolence or had he been beaten up so badly he had to be rushed to hospital and might never be seen again? No-one knew the truth and if John had his way no-one would, he took enough ridicule each day without something new for people to scoff him about.

ya." Mr Milner paused for a second realising that he'd gone off on a tangent.

"So you want to be a bootneck?" he started again.

"Yes sir, more than anything else in the world," replied John. "I know everyone thinks I'm too soft right now sir but I believe I can do it and my mam believes in me too and that's all I need."

"Okay son, let's get you off to the head master. You and I can have a little chat another time if you're serious about this."

Milner escorted John across the yard like a convict heading to the electric chair. He felt nervous because he'd heard of Mr Dobson's reputation and low tolerance for any form of bad behaviour towards a teacher. Teaching was a thankless job but a rewarding one he supposed. John wandered if being a Royal Marine would be a thankless job too, but he didn't care, he had only one goal in life and that was to succeed were thousands of others had failed. With a thirty percent pass rate it was known to be one the hardest military training courses in the world. He was excited about being better than everyone else.

John arrived outside the head masters office and could hear voices from inside; he presumed this was Mr Pearce and Mr Dobson chatting about what to do with him. He heard a woman's voice and his heart sank and panic began to set in. "Oh shit" he thought to himself "that's my mam. She'll kill me."

Mr Milner knocked on the door and entered without waiting for a response. "Sir, young Master Savage is waiting outside for you" said Milner.

"Thanks Brian," responded Mr Dobson. "Send him in and you can leave him with us".

Mr Milner left the room and simply pointed to the room gesturing for John to enter. "Good luck John, I'll catch up with you later."

"Thank you," said John as he entered the room.

Mr Dobson stood across the room behind his desk looking at John, he was an intimidating man. John noticed his mother sitting in the chair opposite him. She didn't turn to face him as he entered the room but stayed looking at the head master as if she didn't want to look at John directly.

"John," thundered Mr Dobson, "Come take a seat next to your mother."

John did so quickly feeling nervous and he glanced quickly at his mother and noticed she had been crying. "Mam," he whispered "are you okay?"

She turned and looked at him with such sad eyes, she got up and went to him hugging him tightly as if this would be the last time he would ever see her. She had never held him so tight and this worried him even more. "Oh son, do you have any idea how much I love you?" she asked while crying.

"Aye mam I do," he replied feeling frightened as to what would follow.

"John, you've never been in my office before have you?"

"No sir, I haven't" John replied beginning to shake. Suddenly he stopped and thought, "if I'm going to become a rock hard marine I'm gonna have to be tougher than this."

"John the reason you have been called here today is because..........."

John interrupted spluttering out his words in a panic "Sir I'm sorry, it will never happen again," he stopped and thought, "so much for tough guy," and he began to laugh in his head.

"Don't interrupt me son when I'm speaking," bellowed the head master. "As I was saying, the reason you are here today is because you had a little outburst and confided in Mr Pearce your PE teacher."

John was confused, did Mr Pearce not explain how this situation came about. Was he in trouble? Or had the dreaded Mr Pearce cut him some slack and simply told the head master about his concerns over the things he said about no-one actually caring about him. John thought silence was probably the best option right now and continued to listen to the head master without interruption.

Mr Dobson continued, "Mr Peace is deeply concerned as are your mother and I about your comments regarding your fellow students and how they make you feel."

"Sir, may I say something please?" asked John cautiously interrupting the head master again.

"Go on," Dobson said looking down at John.

"I didn't mean to worry anyone sir, I lost my temper that's all. It gets to me every now and then, the way people think I am."

"But John why do you think people don't like or care about you?" asked the head looking concerned. "I'm sure your friends like you and care about you."

"They say they do but I know they just use me as a skivvy and someone to make fun of," John felt himself welling up with tears again, fighting to hold them back.

Mr Dobson sat down and began to soften towards him. "John what do you want to get out of your time here at school?"

"Nothing sir, I want to leave and join the marines," John knew this wouldn't be a favourable answer but it was an honest one none the less and he hoped this would be appreciated.

"But John if you have no qualifications, how do you expect to progress with your future? I mean surely even marines needs some form of schooling." He paused and waited a response while trying hard to keep his patience with the boy.

"You don't actually need any formal qualifications to join up sir; you need to pass the basic entry test, its basic maths, English and some problem solving sir."

"So you do need to be able to pass this test though, yes?" he asked hoping to convince the boy to work harder in his final year at school.

It was pretty clear to the head master that this quiet practically unknown child who had resided at this school for the last five years had it all worked out in his own mind exactly what he wanted to do. This was admirable considering most of the students simply looked blankly back at the teachers when asked what they wanted to do on leaving.

John continued to answer the head masters question, "Yes sir, I need to pass this test but I'm confident that I can. I'm not the best in the classes at school but I'm not daft sir."

"No-one thinks your daft son. But I know that you will need this schooling in the future, mark my word. Even commandos need to be trained and educated in how to fight and how to use equipment. How are you going to cope with all that pressure if you have no back ground to think back on?" But the head master knew full well he was wasting his breath on John, he could see it in his eyes, this fifteen year old boy was thinking like a man and was showing determination which many other children his age hadn't even thought about using.

"I just want to be a Royal Marine Commando sir, and I know I can do it or I'll die trying," John said with strength of character that Mr Dobson wasn't expecting. The word "die" jumped out once again to both Mr Dobson and his mother.

"John!" His mother snapped. "Why do you say such things?"

"Like what mum," John hadn't realised how much passion he demonstrated and how often he actually used the phrase "die trying."

"Why would you say you would die trying son? What's going through your head when you talk like that? This is what worries us Jonny."

"Sorry mum, sorry sir, I don't mean I want to die. What I meant is I want it so much that I am willing to make sacrifices to achieve my goal. I dream about being a commando, it's all I ever think about," said John trying to convince his peers.

John's words sank deep into both his mother's heart and Mr Dobson's. He appeared to know what he wanted to do with the rest of his life.

"So John," said Mr Dobson. "What if you fail?"

The question hit him like a thunder bolt and without even pausing to think of an answer he blurted out his response. "I won't, I can't, and I will not accept defeat until I've got a Green Beret on my head."

"I understand what you're saying John and I think it's great you have such determination but you must think outside the box. What will you do if you fail?" said Dobson.

"Okay sir, I'll think about it but to me it's simple. I plan to join the marines on a twenty two year open engagement and when I leave I'm going to open a gym."

"Oh John, it sounds more like a fairy tale than the real world. I hope you succeed son but you must face reality, this is the Royal Marines. I mean, I have no idea what the pass rate is for such a force but it can't be high."

"Its thirty percent sir," John replied thinking suddenly of the one question that had never even entered his head. "What if I fail"?

Mr Dobson sent John home with his mother Rebecca and told him to enjoy his weekend and have a long hard think about what it was he wanted and what would he do if he didn't get in the marines.

Once at home he went up to his room and got out the magazines with information required to join the Royal

Marines. As he sat thinking about what it would be like in training and how hard it was going to be he started to drift into his memories and the reasons behind why he wanted to be a Royal Marine Commando.

Chapter 2

Childhood

His memories flicked back over his childhood and all the times he had been bullied and tormented by the other kids and sometimes by other adults. The taunting of the children over the fact he had no father and the names they called his mother. "She's a bike, your mum," said one older boy. Gordon Townsend from the year above John was a bastard and a bully who preyed on the younger weaker children.

John was nine when it all started in the school yard at lunch time one summer's day. The grass had just been cut so the kids were having grass fights, seeing who could roll up the moist fresh grass and cover their friends. It was great fun and the smell was fantastic. Gordon was doing his rounds in the school yard and over the fields with his bunch of followers who all thought they were tough for hanging around with him.

John was playing and having a great time with his closest friends, Mark, Joanne, Stephen and Ashley. They all laughed and rolled around on the grass playing, harmless fun of the innocent totally unaware of what was coming.

John stood up from the grass laughing when something hit him in the back sending him flying forwards and onto his hands, knees and face; out of breath and almost in tears. He stood up and turned around to find Gordon and his followers laughing.

"What was that for," John shouted angrily.

"You want to fucking fight me do ya, ya little shit!" growled Gordon. He was a nasty piece of work whose father used to box and his mother seemed equally as tough. "You grown a set of balls have ya? I'll fucking kill ya."

John's eyes started to fill with tears stinging his eyes and he fought his natural instinct to run away. "N n n n no Gordon, I meant, I i i i ...." his voice trailed off as Gordon shoved him backwards knocking him to the ground again.

"You pathetic little shit. You want your mummy do ya? The bike!" he snarled

John had no idea what he was talking about. Why would his mother be a bike he thought but didn't dare to ask the question to gain clarity?

Gordon continued nastily, "Do you know why your mummy is a fucking bike Jonny boy? Well fucking answer me twat face!"

"N n n no," John stuttered.

"Coz my dad says everyone has had a ride of her," and the gang of followers burst into laughter along with Gordon.

John still didn't understand and most of the others who laughed probably had no idea what this adult humour meant either but they didn't want to look stupid in front of their bully boy leader.

Play time over and the teacher came out ringing the bell for all the children to line up to go back inside. "I'll get you later twat face," snapped Gordon.

They all lined up ready to go back into school when the teacher noticed John had been crying. As he walked past her to enter the building she stopped him. "What's up with your face?" she asked unsympathetically.

"Nothing Miss," he replied, "I fell over," and he continued into the school. That's pretty much how things went in junior's school for John. He only liked one teacher; Miss Wood was a music teacher with one leg shorter than the other due to a motorbike accident some years earlier. She was a pleasant teacher who always saw the best in people but who didn't suffer fools either.

Miss Wood's class was the last of the day and when she noticed the sad little boy enter her class she immediately approached him and asked what was wrong.

"Nothing miss, I fell over at play time" he said sheepishly.

"John," she said firmly, "I wasn't born yesterday young man, now tell me what's happened."

John started to cry again thinking to himself, "Why can't I be tougher and strong enough to fight all these bastards. I'd teach them."

"It was Gordon Townsend Miss, he shoved me around at play time and called my mum names," he began to sob uncontrollably.

Miss Wood couldn't hide her fury, "didn't anyone witness this happening?"

"Yes Miss, my friends did but no-one dare go against Gordon and his gang," he continued without thinking, "and Miss Holmes said what's wrong with you nastily."

"Oh did she now?" snapped Miss Wood who was now visibly angry and what she had discovered. She had no reason to doubt John's story as he had always been an honest child who she gave a glowing report about what a pleasure he was to teach and that honesty like his was very refreshing in this day and age.

Miss Wood took John out of the class and called to the teacher next door to keep an eye on things while she took him to the head mistress. Mrs Vasey was a tough lady who believed in the old school way of teaching, she ruled with an iron fist and a well worn one metre wooden ruler.

Miss Wood explained the situation to Mrs Vasey and they could both see how scared John was about leaving school at the end of the day for fear of Gordon and his gang catching up with him. Mrs Vasey phoned his mother and asked her to come and collect John from school at home time and explained there had been an incident which upset her son.

When school ended Gordon and his gang were indeed waiting for John but so was Mrs Vasey with her wooden ruler. She saw the boys waiting behind the school wall and charged round after them grabbing Gordon by the scruff of his neck and shouting at the others to get home before she held them back too. They scarpered faster than a speeding bullet, no-one wanted to feel the wrath of Mrs Vasey, not even Gordon Townsend.

The following day John and his mother had to attend school slightly later than the normal start time of ten to nine. Enough time to allow the other children to get into class without seeing something was going on. When they arrived at the start of the head mistresses corridor John could see Gordon sitting outside of Mrs Vasey's office with his mum and dad looking worried. John stopped in his tracks as he thought he would surely be killed after school for causing this much trouble. His mother tugged at his jacket, "You've nothing to be scared of son," she said out loud so they could hear her. "He won't dare lay another finger on you again, I promise."

Both Gordon's parents glanced down the corridor as they heard her speak. John had never seen his mother so angry before, there was hatred in her face and a bravery about her which said, "Don't mess with me!"

They arrived at the office and knocked without even looking at the Townsend family. Mrs Vasey wasted no time in calling everyone into her office. "Thank you for attending this meeting," she said firmly, as if anyone had a choice in the matter.

"You are all called here today because I will not tolerate bullying in my school. Not from you Mr Townsend or anybody else. I have been a teacher for thirty five years and have never seen a young boy so petrified about leaving school as I witnessed yesterday. I am furious about this situation and young Gordon has something to say to you John," her voice rising slightly, "don't you?"

"Yes Miss, I'm sorry for what I said about your mum and for scaring you yesterday and I won't ever do it again. I want to be friends with you." And he started to cry.

John had never seen the bully cry before and hadn't realised what cowards bullies really were before this moment. "Okay," John responded unconvincingly, "but I don't want to be your friend."

You could have heard a pin drop in the room. Gordon's sobbing broke the silence again. Mr Townsend spoke up in a mean gruff voice that scared the living daylights out of his son. "If I find out he's bullied you again you won't need to call the school coz I'll kill him, isn't that right ya little shit!"

Mrs Vasey didn't care for bad language and told the father so, not that he cared, he was as hard as a coffin nail and had tattoos all over his arms, hands and neck. This man didn't really care about his son's bullying antics but was more bothered about the fact that he'd been called to the school to deal with it.

The bullying stopped for a little while but soon enough it returned with a warning of what would happen if Gordon's parents or the teachers got wind of his behaviour. John had his head flushed down the toilet on more than one occasion and was even stabbed in the backside with a needle one day, the blood oozed through his school trousers. His only pair and his mother was furious, of course John didn't tell her about what happened, he simply made up a story about how he had fallen over in the park and some glass had stabbed him. She didn't appear to be convinced but he would never tell her or anyone else again for a long time. He would instead suffer in silence like he did the other abuse he suffered for much of his childhood.

His mother worked occasionally on the fiddle to try earn a few extra pennies without paying the dreaded tax man. She would work as a silver service waitress at the Masons in the City centre a couple nights a week and while she did this she would enlist the services a free baby sitter, Louise the nineteen year old daughter of a friend who lived up the street. A strange girl who didn't go out much, she had been John's baby sitter from the age of six up to the age of eleven when his mother decided he was old enough and trustworthy enough to be left on his own.

Louise went to college through the day and had a couple of paying customers for her baby sitting activities but she liked Rebecca and John and as she was a single mother with an only child she offered as a favour to do this for free providing they never told her other families of the free treatment.

Rebecca would leave for work at around six thirty in the evening to catch the bus at the top of the street. Once she returned at ten to seven not feeling well much to Louise's horror, so now she would wait until after seven before she began to play her games with the young boy. "Right it's after seven so it's time for your bath John," she would say with a smile on her face. "Your mum says I have to make sure you're all clean before you have supper and go to bed. You know I'll let you stay up if you can keep a secret though don't you Jonny boy?" she asked deviously.

"Yes, I know Louise," he replied knowing what was coming. He had mixed feelings about what was about to happen, he wasn't sure if he felt scared or excited by the fact but he knew deep inside it was wrong otherwise why insist on it being a secret. He would play along because that was his routine as it became for most children in the same situation. She never hurt him, shouted at him or told him off which is why she got away with it for so long. Five long years of playing the same games over and over again, sometimes he would say he didn't want to but she'd threaten to tell his mum what they had been doing and she said he'd be taken away and put in a home where men would rape him daily and there would be no-one to protect him. It came to an end when the games started to go a little too far even for a child who knew no better.

She would run a warm bath as she knew he didn't like it too hot and call him into the bathroom. "Take your clothes off now there's a good boy and get into the water, then I'll wash you." She would say to him every single time. She would take the sponge and smother it in soap and wash him properly at first but then she would drop the sponge between his legs, when she went to collect it she would stroke his penis and balls until he became erect. It was a strange feeling for a young boy, it felt nice but very wrong and he couldn't understand why she would want to do this to him when nobody else did. "Stand up now there's a good lad, oooh that looks good Jonny boy. Good enough to eat that cock of yours." She then went down on the boy sucking his penis while holding him by his backside thrusting him into her mouth.

It felt so wrong but it was kind of nice at the same time, he was very confused but after a while it was the same routine and he just went through the motions. Afterwards she would play peek a boo with her breasts, asking him to pull her bra down to reveal her nipples and she would ask him to suck them like a baby, John always wondered if anything would come out of them and that scared him, Louise laughed at his innocent comments and carried on regardless. So long as she was getting her thrills she didn't care about his silly fears.

A couple of weeks before his eleventh birthday Louise said she had a special surprise for him. Rebecca realised that John always seemed clean after Louise had babysat and told her that he didn't need a bath on the nights she wasn't home. She was a little suspicious but thought she was being silly as Louise would never do anything to hurt he precious John. After all she was like family.

Rebecca went to work as usual one Thursday evening and John was playing on his Atari video game his mother had bought him for Christmas with the extra nights she now picked up at the Masons. He was playing Pac man and doing well when something caught his eye. This caused him to lose a life and he turned to see what was going on and there she stood in a bra and a tiny pair of knickers. Twenty three years old Louise was a busty girl, that he already knew as he had been made to suck her breasts many times before but this was different. He knew this wasn't the usual routine, the routine Louise tired of and was getting worried Rebecca would catch her if she wasn't more careful.

"Come with me Jonny boy. Follow me right now" she said.

"I'm in the middle of a game and I'm doing well Lou," he said stuttering a little with nerves.

"I'm not going to tell you twice Mr Savage now get in here, strip naked and lay on the floor on your back," she said in a firm but sultry tone. She knew it wouldn't pay to get angry with him and he always did exactly what she told him to.

John did as he was told, he stripped naked and Louise started to play with John's penis, stroking and caressing him until he became erect, this pleased Louise very much. She saw that as a green light, a sign that he actually wanted to do these things with her. She had convinced herself that it wasn't wrong.

She removed her bra and knickers and sat down on his face and said, "you are going to lick me and put your tongue deep inside of me John and I'm going to suck your cock until we both cum in each other's mouths. Do you understand?"

"No, not really Lou, I don't want to lick you. I don't know what it will taste of?"

"It tastes of me, so will taste so good like you do in my mouth."

"I don't want to," John replied.

"Tough, this is going to happen Jonny coz tonight is the night when we bond forever. You're going to eat my pussy and you're going to fuck me hard and you're going to love it. Is that understood?" she got quite forceful now.

She sat down on his face and was in no mood to take no for an answer. She shoved his penis into her mouth and started to suck hard. He was licking a little bit but it was obvious he wasn't going to pleasure her this way and by now she was so excited she could hardly control herself.

She got up and said, "Stay exactly where you are," she squatted down over his penis and grabbed him with both hands. She placed the tip into her hot wet clitoris and sat down hard and fast and started riding him. John didn't know what to do, he just lay there thinking, "Oh my God I can't believe this is happening to me. Should I stop her? I don't think she'll let me," he was scared to stop her and simply lay back and did as he was told. "Grab my tits," she screamed as she rode him hard and fast. A strange feeling came over him, he shouted, "you have to stop, something weird is happening Lou!"

"You're cumming, yes your cumming inside of me," she screamed

He closed his eyes and scrunched up his face as this strange feeling washed over him, his body released this powerful fluid out of his penis into Louise. He felt weird, disgusted with himself and as low as he possible could. He lay perfectly still saying, "I'm sorry, I don't want to play this anymore," he was ten years old and having his innocence taken like this was terrible.

She stood up off him and the fluid dropped from her onto his stomach, a tear rolled from his eye down his face and she glanced back at him and smirked and wondered off to the toilet to get herself cleaned up. John sat up and gathered his clothes together before heading upstairs to clean himself up, when he got to the top of the stairs Louise was stood outside the toilet door looking out of the window. This wasn't like her to be so quiet and thoughtful and John wondered what could be going through the mind of this bitch, the young lady who had stolen his innocence from the age of six and continued right up until this night a few days before his eleventh birthday. Louise turned and looked at him strangely. "This is it, isn't it?" she said.

John didn't know what to say, "What do you mean Lou? I don't understand what you mean?" He walked into the bathroom to get cleaned up.

"Oh Jonny you are the sweetest boy I have ever known and the only boy who has excited me this way. I'm sorry for everything I have done to you but you have to admit we had fun. It wasn't all bad was it?" She said trying to justify what she'd done.

"I don't know what to say Lou. I don't understand why you've done these things to me and if my mam found out she would kill us."

"No John she wouldn't kill you babe........But she would fucking kill me." She laughed nervously.

"I don't understand Lou, why you and not me?"

"John what I have done to you over the last four years was wrong but I couldn't help it coz I love you and now I'm scared your mam will find out and take me to the Police and that will be the end of me. I can't help the feelings I have for you even though I've always known it was wrong."

"Oh I think I understand. So you mean all this time we shouldn't have been doing these things at all and my mam never told you to bath me every night and do all that stuff?"

"Yeah that's right John, I'm sorry." She looked sad, John had never seen her look so beaten before and he actually felt sorry for her despite what she had done to him.

"Don't worry I won't tell anyone. Our secret will die with me but I don't want you to babysit anymore."

"I'll tell your mam I can't afford to babysit for free anymore coz she hasn't got the money to start paying a baby sitter. Is that okay?" she said nervously

"Yes, that would be good," he said thankful it was over.

Louise leaned forward and hugged John tightly, they held onto each other as if they actually cared about each other for several minutes without speaking.

That's the last time Louise ever babysat for Rebecca Savage and she didn't see much of John after that night, they occasionally passed in the street and a simple hello and a smile was enough to get by each other without entering into a conversation. John feared getting into a conversation in case she tried convincing him to do something else he shouldn't or didn't want to do.

Back at school John continued to blend in with the crowd, he never told anyone of his personal experiences and continued to stay within a small group of close knit friends. Even his friends never seemed to witness the bullying and torment he endured which frustrated him even more. He often wondered if he was imagining things and these occurrences didn't really happen at all or if he was being over sensitive, a question that cropped up over and over again in his final years at school.

The routine didn't change; the boys would shove him around in the corridors, steal his Sunderland football club hat from his head and throw it around the yard and make him run around after it. The ring leaders, a kid named Tattoo and another called Grimesy along with their followers Army (Anthony Armstrong) and (Steven) Humble were the usual culprits who would tease and bully John. The worst part was Army and Humble acted like John's friends and would go around to his house to play on his snooker table with him before they got bored and would start to call him and his mother names in the security of his own home.

Nowhere felt safe to John and his temper started to get the better of him, at home he would lose control and kick or punch a hole in the bedroom walls and his mother would simply see the destruction and ignore it. Rebecca knew her son wasn't happy but was scared to ask him about the problem in case she didn't like the answer or for fear she wouldn't be able to do anything to help him.

On a fairly normal summer's day in 1978 the PE teachers had once again had to cancel the planned outdoor lessons due to rain. With sixty pupils sitting around in the changing rooms messing around, John was laughing and chatting with another boy when he heard Humble and Army whispering to each other. He suspected it would be about him and had a feeling something was about to happen. With sixty other kids in the room why was it always him that had to take the brunt of their crap?

Humble and Army moved up on the bench beside John and started to mock him about his mother. "So Savage how's your mummy? She is a right haggard old cow isn't she? A real fucking slapper as well according to my older brother and all of his mates," the pair laughed as they started to prod at him and kept hissing at him and giving him nasty looks.

What amazed John were his closest friends sat by ignoring the fact he was being bullied right in front of them. John started to cry as anger surged up inside of him; Humble and Army laughed and celebrated their success at making him cry in front of the whole class of boys.

Without warning John exploded into a frenzy of violence, he jumped up and slammed the palm of his right hand under Humbles chin jolting his head backwards and smashed his forehead into Humbles nose splattering the soft tissue across his face, blood gushed down his face and he screamed with pain. John didn't stop there, he screamed at Army, "I'll fucking kill you bastards, I'll fucking kill all of you bastards, I fucking hate you, I fucking hate you!"

John punched Army repeatedly and raised his left arm up high before smashing his elbow down into Army's face, the sound of his nose crunching under the force of the impact. The teachers came running into the changing room shouting at everyone to calm down and they grabbed John by his arms, but John wasn't going anywhere without a fight and hadn't realised the teachers had grabbed him as he kicked and lashed out uncontrollably with his arms and head. Mr Pearce and Mr Milner were the last teachers to enter the room and witness the commotion. Milner leaped across the room and knocked the other teachers away and grabbed him in a strangle hold and spoke softly to him, "calm down John, don't make me hurt you son."

John recognised Mr Milner's voice and realised the teachers had hold of him now and so calmed down immediately. Mr Pearce shouted at the entire room, "Calm down and be quiet or the lot of you will be in detention tonight," he turned to the other teachers in the room and said, "get those two off to the nurse and we'll find out what happened in here." The other teachers did as they were told and removed Army and Humble from the room, they were both sobbing and seemed to be in the place where John spent most of his time......in victim mode.

Once everything had calmed down the deputy head master Miss Turner gathered the three boys in her office accompanied by Mr Pearce and Mr Milner. Miss Turner, a large lady who had never married was a force to be reckoned with, a tough disciplinarian who had an iron finger she would prod you with if you ever crossed her path. Nobody wanted to go see her, she was as formidable as the head master himself, Mr Dobson but she was also a very fair lady who listened intently when students spoke to her and she had a nose for sniffing out the truth.

"Boys," she started, "I am disappointed with what has happened here today and amongst friends. What could have possibly happened to cause such a violent outburst from Mr Savage? I have known you all for the last five years and I have never in all that time seen John behave in this way, I want answers and I want the truth." She paused before continuing, "Mr Humble I would like to hear your version of events first of all but I must remind you we have taken down witness statements from some of the other boys who were present so please be honest."

Humble was still sniffling and looked terrible with cotton wool stuffed up his nose and his eyes red raw from crying, he couldn't look at John he was so upset. "We were just messing around miss, me and Army were making fun of John, but it was only a joke miss honestly. He's our mate so we would never do anything to hurt him."

"Fucking liar!" John jumped to his feet furious at the lies and worried they would get away with it and he would be the one to get into trouble.

"Mr Savage," shouted Miss Turner, "you will sit down at once and if I hear anymore language like that you will be suspended from school immediately. Do you understand?"

"Yes miss, sorry miss."

"Continue Steven," she said calmly

"That's it miss, nothing else. We were just messing around and he threw a wobbler shouting and screaming at us and bashing us up."

"So what exactly we're you saying to Mr Savage that made him throw this so called wobbler as you put it?" she asked with a stern look on her face.

"I don't remember exactly miss, something about him not having a dad I think."

"You think," she snapped, "are you telling me you can't remember what you said to him but you can remember exactly what he did to you?"

Humble sat quietly not knowing what to say next. "So what about you Mr Armstrong? What's your recollection of the whole situation?" She asked firmly.

Army didn't know what else to do but to tell the truth, he thought if they lied to her and she already had the facts she would contact his parents. Army was a spoiled only child but everyone who knew him and his family said you didn't want to get on the wrong side of his dad. Army didn't want to face the wrath of his father and for Miss Tuner to tell them he had tried to lie his way out of the situation, wouldn't be good at all.

"Well, miss it's like this," he began, "we were bored coz class had been cancelled and me and Humble thought we'd have a laugh. We decided to pick on John coz we thought it would be fun to make him cry in front of everyone."

"What!" she said with a raised voice, "you thought it would be fun to make John cry?"

"Yes miss, I'm sorry but I'm trying to be honest with you," Humbles head slouched even lower as Army continued with his confession.

"We started to call him names and we said some stuff about his mam to upset him."

"What kind of stuff?" she asked curious as to the catalyst which caused this quiet well behaved child to explode into a frenzy of violence.

40

"We said Steven's older brother and his friends had all slept with his mam or something along those lines. We kept teasing him and prodding him in his back until he finally started to cry, I think we started to cheer and were laughing at him when all of a sudden he exploded."

"Is that everything Anthony?" she asked with softness to her voice

"Yes miss," he started to cry lowering his head with shame. "I'm sorry John," he spluttered between the sobs.

"Thank you Anthony, I think you can go sit outside now and wait for your mother to arrive. Mr Humble you can stay put for a little while longer and I think you owe someone an apology, don't you?"

"Yes miss, I'm sorry John I didn't mean things to get so bad. I'm sorry," and he broke down again sobbing uncontrollably.

"Okay Mr Humble I think it's time you left too. I must warn you your father is on his way to pick you up and he is not a happy chappy. I wouldn't like to be in your shoes when he finds out about this, he sounded extremely angry. Mr Pearce can you take him out and have him wait separately to Mr Armstrong?"

Mr Pearce took Humble out and sat him down in the corridor to await the fate of his father's punishment. Both parent arrived and took the boys home and they were put on school report for their part in the day's occurrence.   Mr Pearce and Mr Milner returned to the office to speak with John while they waited for his mother to arrive, John sat in the chair opposite Miss Turner wondering what his fate would be for his violent outburst and he was scared of how everyone would think of him after this.

Miss Turner continued, "Why John?   What on earth made you resort to violence?   I can't believe you of all people would resort to this kind of behaviour."

"I couldn't take it anymore miss, I have been bullied most of my life by these boys and plenty of others.   I can't take it anymore, I lost it, I'm sorry......."

"Are you?" she interrupted

"Honestly," he paused, "No.   Sorry, but I'm not sorry. Everyone has their breaking point and they found mine today."

"So what do you think I should do to you for today's outburst?" she asked.

"I don't know miss."

"Well needless to say you will be on report for the next week or so. I wonder what your mother will think about this," she said with a raised eyebrow.

"She'll be disappointed with me miss that's for sure, she doesn't like violence but she knows I want to join the

Royal Marines so she understands I'm going to change due to the training they give."

"The Marines eh, interesting I never thought of you as the soldier type. But I suppose it takes all kinds to be a soldier. Well, good luck with whatever you choose to do but I won't tolerate violence in my school. Do you understand?"

"Yes miss, I understand."

A knock on the door broke the tension, it was Rebecca coming to pick up her son and find out what had gone on. Mr Pearce opened the door and welcomed her into the office and Mr Milner pulled out a chair for her to sit alongside John. Miss Turner explained the day's events to Rebecca and as she explained how the events unfolded you could see the distress in his mothers face. How could her baby boy have become like this, so violent and aggressive? She had a mixture of emotions throughout the conversation with Miss Turner, from sorrow to anger and when asked the same question that had been put to John earlier she didn't know what to say. Miss Turner continued to ask, "so what punishment do you think John should face Miss Savage?"

"I will punish John how I see fit Miss Turner and as you have already put my son on report for defending himself I think this is more than enough. Don't you?" Rebecca had a stern look on her face, a protective mechanism which had kicked in at the thought of her son being punished for defending himself.

Miss Turner agreed as it was John who had been bullied so would leave it up to his mother to punish him.

Chapter 3

Recruitment

April 1979 weeks before John's sixteenth birthday he got out of bed with purpose; he had a steely look in his eye of a young man with determination. He gathered some documentation from the dining room table with signatures on the bottom; his application form for the Royal Marine Commandos. He needed his mothers signature with him being under eighteen and he was to join the as Junior Marine and undergo the same thirty week training course as the adult Marines. He walked around with his head held high thinking about what people would think of him once they knew he had joined and became an elite fighting soldier.

He walked to the top of the street to get the number four bus into town, while standing at the bus stop he saw a girl from school, Joanne and her mother walked up the street opposite the bus stop and they both waved. They had known John since his time at nursery school and her mother had popped in to see Rebecca for an occasional coffee. The bus arrived and John paid his fair and walked half way down the aisle before selecting his seat, he sat against the window looking out thinking of what his future would hold. Although this was the first stage in the lengthy process John felt quite giddy at the thought of his future as a Royal Marine.

His mind wondered having read through the literature hundreds of times and memorised every picture, every article, every word of the glossy catalogue as if it were advertising a holiday resort in Bermuda. Photographs of trainees in camouflage running across the moors with rifles at the ready and fixed bayonets, they looked awesome. Other pictures showed specialised units of the Royal Marines of which he knew he wanted to be part of, rigid raiders, mountain leaders, swimmer canoeists to name but a few. He figured in his twenty two years of service that lay ahead of him he would have plenty of time to train in lots of these roles and had no idea how hard his life would be to get there. He had images of himself running carrying the General Purpose Machine Gun (GPMG) nicknamed the Jimpy into war torn villages in the middle of nowhere, bullets flying all around him and him storming through killing dozens of enemy soldiers. Like a war movie in his head even though he thought the reality would be nothing like the movies he had seen so many times.

John arrived in the town some twenty minutes later and got off the bus, as he walked toward the Royal Navy recruitment office he had butterflies in his stomach. This was it, he was going to join the Royal Marines Commandos, this was his day and no-one could take that away from him.

John arrived at the front door and tried to push it open, it appeared to be locked. He tried twice more before realising the sign "Press buzzer for attention," he laughed to himself thinking that wasn't a very good start. He pressed the buzzer and a small white haired gentleman walked towards the door, "What do you want?" the man snapped angrily.

"I'm here to join the Marines sir," he responded a little shocked at the attitude of the small man in naval uniform. John thought to himself, "who the hell does he think he is?"

The man opened the door and stepped aside, "come on in. What you got with you?" he asked looking at the large brown envelope in John's hand.

John started to speak before being abruptly interrupted, "My joining......"

"Put it down over there," he snapped pointing to his desk, "and get your arse on the pull up bar. I want at least three reps."

John looked at the bar rigged between the two partition walls dividing the Royal Navy section and Royal Marines section and walked under the bar, he jumped up and grabbed the bar with an under grasp grip. "Get the fuck down and do it properly!" snapped the white haired man.

John dropped back to the floor and stared at him confused as he didn't understand how else to do a pull up. "Over grasp grip and shoulder width apart. If you can't even get this right how the hell do you expect to be one of this Country's most intelligent fighting men?"

John glanced at him and hopped back up onto the bar, this time with an over grasp grip shoulder width apart and started to pull his eight stone of body weight up towards the bar. John thought this would be easy as he had been practicing pull-ups at home albeit under grasp. John was shocked at how hard this was and struggling to reach his goal of three repetitions before dropping back off the bar to the ground huffing and puffing.

"Is that it?" he snapped

"Yes sir, you said you wanted three reps."

"I said at least three reps sunshine. Three fucking reps faggot!"

John felt uneasy in this guy's presence and started to wonder what he was letting himself in for. "Okay sit down and we'll go through your paperwork."

They sat opposite each other, "My name is Chief Petty Officer Stone, you can call me Chief is that clear?"

"Yes sir," John said nervously.

"What did I fucking say to you? Are you stupid or something? Chief, chief is that clear enough for you or should I write it down?"

"Sorry Chief," John responded.

"Right young man what's your name?"

"John Savage, Chief."

"Okay son listen to me carefully. I can tell you're a little shaken up by the way I'm talking to you but you better get used to a lot worse before we send you to CTCRM I can tell ya. If you can't handle a bit of verbal banter then you got no fucking chance as a bootneck you understand?"

"Yes Chief, I understand I have to get used to taking orders."

"Orders are one thing but you're going to get a whole world of shit thrown at in Lympstone and you better be mentally prepared or you won't last a week."

Chief Stone glanced over John's paperwork and said, "so you're not quite sixteen yet. I noticed your mother has signed the permission sheet, what does your father think about this?"

"I don't have a father Chief. Never met him and have no idea who he is."

"Oh okay, what does your mother think about you becoming a Royal Marine?"

"She's okay, she bought me a pull-up bar and a punch bag to train with and she encourages me to go for a run when I don't feel like training. Yeah she's good Chief," he responded proudly.

"Glad to hear it son, but there's one thing jumping out at me in that last mouthful and that's when you said she tells you to go when you don't feel like training. Self discipline and determination are the biggest values you will need as an aspiring Marine. It's up to you to get your arse out of bed when its pissing down and the temperature is close to zero, when the wind is in your face on a long uphill section of a run, she won't be there to chase you up that hill will she."

"No Chief, I am determined and I do get myself up in the morning etc, I meant to say my mam is behind me and supports me 100%."

"Okay, good coz when your away from home for months on end without any contact with your pals back home its gonna get tough and your gonna get homesick from time to time and that's when you need a strong family member on the other end of the phone to tell you to grow a set of balls and get on with the job."

The Chief continued to talk John through the documentation and booked him in for the following week to come and do his aptitude tests. "You must pass basic Maths, English and problem solving to get in. Are you okay with these things?"

"Yes Chief I should be fine."

The Chief booked John in for the following Monday and then continued to inform him he would have to go the Newcastle office for his medical examination with a Royal Navy Doctor and if he passed the medical he would arrange for his Potential Recruits Course (PRC) in Lympstone, Devon.

Commando Training Centre Royal Marines (CTCRM) is based on the River Exeter and has its own railway station called Commando Halt and this would be where John would spend three days undergoing the physical and mental tests which would decide if he was good enough to attempt Commando training and become a Royal Marine Commando. He talked him through each day step by step and explained how tough it would be, he emphasised this point over and over again as if trying to put him off.

Once they had finished going through everything Chief Stone stood up and handed more information to John about training, pay, promotion and all the general information that would be required should he succeed and gain entry. He gave him some off the record info such as the nick names used for the Marines, such as 'The Corps', and explained how marines were often referred to as 'Bootneck' or as 'Royal' for short, John liked this and it was apparent by the happy look on his face nothing the Chief had said was going to put him off his goal to become a Royal Marine Commando.

Chief Stone shook John's hand and opened the door and wished him well, "Take a good hard think about this son, it's a big decision. Don't think it's all John Wayne bullshit, there's a lot of hard graft ahead of you. Good luck and I'll see next Monday for the test. Take care."

"Thanks Chief," he walked away feeling ten feet tall. John walked to the bus stop and when he sat down on the bus he couldn't wait to open up the new recruitment magazine and a copy of the Royal Marines monthly magazine the 'Globe & Laurel'. He also had the pamphlet regarding his PRC which he couldn't wait to read as he was informed the entry tests had recently changed to make it tougher. He opened the PRC pamphlet up and began to read the requirements; his heart began to race as he read through the 'new' tests.

The days started at 0600 hrs and went on till 2100 hrs; it included physical and mental tests along with information videos and talks with new and senior recruits currently undergoing training at Lympstone. They would also chat with Marines with trades which could be used later in life when they returned to civilian life, like payroll, signallers, heavy goods drivers, computer technicians and chefs. The days would be long and hard and attendees would be required to live life as a recruit wearing uniform and making beds and cleaning the barrack blocks on a daily basis and would be subject to inspections to give them a taste of things to come.

John read this part without any concern, it was the fitness tests that shocked him compared with the previous literature he had received. Tests such as the a mile and a half jog to warm up before running it again with a target time of under ten minutes thirty seconds, an acquaint on the Tarzan Assault Course, Endurance course, Log run, Rope climbs, Fireman's Carry over 200 yards in under 90 seconds, a swimming test which John didn't look forward to as swimming wasn't his strong point. This along with the United States Marine Corps (USMC) test which consisted of 85 sit ups in 2 minutes, 36 burpees in 1 minute, 60 push ups and 18 over grasp pull-ups, followed by some short sprints and some gym work.

A brutally tough week by anyone's standards and John knew he had to up his training if he was going to become an elite soldier. The reality dawned on him things were going to be a lot tougher than anticipated and there was obviously a lot more to becoming a Royal Marine than the glossy catalogues made it out to be. He wanted it more than ever.

When he arrived home he couldn't wait to show his mother the pamphlets and magazines and get started on his training. They sat for hours talking about everything and Rebecca sat and listened to her son, he got so excited, she had never seen him happier than when he was talking about his future as a Royal Marine. After reading through the info she too hoped John would be fit enough and strong enough to make it through selection let alone the longest basic training course in the world. She said a silent prayer for her son and realised he would need more support than ever before as he embarked on this new adventure.

She sat and watched his expression as he talked about every last detail of his experience at the careers office and how he obviously exaggerating as to how calm he claimed to have been when confronted by the Chief Petty Officer. She smiled at her son as he tried to act all macho and she knew he wouldn't know how to take such an abrupt introduction. She loved her son and was glad he had something to focus on; she believed he could do it; he gave her no reason to think he wouldn't. John went to bed with new determination in his mind. He would do it if it killed him; he had the best sleep in a long time that night as he prepared for his first day of training in preparation for his PRC.

John's sixteenth birthday came and went and he received the news he had passed his written test and medical examination. It was a Thursday morning; John had just returned home from a five mile run and was stretching his legs out in the passageway when the postman dropped the day's mail through the letter box. John picked the handful of letters up and walked into the living room and placed them on the small table on the left side of the room when he noticed his name on a brown A5 envelope, his heart skipped a beat and he quickly forgot about the heavy breathing and pain of the run as he picked up the letter.

He held his breath as he opened it and as he unfolded the sheet of paper a huge smile widened his face as he noticed the date of his PRC at the head of the letter, Wednesday 4th July 1979 his three day adventure would begin and his life would take on new meaning, all he had to do now was pass the course. He had six weeks until the potential recruit's course and he knew he had a lot of work to do; he stood in the living room and said out loud to himself, "efforts must be doubled."

He got up at 7 am the following morning and started his day as if his life depended on it; he stretched a little as he always did. Not too much, John didn't need to stretch before exercise as others did. His legs were strong and supple and his greatest asset considering his small frame and eight stone body weight. He left the house and slipped his front door key inside a small pocket on the inside of his Ron Hill Tracksters, a pair of running tights favoured by runners and outdoor enthusiasts, he checked his laces one last time prior to setting off on his run.

He set off like a bat out of hell down the road in which he had lived his entire life, the start of a ten mile journey via the coast of Seaburn, along the sea front and through the village of Whitburn before turning towards Cleadon Village and back towards his own estate again, long straight roads that seemed to last an eternity with steady climbs. He arrived back home in 70 minutes breathing heavy and disappointed with his time, "bastard" he shouted at himself as he looked down at his watch, he had felt good on the run and thought he was flying and expected a much faster time, he wondered if the mileage was correct but it was estimate based on how fast he thought he could run. He went into the house and headed straight upstairs to begin his next part of the workout. Fifteen minutes on the punch bag, constantly punching for the full duration varying between fast minutes and slow steady three minute intervals, his arms and shoulders felt like lead but he had to be tough if he wanted to be a Royal Marine, in his head being the best meant everything after the childhood he had endured.

He finished his boxing workout and went and lay down on his camping mat in his bedroom and put his feet under the barbell filled with weight discs giving him the support he needed to hold his feet down while he did his sit ups. He began without hesitation to crank out the sit ups, one after another, boom, boom, boom he ploughed through them as if they were nothing. 50, 75, 100, 125, 150 done, he sat up, his stomach was red raw from the blood flooding his muscles, but it was a good burn. With a slightly sadistic smile across his face, he felt good and he knew he'd completed a good workout which would stand him in good stead for his PRC in a few weeks time. His day's consisted of similar routines six days a week and he always took a Monday off to give his body time to recover, running, circuit training consisting of push ups, variants of sit ups, pull-ups, burpees, squats, and boxing along with a one mile swim twice weekly and hill running, short distance fast and furious and longer runs up to 13 miles at a fast but steady pace. He felt strong and fit and was becoming more and more confident in his own abilities; he was ready for the PRC.

Chapter 4

Potential Recruit Course (PRC)

Six young men stood at platform four in Newcastle rail station on the morning of Tuesday 3rd July 1979 when the train arrived they eagerly climbed aboard. It was the express train to Exeter St David, an eight hour journey by rail where these men aged between 16 to 25 years old would get to know each other a little better and test each other's knowledge on the history of the Corps.

The birth of the Corps 1664, the title Royal denoted in 1802, and so it went hour after hour the young men discussed their plans. They all spoke without any doubts about their ability to pass the PRC and go on to complete Royal Marines training, all except one guy, Mike, a 24 year old plumber who had tried once before some five years previously. He made it to week 8 in training and quit due to the pressure on what the forces called 'admin' duties. Admin was basically cleaning their equipment, barracks, toilet's known as the head in Naval speak, and the main part, taking care of themselves and their uniform. Some of the men laughed when he said he quit because of the admin but John sat listening intently and wondered how hard the other parts of military life would be, he had never thought about the washing and ironing as being something you could fail and the drill sounded a doddle in the magazines.

"So you polish your boots everyday and iron your clothes," said a young ginger kid sitting opposite Mike, "What's the big fucking deal?"

Mike looked at him with a wry smile across his face, "You'll see soon enough, if you pass the PRC that is. It aint as easy as you think sunshine."

"I'm not fucking worried about any of this shit. I'm fit as fuck and I can do all them daft fucking commando tests with my eyes shut," he laughed, "the names Ginge by the way."

"Its kids like you who don't make it past day one of the PRC. Full of yourself but end up crying like a baby begging to pull out of the run or the endurance course acquaint," Mike laughed.

"So what's it like Mike," John piped up wanting to change the subject as it was obvious that Ginge was starting to wind Mike up and this wouldn't be a good start if they ended up thumping each other before they got there.

"It's nothing like the magazines say it is mate I can tell ya. The PRC is hard as fuck lads; seriously you are going to have to dig deep to pass these three days."

The group of men sat listening intently now they knew someone had inside information about what they were about to face. Even Ginge stopped his gobbing off to see if he could pick up any tips to help him get through the next three days.

Mike started to describe the old PRC he had undertaken and explained that it was a lot harder now and he knew a few guys who had already failed this year. They couldn't handle the mental and physical pressure applied during their three days in hell as they described it. He had their attention and you could see one or two of the men starting to have doubts, they weren't so cocky now.

Mike started to tell his story, "The PRC was pretty easy when I did it but I wish it hadn't been coz I got one hell of a shock three months later when I walked through the gates of Commando halt and began basic's."

"The first day was a fucking nightmare, we got off the train and the Drill Instructor was waiting for us on the station with his drill stick tucked under his arm. Corporal Davison was his name; he'd been in the Corps 15 years and was hard as fuck, one scary bastard. I was pretty cocky so as soon as I got off the train I walked over to him and said, "hello mate, I'm here for training." And boy did he fucking scream at me."

"What did he say," John asked.

"He said I don't give a fuck who you are nancy boy now get in line with the rest of these retards and shut that fucking hole under your nose before I ram this in it and he waggled his stick at me," they all began to laugh as did Mike as he relived the experience, "actually what the fuck am I doing going back," Mike asked as he burst into laughter.

"So what else happened?" asked John feeling nervous and wondered how much of this was being said for effect and how much actually true, surely if it was that bad Mike would never had returned. Mike continued to tell his story.

"We got marched everywhere even when in civvies (the name given to all civilian clothing) and we went straight up to the Induction Centre where you spend the first two weeks of life in the Corps. The instructors sent us for a hair cut even if we didn't need one and we collected our kit from the stores, none of it fucking fit but they just threw it at you and told you to piss off and it would get sorted later. We all stood at the end of our beds and had to swap everything round until we had kit that fit us and anyone who didn't get everything had to go back to the stores and get a gob full of abuse from the store man."

"The first week is a piece of piss really it's all admin stuff and a bit of basic phys in the gym with the PTI's, the first week finishes with Exercise First Step which is a couple of days in the field learning basic field craft and how to move if you get attacked during the night, they call this a 'crash move' and when it happens you shit yourself," Mike laughed again and once again said, "I have no idea what I'm doing here again. I must be fucking mad," the whole group laughed at his story but everyone was secretly thinking that they didn't like the sound of what he was saying. Even John started getting worried, he sat there thinking of all the preparation he had done and how none of it could prepare him for what was about to happen.

"Mike," John interrupted, "if it was that bad surely you wouldn't have come back mate."

Mike stopped, a serious look on his face before speaking again, "this is what I have dreamed about my whole life, I can't go through life knowing I didn't give it one more try before I have to call it a day. I mean I'm 24 years old man, I don't have forever, I'm the pensioner of the group," they laughed again and it had become apparent his humour would come in handy over the next few days.

"So come on Mike tell us about the phys, I've trained hard for this so I guess I'm wondering if I've done enough after listening to you mate. If I'm honest mate you've scared the shit out of me" they all laughed at John's honesty. They all felt the same way but no-one was willing to speak out about it, after all they're supposed to be big tough hard men joining the Royal Marines.

The hours passed with conversation about what each of them expected of life in the Corps and what they wanted to be, some simply wanted to pass out of basic training and then think about what direction to take, while others knew exactly what they wanted to be. Ginge wanted to be a swimmer canoeist (SC) which was the specialist qualification of the Royal Marines Special Forces (SF), the Special Boat Service (SBS). A marine must have served for 4 years prior to application according to the pamphlets given out in the recruitment office but Mike claimed he knew of people who had gone straight from basic training, how true this was nobody really knew. The training for the SC course was 12 months long and said to be the hardest training in the world, an amphibious version of the Army's Special Air Service (SAS), the most feared military force in the world. The SBS were a little more low profile than their Army counterpart and didn't enjoy the publicity the SAS did. Mike said he wanted to become an Assault Engineer; they trained in explosives and to blow shit up as he put it. John stayed out of the conversation until the end when Ginge realised John hadn't contributed to the conversation. "So what about you John?" he asked.

John responded without hesitation, "sniper," and the guys fell silent.

"What's that?" asked Ginge looking completely puzzled. He had heard it was part of SBS training but didn't actually understand what it entailed and he also assumed as it was only a small part of SF training it couldn't be too hard.

He answered in his head before answering the question, "only the most feared man on the battle field," and then he spoke out, "it's a marksman but he's more than just that, they specialise in long range reconnaissance and camouflage and concealment. They're the dog's bollocks," he laughed out loud. The guys joined in with the laughter and they were all impressed with the macho talk being bantered around the group, there was a whole lot of testosterone in that train carriage.

The train arrived at Exeter St David's railway station and they heard the announcement for their next train and they quickly exited the train and jogged to the next platform to catch the next shuttle train to Exmouth stopping at Commando Halt. As they sat on the train they could see several young men with shaved heads who were obviously in the Marines. Mike said hello to one of them in the hope of striking up a conversation but the young guy looked at him and then looked away as if to say, "I'm too good to speak to you."

It took ten minutes for them to arrive at the platform of Commando Halt and as they exited the train they were shocked to see no-one there to greet them. There was ten guys stood around looking lost on the platform and Mike walked over to the Marine who was standing on guard duty at the gate beside the platform and said, "Hi mate, we're here for the PRC. Do you know what we do now?"

The Marine stood tall and proud wearing his green beret and holding his 7.62mm self loading rifle (SLR) across his chest, he looked tough and didn't smile or show any kind of emotion which was a little unnerving. "Wait there and I'll get someone from the guard house to come down and show you where you'll be sleeping tonight."

They stood at the entrance for the next five minutes not knowing what to do as they waited, then a short stocky guy came striding down the walkway to the platform. He looked to be around 5ft 6 inches tall and the same width; he was wearing his lovat green uniform and Green Beret upon his head, he looked like one mean mother fucker. He arrived and spoke firmly and with confidence, "right lads follow me to your digs for the night and we'll grab you some bedding. The rest of the course won't be here until tomorrow so you can get some rest and tomorrow the fun begins," he smiled as he turned away from the group and started off as if he was on a mission.

The group followed him to the barracks and were told to stay in one room rather than split up as the rest of the course would soon follow, they were shown where the take away van was situated on base, it was called 'Dutchies" and little did they know it had a long successful history as it would feed the recruits every night outside of their normal meal times. They collected their bedding and walked across base back to Dutchies to get a burger and some chips before bedding down for the night, none of the potential recruits slept much that evening as they all lay contemplating the next three days.

0600 hrs the door to the room came crashing open, "who the fuck are you lot?" screamed the Marine stood in the doorway. "Are you the wankers on the PRC?"

"Yes sir," said Mike jumping to his feet butt naked in the middle of the room.

"Sir, fucking sir, I work for a living you little shit. My name is Corporal Davies and I'll be spending the next three miserable days with you lot, now get the fuck out of bed and hit the showers. I'll be back in 15 minutes to inspect this place so it better be fucking tidy! Anyone here been in the forces before?"

"Yes Corporal," said Mike nervously.

"What were you in?" the corporal demanded.

"I was here about 5 years back Corporal."

"Good man, right, once you've been showered show this lot how to make their beds with hospital corners and tidy the room. Any questions, no, good!" He left the room as fast as he had arrived and the young men of this PRC started running around like headless chickens to get showered and make their beds before the terrifying corporal returned to carry out his inspection.

The first day of the PRC consisted of lectures about the Corps, marching around on the Parade Ground with a Drill Instructor who commanded respect with just the sound of his voice, followed by a 3 mile run, the first 1.5 miles was done with the PTI in less than 12.5 minutes followed by the timed event which had to be completed in less than 10.5 minutes, fail here and you were sent home without completing the rest of the PRC. This was followed by chatting with some of the senior recruits on base known as the Kings Squad, an honourable name given to recruits in the last two weeks of their basic training, men who had completed the 30 weeks of training and successfully completed the commando tests, these guys were at the end of it all and ready to join the elite force at their chosen commando unit.

The two guys who came to speak to the PRC were both heading to Arbroath in Scotland to join 45 Commando. The spoke frankly about the training and made no secret of how tough it would be but also made it clear that if you wanted it enough anyone could make it, all it took was balls of steel and a bit of fitness, the PRC laughed at this comment and it was obvious there was a certain type of sense of humour required to be a Royal Marine.

On day two they were up at 0530 hrs and rallied outside of the barracks in gym kit, "morning ladies," called out the course Sergeant. "This morning you're going straight to the gym to carry out the USMC test followed by breakfast before more lectures, drill and then we're off to the bottom field to do a little bit of the assault course, some rope climbs and fireman's lift any questions?"

"No Sergeant," came the response of the whole course.

"Right follow the PTI's in double quick time and I'll see you men later," he stood still while the PTI called the course to attention before heading off towards the gym. The PTI's wasted no time in showing these young men what training was all about, they immediately had them sprinting from wall to wall in the huge purpose built gymnasium, running around being told to touch the floor with the left hand, both hands, forward roll, backward roll, dropping to do 10 push ups, 10 sit ups, 10 burpees and so it went for around 10 minutes until some of them were feeling sick and the test's hadn't even begun. They grabbed the mats from a huge pile in the corner of the gym and laid them out in a long line, the men were paired off with people of similar heights ready for the tests.

"First things first gentlemen," called out the PTI, "one man down on the mat and the other sits on his feet, two minutes is all you get ladies and I want 86 sit ups to achieve maximum points on this exercise."

The young men jumped to their positions, John was sitting on feet duty first, he held the feet of ginger haired boy who appeared even younger than he was. His name was Simpson, they never found out each other's first names unless specifically asked. It was the longest two minutes in the world to the guys on the floor, the PTI called out when it was time and the first man jumped to his feet and was told his score by the man sitting on his feet.

Simpson jumped to his feet and John said, "70, well done mate," he immediately dropped to the floor in the lying position to prepare for his two minutes. The PTI called out again to signal the start of the next two minutes, his muscles screamed the whole time and it was a relief when the PTI called time again. John sprang to his feet and Simpson said, "80 fucking 6 man, that's amazing," and they stood in silence waiting for the next command. The PTI asked each man to shout out his score so it could be recorded by another instructor and John was only one of five men to achieve maximum score on the sit-ups.

The same protocol applied for the one minute of burpees of which John achieved close to the maximum of 36, he got 34 reps and was now under the watchful eye of the PTI's as they searched for people who showed potential in the fitness tests, then came the press ups where you aimed for the maximum number of 60 with no time limit but if they saw someone struggling they stopped them and told them to stop being so dramatic with all the grunts and groans that came from the whimpering men on the floor. Again John did reasonable well on this but was nowhere near the 60 for maximum points; instead he achieved 45 which wasn't bad for an 8 stone, 16 year old boy. Pull ups came next; John achieved 13 out of the maximum 18 required. Then came the sprints which wasn't John's strong point but he didn't come last so he was reasonably happy with his overall performance of the morning.

They rushed back across base to the barracks to get showered and ready for breakfast, they were doubled to and from breakfast to get ready for the next set of lectures and a bit of range work so they could all have a go at shooting the SLR (self loading rifle) and the new rifle which was under test at the time, the SA80A1 had been fitted with a .22mm conversion so the potential recruits could get a feel for the rifle, this was followed by more marching before being taken back to the gym for the dreaded swimming test. Dreaded by those who wanted to be an amphibious soldier who weren't the strongest swimmers, they were each asked to do a backwards summersault off the 10 foot diving board followed by a two length swim using breast stroke followed by treading water for two minutes without touching the side of the pool before being allowed to climb out and go get showered and ready for the next session on the agenda.

It was mid afternoon when they were told to climb into the back of a 7.5 tonne Bedford military truck; this was driven at brake neck speed across Woodbury Common to the start of the infamous Endurance Course. Infamous because of its long dark tunnels and it's fully submerged tunnel which required recruits to trust their oppo's to push them far enough through the tunnel so the other man could catch them and pull them through the other side. This was scary stuff and everyone felt nervous about this part of the course, as soon as the truck stopped the shouting began, worse than in camp as no-one could hear them out on the Common.

More push-ups, sprints up and down hills and bodies held in the half way position of the push-up, their bodies cried out as did some of the young men on the course, "Shut the fuck up!" screamed the instructors, they showed no mercy out there, this was their world, a Marines world where only the fittest and strongest survive. John knew this was make or break time for him and even though many of the potential recruits felt reasonably confident the instructors constantly told them none of them had done enough to pass yet and so the seed of doubt was set in their minds, more mind games to see if they had what it takes to become one of the nation's finest soldiers.

They started off around the Endurance Course following the Sergeant and followed by the course Corporal as the PTI's watched from the banks to monitor the performance of the potential recruits and to watch for anyone showing either signs of strength or signs of weakness, they wanted men with steely eyed determination to carry on when their bodies and common sense was telling them to quit, they wanted men who they would trust to stand side by side in a war and know they wouldn't let them down no matter what the odds. They ran down a mud gully and into Peter's Pool holding onto a rope and trying to run through the pool of water while gasping for breath as the cold water hit their nether regions, half way across the Sergeant stopped and told them all to duck their heads under the water to acclimatise them to the temperature, they continued up and out of the pool and through several tunnels of varying length and heights all to test a man's ability to move quickly and to test for any signs of claustrophobia.

Then they came to the real test as they arrived at the submerged tunnel. A demonstration was given before attempting it themselves, three at a time they went through the tunnel and two of the potential recruits failed to go through the tunnel and were told to carry on regardless. At the end of the course they gathered along side two telegraph posts lying on the road, "right men, in teams of four pick up the log and run with it until we shout change. You'll be carrying it for the 4 mile run back to camp unless anyone wants to quit now?"

The hearts of some of these young men sank at the thought of a four mile run back to camp carrying this full size telegraph post, John was at the front of the first log having completed the Endurance Course near the front and heard a single voice amongst the commotion.

The voice said "I can't do it, I can't go on, it's just too hard, I'm not cut out for this," it was Ginge from the earlier train ride; he was done, his mind broken from the rigours of the last two days. He had wrapped as they said in the Corps when someone quit or gave up on something. Ginge was told to get in the back of the 7.5 tonne truck parked alongside the road where the logs lay and soon after this the domino effect they had heard about came into play, one by one they began to fall as the log race went at full speed along the road back to camp, the screaming of the instructors didn't let up for a minute, the physical pain was visible on these young men's faces as they trudged along the road

"Change!" screamed the Sergeant as the four men swapped with what should have been another four, John glanced over his shoulder as he went to hand the log to another recruit only to find two people left to hand over to.

"Where the fuck is everybody?" shouted John to the other men who had carried the log with him. He kept hold of the log changing to another shoulder as his left was now raw where the log had rubbed against his skin, he had never felt pain like this but something came alive inside of him and he felt strong, happy and tough as if he had already passed the training and this was his moment to show he was worthy of joining this elite force.

The three remaining recruits continued along the road for a few hundred yards before the instructors shouted for them to halt, they were told to get the logs in the back of the trucks and climb in behind them. John was puzzled, was it because too many had quit or had they actually finished the exercise and passed this part of the course?

"Well done to those who didn't fucking quit on us today," said the Sgt, "and for those who gave up we'll just have to wait and see what the result is won't we."

As the truck sped down the country lanes towards camp no-one spoke for what seemed an age until Mike finally turned to Ginge and said, "You never know mate, they might not fail you. You finished the endurance okay didn't ya, keep your chin up Ginge my old boy, that's what Commando spirit is all about," and he sat back smiling.

"That was fucking mental." John said laughing about it almost deliriously, "and I fucking loved it!"

A big grin spread across his face and a real feeling of achievement after what he had just completed. When they got back to camp they cleaned out the truck and washed down the logs before going off to an old shower block to clean off all the mud from their clothes before showering themselves down properly and heading back to the barracks. They hung their wet clothes up in the drying room and went for some scran, more Marine speak meaning food. They shovelled the scran down them as if they hadn't been fed for a week and it didn't matter that it wasn't the kind of food John normally ate, rice, chicken, some kind of mixed vegetables that he wasn't quite sure about, covered in gravy, followed by rhubarb crumble and custard, a huge portion washed down by a pint of tea, mopped up with bread.

Full to the brim they went off to meet the recruits who had reached the end of week two of basic training, they were in the Induction Block, the place every recruit spent the first two weeks of their life as a soldier. It reminded John of an old American war movie, boot camp as the American's called it, simply induction to the Royal marines. They chatted for an hour with recruits who seemed nervous and scared at what they were doing, some tried to look hard in front of the potential recruits.

By the time they returned to the barracks for the night it was 2130 hrs and lights out was 2230 hrs sharp. They slept well after the day's activities they had endured and they went to sleep wondering what day three had to offer.

Day three, 0530 hrs the doors crashed open and the shouting started as the remaining men jumped to attention at the end of their beds. The Corporal looked happy and was smiling as he gave his next order.

"Everyone into the corridor now!" The bodies piled out into the corridor not quite sure what was going on. They stood with their backs against the wall to attention awaiting further instruction; he left them standing for several minutes in total silence, the cold floor chilled their feet and the cold wall behind them sending a chill down their spines, waiting, listening, and breathing.

"Three minutes gentlemen, that's exactly how much time you have to get into full uniform and outside on parade ready for the bottom field," he paused before giving the deafening command, "NOW!"

The men ran to the drying room scrambling to grab what they hoped was their clothes from the day before only to find the drying room hadn't been on during the night. The clothes were still wet and cold and everyone stopped and looked at each other before Mike shouted, "just get them out of here and get them on your backs lads."

Everyone did as Mike ordered; they rushed around pulling on the damp, cold clothing which chaffed at their legs as they pulled them up and over their thin lean wastes. "Ten seconds," came a shout from the end of the corridor, it was the Corporal again and he seemed angrier than ever before "move your fucking arses ladies, this is not the fucking Salvation Army!"

The terror could be seen in the young men's faces as they scrambled to get ready and outside on time, they poured out of the building as the Corporal said firmly "press up position, down," he paused to wait for the remaining potential recruits to arrive and as they were late they all knew they would be punished. Once the whole course was present the Corporal spoke only briefly before giving his simple commands, "I will teach you ladies to be late for one of my parades, do you fucking understand?"

"Yes Corporal," came the united response of the course.

His commands followed and were repeated until he was satisfied that none of the recruits could do another press up, "arm's bend, and stretch," he would of course pause for up to a minute in the arm's bent position until every mans arms trembled with pain and the stress of which their muscles had never felt before. "Right, stand up," and every one of them jumped up faster than ever before fearing what might happen if they didn't react quick enough.

"In single file, follow me to the bottom field and let's get this show on the road," he took off at a fast pace and everyone ran behind him hoping to keep up with this lean green fighting machine.

They arrived at the bottom field and after a few sprints and more press ups, sit ups, burpees and generally being exhausted prior to the tests they stood at the bottom of the 30 foot ropes ready to climb them to the top. For some this would be the first time they had climbed ropes since gym class at school, for John this wasn't so long ago and as such he wasn't nervous about this next test, nor was he worried about the aerial obstacle course ahead of them. He climbed the ropes with ease, went on to complete the next section of the aerial obstacle course before getting ready to do the dreaded fireman's carry over 200 yards in under 90 seconds, John was partnered with another 16 year old boy from London whose name he didn't remember and so he called him Cockney.

Cockney had done quite well so far and hadn't wrapped on any of the tests, he seemed fit and strong for his size and was of similar build to John. Cockney took John by the wrist and placed him over his shoulders as shown by the instructors, his shoulder jammed into John's crotch and with John's right leg hanging in front of his body, he grasped the leg and the wrist in his right hand and when the order came, "Go!" They were off like a Grey Hound out of its box on a race course, Cockney was going great guns but the pain in John's stomach and crotch was not so great, 87 seconds came the shout as

Cockney crossed the line and threw John to the floor face first.

"What the fuck is the point of carrying the casualty off the battle field and then dropping him on his fucking face?" screamed one of the PTI's, "now get up and get into position and you better hope he's got more fucking control than you."

John got up and took Cockney in the same position as shown by the instructors and got ready for his turn, "Go!" came the command and off they went again, John struggled with this test with him being so light and although Cockney didn't look much bigger, when John crossed the line and placed his partner down to the words 90 seconds he wasn't happy.

"How fucking heavy are you?" asked John snappily

"I'm about 10 stone why what are you?" asked Cockney

"Eight stone, no wonder I fucking struggled," John laughed at the situation.

The instructors wasted no time in getting the potential recruits ready for the Tarzan Assault Course acquaint, they didn't plan on doing the full course, this would have taken too long and the morning drew to a close and the potential recruits were eager to receive the results and to find out who would be invited back to attempt the 30 weeks of training required to become one the elite. They were given five minutes to get around a selection of the apparatus which made up the Tarzan assault course and they were expected to show the kind of determination required of a budding Royal Marine Commando.

Over the wall's, across the jumps, under the scramble net, across the zig zag walls, over the rope and across the swing bridge, up a killer 100 yard hill sprint to a fence made up of scaffolding pipes, up and over they went before heading to the tunnels before emerging and climbing over the wall with the knotted rope and down the steps on the other side and a last 20 yard sprint to the finish line in the form of a PTI with a stop watch.

John's lung's burned like never before as he emerged from the tunnels and climbed over the wall, he almost fell down the steps on the other side and staggered past the instructor as he called out, "4 minutes 35 well done son, now down to the flat area and keep running round in a circle."

John didn't respond, he just did as he was told and staggered on to the flat area and continued to trot in a circle with the other two young men who'd beaten him to the finish line. He didn't like coming third but at least he was nowhere near the back of the group, those guys were getting some serious verbal abuse right now, "move your arse," screamed the instructors, it was there way of encouraging the young men who wanted to join their ranks, it didn't always feel like it when they were screaming at you six inches away from their faces.

As the remaining 25 men jogged in a circle at the end of the assault course the instructors called them to a halt and told them to face 'The Tank', a huge tank of murky cold water with two ropes going across the length of the tank where the marines would practice rope regains if they were successful in gaining entry to the Corps.

The Sgt stood in front of the gasping men and spoke with a jolly voice, "Okay men, good effort on the bottom field. It's time for you guys to cool off a little before heading back up to the barracks to clean your kit away and prepare for your leaving routine. On my command.......GO!"

The men bolted towards the water tank and threw themselves in head first for the most of them but some climbed onto the wall and jumped in feet first and a couple dived in, they came up gasping for air as the cold water took them by surprise. They came up laughing and happy as they all knew it was almost over and the tests complete, it was just a case of getting ready for the results and at least half of the young men were confident they had passed and would be back here in a few months time and their journey to become a Royal Marine would finally be under way.

The young men stood to attention in a small office with CTCRM Regimental Sergeant Major (RSM) standing at the front of the room alongside the course Corporal and Sergeant, they looked stern, the young men of the PRC felt nervous and John could feel the pressure around him in the room. He kept talking to himself in his head, "I have to pass this, I can't fail, I want this so much."

"Right!" Snapped the RSM, "My name is Sgt Major Savage," John's heart skipped a beat as he suddenly had a very strange thought that the man with the same name at the front of the room could be his father. No surely not, surely his mother would have told him if he was worth knowing and especially knowing that he was joining the Royal marines.

"I have to tell you girls that I have never seen such a pathetic bunch of losers in my 20 years in the Corps. I'm here to tell each and every one of you that you have failed!" The room fell totally silent and the hearts of the young men crushed. "Which is why none of you are going home today? You will all do the three days again starting right now!"

The words of the Sgt Major shook the very ground they stood on and every man in the room was terrified, not one of them knew what to say or do. The course Sgt stepped forward and spoke next, he screamed his order like a maniac, "Get your arses back into barracks and get your fucking PT kits on. I'm going to run you till you puke, now fucking move!" The young men sprinted out of the office and back to the barracks to get changed but three of the men stood still and all struggled to be heard as they all spoke at the same time, "I can't do it again sir."

The voice of the Sgt Major shook the corridor, "STOP! Get back in here now."

The men ran back into the room and you could see many of the faces were of beaten men who would have had no chance of going through another three days like they had endured. The instructors were laughing at the front of the room as the men stood back to attention wondering what the hell was going on and if indeed this was the sense of humour of the Royal Marines.

The Sgt Major had a wide grin across his face, "Ha ha you should have seen you're faces," he laughed at the petrified look on their faces. "The following people have achieved a superior pass and I would like you to step out to the front of the room and face the rest of the course. Smith, Callahan, French and Savage, well done men, I look forward to welcoming you to join basic training earlier than the rest of the people who have passed the course."

There were huge grins around the room now as everyone in the room assumed they had passed the course. "The following people have failed and will be spoken to separately. Green, Stevens, Barrow, Hall, Mellroy and Charlton."

Smith was the kid previously known as Cockney, Mike Callahan a fellow Mackem on his second attempt, French an England boxer also from London and of course John Savage had achieved superior passes and were ready to become recruits in Royal Marine basic training, they couldn't have been happier.

Stevens better known as Ginge, the cocky Geordie from Newcastle was devastated at the thought of failing and wished he hadn't have pulled out of the log run, he was spoken to and they told him he had failed because he didn't show enough determination when faced with adversity. The other fails were from the Midlands and North West areas of the country and all given the same speech from the Sgt Major.

"It's better to have tried and failed than not to have tried at all."

These words were painful to hear for these young men who came to Lympstone with high hopes of becoming commando's and for them the journey was over despite been given the opportunity to return in six months time. If they dared to face the PRC all over again, a thought far from their minds right now.

The Sgt Major gathered the four men who had achieved a superior pass and spoke to them as if already Royal Marines, "well done guys, it's good to see there are some young men out there with the determination and guts needed to join our ranks and hopefully become Royal Marine Commando's."

They left Lympstone that afternoon on the train back to Newcastle and for most of them it was a joyful journey back home to tell their families and loved ones the good news, but not for Ginge. He was gutted but still joined in the celebration with the others and gave congratulations to those who had succeeded. John was in a good place and felt proud, plus he had found a new friend in Mike Callahan and had every intention of getting as much knowledge about basic training from Mike as he possibly could. They would become training partners and although they lived at different sides of the town they would run to meet each other and train hard together, push each other past the point where most would quit and they hoped to gain entry at the same time so they would at least know someone in basic training.

John returned home on the Friday evening at around 8 pm, as he walked through the door his mother leapt out of her chair to greet him. He had a huge smile on his face. Rebecca spoke first, "well, come on tell me how it went. I can see it must be good news and it wouldn't have killed you to have rang me ya little bugger," she was grinning and so happy to see her son back.

"I got a superior pass mam, a superior pass, can you believe it," he laughed as he spoke.

It only just started to sink in; he would be heading back to Lympstone sooner than he thought. His mind was already filled with training plans to ensure he was even more prepared by the time he got back and he wanted to ensure he stayed at the front of the Troop.

"A superior pass," shrieked his mother, "that's fantastic news son. I knew you could do it and I'm so proud of you," she began to cry with happiness and John stepped forward and gave his mother a hug. He held her tightly, they both knew the day would come when they would hug each other for the last time in a while.

John spent the rest of the night telling his mother every last detail about the PRC and every detail about the new people he had met. He told her about his new friend Mike Callahan and the sorry look on Ginger's face after all his macho talk before they arrived and all that talk about becoming a swimmer canoeist in the SBS. John wondered how Ginge would explain his failure to his girlfriend back at home and his father who had tormented him before he left saying, "you, a fucking marine. That'll be the day," and he would laugh in his son's face. John didn't want to be in his shoes when he returned home a failure with nothing to celebrate and he realised how lucky he was to have made it through the toughest three days in his life. He felt happy and content when he eventually went to bed that night.

Only two weeks had past when the letter landed on the passage floor, a brown A4 envelope with the stamp of the Royal Navy in the top tight hand corner. It was the best letter to have ever arrived for John and as he opened it his eyes lit up while at the same time his heart almost stopped when he saw the entry date.

Dear Mr John Savage, Commando Training Centre Royal Marines invites you to join 501 Troop on Monday 14th January 1980. The training will last 30 weeks and you will be given leave at set times throughout the year an your pay will be ....the standard enrolment letter continued to give John all the necessary information he required but the date was a huge shock to him. He had taken a Youth Training Scheme (YTS) at the Sunderland Outdoor Activities Centre as a trainee instructor and was learning skills he believed would stand him in good stead for his future. He learned navigation skills, rope work and knot tying, mountain first aid, kayaking and climbing all of which would help prepare him.

Rebecca came home from work in a cheerful mood and as she walked into the living room she caught sight of the brown envelope on the table and called out for her son. "John, are you here son?"

When no response came she took the letter from the envelope and read the details, as she read the date her heart sank knowing this would be the last Christmas she would spend with her son and it hit her like a sledge hammer........These next few months would be the last with her son living at home and then he would be gone for months at a time, maybe even years depending on where he was based.

When John returned home from a long training session with his new friend Mike his mother was sat in her armchair crying. John rushed to her side, "what's up mam? What's happened?"

He noticed the letter to her side and knew what it was that was bothering her. They both knew the day was coming for her little boy to leave home to become a man and that fact had finally become a reality which had hit them both a little more than they expected it to.

"It's okay mam, I'll be home every time I get leave and I'll only be gone 10 weeks before I'm back again and then you'll be able to come down at week 15 to see my halfway pass out parade," John said positively.

"Ten weeks," she said, "I've never been away from you for more than four days since the day you were born and that was for your PRC."

"I know, but it'll be okay, honest. Just think what it'll be like when you see me after 10 weeks, how different I'll be and how much training I'll have received. I'll already be a soldier the next time you see me, isn't that great?"

"Yeah, I suppose so. I'm already proud of you ya know, and I love you so much. I always knew this day would come but I guess I never thought about what it would be like to not have you around every day. I'm gonna miss you."

Chapter 5

Preparation

John continued to train six days a week, the days were long and he didn't stop at one activity per day, his job at the outdoor activities centre gave him plenty of opportunity for extra ordinary training facilities. He would run the 3 miles to work every morning and get washed in the tiny bathroom cubical prior to starting, the mornings were usually pretty boring but his boss was a good bloke and ex Royal Marine Reserve with years of mountaineering experience and who had once been an SBS reservist. He organised a swimming session once a week at the local Polytechnic swimming baths behind the centre where they would practice for 90 minutes for their latest qualification, the Bronze Medallion Life Saving Award. It was a requirement of all pool attendants and life guards alike and was not an easy test to pass; John passed it with a struggle as swimming wasn't his favourite thing but he did it all the same, after all it wouldn't do him any harm in the marines.

He took a couple of classes down to the docks where a few walls gave the centre the grounds they needed to take small groups of school children and the disabled, John would come back to the centre and climb for at least an hour, testing his body every step of the way, leaping for barely reachable handholds and stretching his leg length beyond their normal capability, he loved it. This would be followed by a lunch time run to the local ski slope; a 3 mile round trip with some very interesting hills on and around the slopes, Silksworth was also the home of the Sunderland Harriers running club. John had visited once to show an interest in the hope of them pushing him to new heights of running but he didn't like their attitude, an elitist group who didn't welcome outsiders unless they had been recommended by one of their own. He had entered a few road races for pleasure and had beaten some of the Harriers at their own game; John felt good passing those pricks on the long hard uphill sections of the races.

After his lunch time run there might be one or two more classes if he was lucky or else it was time for the boring job of rubbing 'dubbing' onto the walking boots which the centre hired out to members of the public. Sitting down was not a pass time John enjoyed and he struggled to stay focussed when confronted with boredom. At the end of each day John walked home at a good speed, he figured this would prepare him for speed marching and he often carried a small day sack with him and filled the pockets with his home made weights, sand bags taped up and weighing around 5 kg each, he rarely carried less than 20 lbs on his back and was building strength in his legs as a result.

He arrived home and went straight upstairs to begin his circuit training, pull-ups, push ups, close hand push ups, sit ups, V sits, crunches, burpees, squats, squat thrusts, mountain climbs (an alternate leg squat thrust), leg raises, calf raises and then some light weights with high reps to burn his muscles out totally, this was usually followed by another 5-10 minutes of punching on the bag.

The weeks went by and John grew stronger and fitter, his 10 mile time now under 60 minutes and he could smash the 1.5 mile run in less than 8 minutes so he had no worries about the tests he had already undertaken and he felt ready for the rigours set to come.

John met a young lady in the December; Amy Walsh was 6 months younger than John and from a big family on the same estate. They didn't know each other despite going to the same school and having some of the same friends, John was a shy lad who had low self esteem when it came to the opposite sex.

The winter was tough, bitterly cold with strong winds and plenty of sleet and snow to contend with. The winters never seemed to bother John, he actually preferred them to the summer as he wasn't very comfortable in the heat, this would change in time but right now all he had in his mind was to become a Royal Marine, an Arctic Warfare Specialist and serve many months in Norway fighting the elements.

Amy was a well educated girl sitting her A-levels and had aspirations of becoming a Doctor one day, this suited John just fine, a nice trustworthy girl back home to write to and who had a determination all of her own, he liked that about her. She had three brothers so was used to the male sense of humour and banter which was just as well as John liked to play games and make fun of people, he was sarcastic but not in an offensive way. Most people understood his wit as harmless banter and weren't offended by it, Amy loved to be around him, he had such energy and passion and he never shut up about his life in the marines, what he was going to achieve even before he had left for basic training.

He would talk about exactly how long it would take him to pass out of training and to reach each promotion, "I'll make Lance Corporal in 2 years, Corporal in 4 years, Sergeant in 7 years and then we'll just see where I decide to go after that," it was as if it was all pre-defined and couldn't go wrong, as if he knew something no-one else did. John brimmed with confidence and Amy loved this about him, Amy was anaemic so would get tired quite quickly and would regularly want to nap as soon as she got home from college, but as soon as John arrived she didn't get much time to rest.

"Let's go for a walk to the beach," he would say as if it was ten minute stroll away. In fact the beach was a six mile round trip but they knew they would get fed for free as his friends mum worked at the fish and chip shop on the sea front. Proper fish and chips cooked in beef dripping, served on a piece of paper and smothered in salt and vinegar, just the way they were meant to be eaten, they walked along the coast line chatting about what Amy had been up to at college that day and she would always ask what training he had done and once again he would come alive with motivation as he described his days exercises and they would chat about their future together. John made no secret of how much he loved Amy and she reciprocated this back to him, they talked about how they would marry and how John would wear his dress blues, the Corps unique uniform which showed their ties to the Royal Navy, they would get very excited at the thought of a life travelling around the world together.

Sunday 13th January 1980 was a strange day in the Savage household; Rebecca made sure John had everything listed on the sheet the Royal Marines recruitment team had sent him, boot polish, parade gloss, spare laces, towel, flip flops, sewing kit and so the list went. Mike had also given him a list of things to buy that weren't on the enrolment list.

Everything checked and accounted for and she sat alone in the living room as John spent his last few hours upstairs cuddling and kissing his beautiful Amy, oh how he would miss her, yet another obstacle he hadn't considered when he dreamed of life on the ocean wave. They went downstairs to have supper with his mother and the two ladies acted as if everything was normal but John knew they were putting on a brave face to make things easier for him, he felt a mixture of nerves and excitement as he ate his last supper as a civilian.

At around 11 pm John and Amy went to bed together for the last time; they lay in each other's arms and kissed and caressed each other. They made love as if for the last time in their lives and as John got up to turn out the light he noticed it had begun to snow, they sat together in silence watching the snow fall outside his bedroom window before lying down together and drifting gently off to sleep.

Chapter 6

Welcome to CTCRM

John arrived at Commando halt late on the Monday afternoon, just in time for the last scran of the day. The Drill Leader who met them escorted the new recruits of 501 Troop to the Induction block to drop off their civi gear before taking them for their first taste of Royal Marine scran as a fully fledged recruit, then they collected stores, everything they would need for the next 30 weeks of basic training. Boots DPM x 2, lightweight trousers x 2, jersey x 1, shirts green x 2, shirts kaki x 2, parade boots x 1, dress shoes x 1, belt green x 1, belt Corps colours x 1 and so the list went on until they had everything from laces to respirator, magazines to helmet. This was the point of no return, these boys began their journey into manhood, their faces was a mix of raw nerves to fake confidence and the instructors could sense it, they had seen hundreds, some had seen thousands of recruits walk through those doors and only 30% would make it.

Fifty two new recruits stood present on day one, around 20 would make it through training with their original troop. Many would fall behind or fail to meet the grade first time and would face the humiliation of being back trooped. A new troop would arrive every two weeks so for most they would normally be sent back to the following troop but for others who suffered injury it could be much longer and no recruit wanted to spend any more time than they had to at Lympstone.

They spent the first few days learning everything from how to wash and shave properly to cleaning their boots. The floors had to be polished on a daily basis and buffed with a broom like device made up of a steel weight weighing around 5 kg on the end of a broom stick covered in a soft cloth. Toilets had to be scrubbed and brass pipes would gleam, many hours would be spent with tins of brasso in hand scrubbing the pipe work until everything was like a shiny new penny. No stone was left unturned on inspection and this the starting point of which their future inspection would be based on, bed blocks had to be made to the perfect size of two Globe & Laurel (G&L) magazines, every shirt, jersey and trousers would be the size of the G&L, black leather gloves would be polished and folded so the padded knuckle guard would gleam. There wasn't just the simple bed block to contend with either, two other ways of making the bed existed depending on the day of the week.

It all seemed pointless to the recruits at this stage, they simply wanted to become commandos and didn't understand why all this cleaning was necessary, but necessary it was and they would do it over and over again until they could do it with their eyes closed and heaven forbid any man who failed to take on board the instruction given by the Corporals of 501 Troop.

Lieutenant Wray was troop commander and Sgt Mallaney was the troop sergeant, there were four Corporals in the troop, two of which were very experienced instructors with 40 years' service between them. Corporal Goode had been in the marines for 22 years and was the Platoon Weapons Instructor (PW) class 1 which was the highest qualification in the field, they specialised in every type of weapon in the Royal Marines armouries and tested all new weapons prior to them gaining approval, they also delivered Sniper training and certain aspects of SF training courses. He was a hard man who didn't suffer fools, he was a bootneck through and through and had given his life to the Corps and expected only the highest standards from his recruits, it was said that any man who passes in his section would be a top marine by the time they hit the commando units.

The other Corporals were Cpl Shaw with 18 years' service, Cpl Dunn with 8 years' service and Cpl Wright with 7 years' service, working alongside this and other troops was Cpl Garver the Drill Leader who taught the recruits the basics in weeks 1 and 2 before handing them over to their Section Commanders.

At the end of week one the recruits were taken out on what the Cpl's described as a camping trip, Exercise First Step was the easiest of the coming field exercises and lasted only 36 hours. They travelled out by bus to the drop off point and they set up camp, the Cpl's showed them how to set up the instructors camp first, a tent and camping beds, a toilet in a separate smaller tent, a big stove with gas bottles and even a gas fire to keep the instructors warm on these cold nights and then each Cpl showed the recruits how to set up their bivouac (BIVI) and sleeping area, how to cook using the hexamine stove and took them through each item of their ration packs known as the ratpack. A small tin of sausage and beans, steak pudding, a tin of meat paste, biscuits brown, biscuits fruit, fructose tablets, water purifying tablets and some tined peaches for desert, this made up the 24 hr ratpack that each recruit would have to live on in normal conditions. For those who made it to the commando units they would all at some point serve at least one draft in Norway doing Arctic Warfare Training and here they would be given dehydrated rations due to the freezing temperatures. They were usually Mutton granules and dried peas with dried apple flakes for desert, not very appetizing at all but it was hot food and that's all that mattered out there.

Once settled into their sleeping area the recruits were shown how to carry out a guard duty and monitor the perimeter, this was the first time they had been out in the field and as John walked slowly through the night watching for the fake enemy he felt good, he was walking with his rifle at the ready, it didn't matter that his magazine was empty and that he knew nothing was going to happen to them on this first exercise, he felt like a marine already and was enjoying his first night out in the field.

This was a good sign as he intended on becoming a Royal Marine Sniper in which his world would become the field and he would have to become one with the terrain and its elements in order to survive, after all the sniper is not only the most feared man on a battle field but also the most wanted by the enemy, to be captured by the enemy would mean torture and a terrible death as he is a specialist in gathering intelligence information on the enemy and does so without writing the information down on paper. If a sniper was to be captured they would almost be expected to commit suicide rather than face the wrath of the enemy in some third world country.

John slept well in his bivi that night, the cold didn't bother him as it did some of the others, soft Southerners he thought to himself when he heard the complaints. It was obvious that for some of these young men they were not cut out to be marines and would soon be put to the test in true marine fashion. The recruits were told to be ready for inspection by 0600 the following morning, all of their kit laid out as shown the night before and everyone had to be the same, kit laid out, clean shaven, boots polished but not bulled to a shine when they were in the field and stood to attention for the inspection by the Troop Sgt. Sgt Mallaney was a thin rugged looking man, his face was dark from the sun and weather beaten; it showed that of a man who'd had a tough life with a few scars on his face that everyone assumed was from war, he too had served 22 years in his beloved Corps and he had a good reputation for turning out top quality marines and that wasn't about to change.

He walked silently amongst the three rows of men and their kits lay out across the damp ground on Woodbury Common, he stopped at one of the sets of equipment and picked up the black plastic mug that fit on top of the water bottle, "what the fuck is that shit!" he screamed at the boys face, "answer me."

"I don't know Sgt" came the feeble reply of the young recruit, he was a Scottish lad who hadn't said much since joining the previous week, maybe he was shy, maybe he was scared, maybe he was just plain out of his depth.

"There's fucking grass and mud in your fucking mug you dirty little bastard," the Sgt bellowed at him again as he began to kick the boys kit across the common.

It went everywhere, his sleeping bag was thrown into a gorse bush and his mess tins were thrown a good 50 yards away into the field as he demolished the young Scottish boy's kit. "I will fucking teach you to turn up for inspection with dirty gear, and that goes for every man jack of ya. You can all fucking stand by!" His words terrified the whole troop, why would he punish us they thought just coz of that knob head, but that was life in the forces, if one person fucked up then everyone got punished to try make the weaker recruits work harder or face the wrath of their fellow recruits.

The Sgt continued to inspect the equipment and all four Cpl's joined in tossing peoples kit into the many gorse bushes that surrounded the area and then it happened, the Sgt's voice shattered the silence of Woodbury Common as he found an electric shaver in one of the kit bags, hidden away deliberately in an attempt to outwit the instructors at their own game, big mistake.

"WHAT THE FUCK IS THIS!" he screamed, holding the electric shaver in his right hand, his face one inch from the young man's. John quickly sneaked a glance to his left to see who it was; "shit" it was Mike Callahan. Mike had learned a few tricks in his 8 weeks at Lympstone last time but hadn't vouched on his new instructors catching him out so soon and boy were they going to pay for it.

The next hour was spent crawling in the gorse bushes, needles stabbing at their legs and bodies, ran up and down hill after hill, fireman's carries up the hills and sprints back down, press ups being held in the half way down position for minutes at a time until no man could hold his own body weight, more carrying techniques and then they ran to a small stream and had all of their kit thrown into the water and then they had to climb in after it on hands and knees.

Freezing cold, soaked to the skin the men stood to attention on the side of the road where the bus awaited them; their wet kit had been shoved back into the small pack and their 58 pattern webbing, they stood there shivering for what seemed like an eternity.

The Sgt was not a happy man, "right men, I think you all know what happens if you try to outsmart us. I will not fucking tolerated anyone taking the piss out of me, this is my troop and you will have an electric shaver when I fucking tell you, you can. Is that clear?"

"Yes Sgt," came the unified shout of the troop. No-one dared do anything other than stand and listen to the Sgt for fear of making him any angrier.

"You can throw your small packs into the vehicle and keep your webbing on. You're running back to camp, it's a 4 mile speed march and you will make it in 40 minutes and not one second longer, fail this and I'll send you back to your mummy with my size 9 boot stuck up your arse."

They got their kit onto the floor of the bus and stood back on the road in three ranks awaiting their orders, the Scottish kid couldn't take anymore, he walked up to the Sgt much to the horror of the other recruits and said out loud, "Sgt I want to quit, I can't do this, I'm just not good enough to be a marine."

The Sgt didn't batter an eye lid as he turned to look at the recruit, "Fine, get on the bus and when you get back to camp get a shower and changed into your civi's and wait outside my office. Now fuck off."

He turned and looked at the rest of the troop before speaking again, this time he was calm but still scary, "anyone else want to fuckoff home to your mummy before the bus leaves?" In case you hadn't realised yet, I didn't fucking invite you to join the Royal Marines, you asked me if you could join my Corps and I won't pass any wanker to go stand on the battle ground if you're not up to the standard. 30 seconds till the bus leaves so make your fucking minds up."

You could tell there were several recruits contemplated wrapping that day but only one other stepped forward; he was one of the older guys in the troop and he was one of Johns neighbours in the induction block. His name was Alan Sanders and as the induction block was laid out in alphabetical order he was in the next bed to John. He was a big guy, very strong but quiet, he had a wife back home and a young son who he was already missing, Alan was 29 years old which made him the oldest recruit in 501 Troop but it was still a shock to everyone when he just walked towards the bus and climbed into the warmth alongside the Scottish guy.

Cpl Goode took charge of the Troop without warning, "Troop, left turn. Forward march, left, right, left, right, left, right, left.............." They marched for around 100 yards before breaking into double time and the Cpl introduced the troop to a marching song, "who's that man with the big red nose," to which the recruits responded, "hoo harr hoo hoo harr."

"The more he wanks the bigger it grows"

"Hoo, harr, hoo, hoo, harr" and so the song went.

It took their minds off the aches and pains for a short while, the pace picked up towards the end as the Cpl notified the troop that they had three minutes to make it into the camp gates and be stood in three ranks on the other side of the road. The men of 501 Troop ran for their lives up and over the footbridge to CTCRM and in through the main gates and fell in on the other side within the allotted three minutes. It was amazing what could be achieved when you knew the consequences of failure.

At the end of week two the recruits faced their assessment and this time it was on the parade ground, basic drill must be passed prior to any recruit going onto phase one of basic training. The remaining 50 recruits passed the drill test and got to remove the orange tabs from their epaulettes denoting induction recruits and they spent the Friday afternoon moving from the induction block to their new accommodation blocks on the other side of camp. They were like a block of 1970's flats, four stories and housed 2 troops at a time with 6 men to a room and two rooms making up a section.

Before leaving the induction block Lt Wray briefed the troops, "well done gents on passing the induction phase and making it so far. That's the easy bit done and now the real training begins, so without further a due I will call out the names of each Section Commanders name and section number. As you have already been told which section you now belong to once we're finished here you will go direct to your new block and await an intro from your new section commander. 1 section Cpl

Wright, 2 section Cpl Shaw, 3 section Cpl Goode and last but not least 4 section with Cpl Dunn, Dismissed."

The recruits went off to their new accommodation blocks and stood on the landing area awaiting their Cpl's arrival, ground floor was sections 1 and 2 and the first floor was sections 3 and 4, they all waited patiently. Cpl's Wright and Shaw were the first to arrive and they each called their sections into one room and started chatting quite pleasantly with them about how they did things and what they expected of their sections. It was about 10 minute later when Cpl's Goode and Dunn arrived; they did the same as the others, called their sections into one room. Cpl Goode wasn't exactly the warmest of characters but the 12 men of 3 section knew that they were about to be trained by one of if not the best section commanders in the Corps.

"Right lads I don't fuck about I am firm but fair. You may not like me to start with but you will learn how to be a Royal Marine Commando of the highest standard, anyone who can't give me 100% can fuckoff right now. I'm not bothered about what the Corps wants regarding its numbers of expected pass marks in each section, I will fail every fucking one of you if you don't meet my standards. If you have a real problem you can come and speak to me but I'm not into having Jackanorie so don't come for a fucking moan about how hard your finding it, this is the Royal Marines not fucking summer camp. Good luck lads, now go get some scran and then get your kit squared away ready for Monday. Go to town tomorrow on your first leave and don't make a knob of your selves. See you at Church on Sunday, any questions?" there was no response from the section.

"Good, crack on," he dismissed his section and headed off to his car to leave for the weekend, the recruits did as they were told and went for scran before preparing as much of their kit as they possibly could for the following week, week 3 of basic training was where the real training began.

The whole troop went into town on the Saturday morning after breakfast; they had things to buy for their next exercise, secateurs to help cut the foliage down and help create real camouflage, lots of paracord and a couple of bungees along with some other bits and pieces. The young men started drinking at around 1300 hrs and for some this was the release they had been waiting for over the last two weeks, they continued throughout the night without giving much thought of going back to camp.

John wasn't much of a drinker and at the age of 16 he had to be careful that he wasn't caught for underage drinking as this wasn't just a civilian offence but a military one which would be punished should he get caught. The majority went to what the recruits called the Nods Head, 'nod' was the nickname given to Royal Marine recruits in basic training as they were always falling asleep no matter where they were, no-one asked John for any identification and he drank four pints of larger before calling it a day and agreeing with a couple of the other guys to go back to camp early so they weren't too hung over for church the next day. Not that they were a religious bunch but the first couple of weeks in training they were made to go to church to see the Padre and hear him talk about why it was okay for the marines to kill the enemy, an interesting combination John thought, religion and the marines.

He arrived back at camp at around 2100 hrs with Mike and a couple of other guys from 1 section, they went to the main bar on camp and had a couple of drinks there to pass some time and then got back to the barracks around 2300 hrs and went to bed.

The bedroom door came crashing in and John leapt out of bed thinking he must have slept in for inspection on Monday morning; he looked at his alarm clock and saw 0300 hrs on the face of the digital clock, "what the fuck is going on?" he shouted to the drunken recruits.

"Mills is fucking pished," slurred John's roommate. His name was Keith Fentiman and he came from a small village in North Yorkshire, he was 19 years old, a fit young lad who was oozing confidence about passing basic training and going onto bigger and better things in the future. Mills however was from 2 section and if word got out that one of Cpl Shaw's lads had been causing trouble there would be hell to pay, some of the guys in the troop had Mills under a cold shower trying to get him to snap out of his drunken stupor without much luck. In the end they stripped him off and got him into bed to sleep it off and as they did this they told John the story of the night.

The majority of the troop was in a night club in Exeter when Mills started getting a little rowdy and drawing the attention of the door staff. They threw Mills out and asked a couple of others to leave quietly, which they did but when they got onto the train a man claiming to be a Cpl in the marines told Mills to calm down and behave himself, the next thing they knew Mills was on top of the guy punching him in the face several times and the guys had to drag him off. They also added that they weren't convinced he was a Cpl as he didn't fight back and stayed on the train after they had gotten off. John was mortified by the story and as he was one of the few sober people in the troop that night he started having thoughts about what punishment they would all receive because of Mills antics. John did not sleep well that night and was dreading Church the next morning.

Thankfully nothing ever did come of Mills antics on their first weekend ashore, but the young recruits did learn a valuable lesson about staying in control on a night out after seeing the state Mills had been in and what the others had done in an attempt to sober him up, that cold shower was enough to put anyone off.

Week 10 was a point all of the recruits had been looking forward to, two more exercises under their belts, Exercise Gruesome Twosome at week 4 and Exercise Hunters Moon at week 8 both of which were very tough and kept pushing the recruits to the maximum physical and mental limits. Twosome was the exercise all recruits talked about throughout training, it wasn't nicknamed gruesome for nothing and boy did it live up to its name, it all started on the first night when the recruits bivied up, they had been asleep for an hour when it happened, the thunder flashes went off, CRASH BANG, and the whole camp lit up like a fire work display, the recruits jumped up and grabbed their kit and rammed it into their packs, people were running everywhere and the poor bastards on guard duty were still trying to hold the perimeter while their kit sat back in the camp with no-one bothering to get it together for them.

The Cpl's were screaming at the recruits but they could hardly hear a word for all the commotion, "move your fucking arses, you're under enemy fire."

John was in a state of total panic as he fumbled to get his kit into the small pack, he hooked the two clips to the front of the webbing and threw the pack over his head, he didn't try to attach the bottom clips, he just put his helmet on and started running towards the rendezvous (RV) point 400 yards away.

As he ran at break neck speed across the moor, through the gorse bushes and thorns he noticed a couple of guys fumbling around trying to gather their equipment, it was Hawkins and Smith, the two guys who had been on guard duty and they were flapping big style. John ran over to them and started to help Hawkins pack his gear, Cpl Dunn saw this and ran towards them, "get a fucking move on!" he screamed at them. Smith just jumped up in a panic and started running without half of his kit but John stayed calm and carried on helping Hawkins.

"Oi you fucking idiot," screamed Cpl Dunn at Smith, "get your arse back there and get your kit together."

The Cpl couldn't believe that Smith was actually going to abandon his kit. John and Hawkins had now got his kit together and started heading to the RV, they left Smith behind with the Cpl to deal with his own stuff, the Cpl was giving him a hard time over it and they didn't plan on hanging around any longer. The next three days was spent being constantly bumped, every time they settled down to get scran the thunder flashes would come flying in and BOOM off they went again and it was panic stations again with everyone running around like headless chickens, the instructors were obviously enjoying themselves and when they weren't being bumped they were being 'beasted' a term used for the unofficial exercise programme that all soldiers had to endure. It was said that it wasn't the basic training that got soldiers ultra fit but the beastings they received. There was a lot of controversy surrounding this method of training which was being discussed at the highest levels, even politicians had got involved after some Army instructors took it a step too far resulting in a couple of suicides of some young recruits in basic training.

The marines didn't have a high level of bullying despite its harder than average reputation, it was due to the fact that the training was hard enough without some sadistic instructor getting pleasure out of seeing a recruit crack under the pressure.

The exercise was finished off with the usual 4 mile speed march with full kit, the webbing weighed 30 lbs dry, 40 wet and their personal weapon weighed 10 lbs so needless to say these were not easy at the end of a week in the field, the weather at this time of year was not favourable and everyone felt constantly cold and wet, all part of the toughening up process and a very necessary part of the training.

Week 8's exercise Hunters Moon was a little easier in the sense that they didn't get beasted as much, unless of course they got something wrong or someone got picked up on inspection, which someone always did at this stage of training. This was a 3 day navigation exercise which did just that, they navigated across Woodbury Common day and night between the different check points and were given time scales to get to each location, so they were expected to Yomp from check point to check point in full kit.

This exercise didn't finish well at all; one of the recruits had fallen asleep while on guard duty, a big no no in a soldier's world. While the young Welsh recruit slept in his fire position Cpl Goode came across him and decided that rather than wake the whole camp up and beast everyone he would see what the recruits reaction would be when he woke up and his rifle was gone, he slipped the rifle from his hands and took it back to the

Cpl's tent and waited for the recruit to come over cap in hand and explain the situation to his instructors, but it didn't happen and the Cpl was puzzled as to what was going on. Instead at first light, some two hours later Recruit Mike Callahan turned up at the Cpl's tent and asked for permission to speak to Cpl Goode, he was physically shaking when the Cpl came to the entrance of the tent.

"Corporal, I am PO66649Y, recruit Callahan of 501 Troop requesting permission to speak."

"What the fuck do you want Callahan?" asked the Cpl not expecting to hear the next sentence.

"Cpl Goode, when I woke up about 15 minutes ago my rifle was gone. I assume one of the instructors has taken it as I didn't wake up, I'm sorry Cpl I don't know how it happened."

"Your rifle is gone?" questioned Cpl Goode

"Yes Corporal," Callahan could tell from the look on Cpl Goode's face that it wasn't an instructor that had taken the rifle and the Cpl exploded into action and ran across the camp screaming at the top of his voice, "Fall in, in three ranks at open order right fucking now!"

He was furious and Mike could tell that it wasn't him that was in the shit for this, someone else had done something terrible and was about to pay for it dearly.

"Now I want every man in this fucking troop to hold his rifle out in front at arm's length. It appears that we have a fucking thief in camp," screamed the Cpl.

The hearts of every man in the troop sank as they knew that theft was one of the worst things anyone could do. It meant that one of our own lads had taken Callahan's rifle and were in for a world of shit once they were exposed, not only from the Cpl but also from his fellow recruits, if you can't trust the man next to you, then who could you trust?

Cpl Goode and the other instructors had gathered in front of the troop and they looked mad as hell. Cpl Goode spoke out in a firm tone, "I want the thieving bastard who took Recruit Callahan's rifle to step forward and own up right fucking now."

There was silence and no-one moved, everyone started to flinch and look to their sides at each other, "stand fucking still!" shouted Sgt Mallaney who was now virtually frothing at the mouth with anger, "you've got one fucking minute to step forward or you can all fucking stand by," and he meant it, he was blue in the face and the veins stood out on his forehead. Still no-one moved and as the pain of holding out their rifles started to kick in, the recruits broke silence to try to get the culprit to go forward.

"Come on," came the cry from most of the men in the troop as the winces of pain swept across their faces. Still no-one came forward and the patience of the instructors was now being tested, as was the patience of the men in the troop.

As the minute came to an end Sgt Mallaney stepped forward, "No-one eh? Not one fucking man of you brave enough to come forward and admit that you stole Callahan's rifle. We know you fucking have it and we know who it is! We know coz Cpl Goode here took it from you while you were asleep on guard duty and we know it wasn't Recruit Callahan."

Right then the young Welsh recruit stepped forward and spoke out, "It was me Sgt," he was trembling for two reasons, one he had stolen from a fellow recruit and two he had put the other recruits through all this shit and only admitted it when the Sgt told them he knew who it was.

The Sgt exploded, shouting and screaming at the boy, "Gallagher you fucking wimp, why the fuck didn't you just come to the fucking tent and tell us what happened?"

"I was just shocked Sgt, I don't know why I did it."

Recruit Gallagher was not only in the shit with the instructors but the lads in the troop would not let this go unchallenged either and Gallagher knew it.

"So you fucking went off and stole your oppo's rifle, you cunt!" The Sgt was one inch from his face and screaming at him, the troop actually started to feel sorry for him but that wouldn't last long when the punishment was dished out to everyone. "I will fucking teach you to steal from your oppo's and waste my fucking time. I can't fucking believe you actually went searching for and took someone else's rifle. What have you got to say about that?"

"Nothing Sergeant," Gallagher responded feebly.

"Right lads, get your fucking kit together and get fell in on the road in three ranks facing up the hill. You can fucking stand by!" The Sgt and Cpl's went off to get ready, "3 minutes," shouted Cpl Goode as they walked away.

The whole troop ran off and got their kit ready, Gallagher walked over to Callahan and showed him his rifle was safe before handing it over. Mike didn't speak to him, he just nodded to acknowledge it was safe and took it from him and left Gallagher to go see the Cpl to collect his rifle. As they got close to the tent everyone heard the Cpl shouting at him, "What the fuck do you want ya little bastard? Fuckoff and get your shit together, you'll get your fucking rifle when I see fit to give it back to you, now fuckoff before I wrap it round your fucking big ears!"

Gallagher ran off to get his kit ready and was now in tears, no-one cared that he was upset, everyone was angry at what he'd done. The troop fell in on the road as they were told to and were waiting for the instructors when Cpl Goode and Cpl Shaw appeared.

"As a result of fuck wit Gallagher's unacceptable behaviour the entire troop will be yomping back to camp; there will be no back up vehicle, no dropping out and no fucking stopping until we get back to camp. Is that understood?" Said Cpl Shaw.

"Yes Corporal," came the united response and off they went, the forced march was harder and faster than they had been pushed before in the previous 8 weeks. Cpl Goode took the front of the troop, Cpl Shaw at the rear and they were taking no prisoners, the corporals constant shouts of, "close up to the man in front, get in time and keep fucking moving."

A six mile Yomp at a fast pace with full kit weighing around 60 lbs was not on the scheduled plan for the end of the exercise, and everyone made it, they were in bits by the time they got back and it wasn't going to stop there. It had taken 70 minutes to get back to camp which was good going considering the weight they were carrying. They were given one hour to clean their kit and get it all squared away before scran, it was the last scran of the day on a Sunday, breakfast and lunch and that was it so if you missed it you'd be going hungry until Dutchies opened later that evening. They had just got their kit away when Cpl Goode turned up at the block, "landing," he shouted and everyone had to drop what they were doing and get to the landing and stair well.

"Right lads, a piss easy exercise ruined by that fucking tool," he said pointing to Gallagher, "I wish I could say that was the end of it but it isn't, so get your PT kit on and meet me at the tank on the bottom field in 3 minutes. GO!"

The men of 501 troop missed lunch that day and were put through another 2 hours of phys on the bottom field as other recruits walked by on their way to and from the train station heading for town, they had a smile on their faces as they walked on by.

Cpl Goode didn't mind humiliating his troops but he wouldn't have another recruit have a dig at them when they were suffering as one recruit from a senior troop shouted out, "Enjoy your phys boys, don't get too dirty now will ya," as he walked by.

"Who the fuck are you talking to?" shouted Cpl Goode, "get your arse over here."

The recruit walked over calmly as if he was above the Cpl's authority, "yes Cpl."

"Who the fuck are you sloping over here like you couldn't give a fuck? I'll rip your bollocks off sunshine and set up a private session of our own, how do ya like that fuck wit?"

The recruit went red in the face as he was put back in his place; Cpl Goode took the recruits name and the name of his section commander. Cpl Goode didn't take to people being cocky with him, especially a recruit who hadn't even earned his Green Beret yet, "cheeky twat," the Cpl said under his breath as the recruit walked away. He finished putting the men of 501 Troop through their paces and then sent them off to get cleaned up and put the whole troop on inspection at 2100 hours at the guard house. They were pissed off at just how far this punishment had gone; they were furious and couldn't wait for it to be over so they could enforce their own revenge on recruit Gallagher.

It wasn't until the Friday night of week 9 when the lads went out to town on the piss that it happened. They were standing in the Nods Head when Hawkins a huge lad from Port of Glasgow followed Gallagher to the toilets, no-one knew what was going to happen, just that Hawkins had made no secret of how pissed off he was with the extreme punishment the troop had suffered because of his stupidity. Hawkins walked into the toilet, Gallagher was at the urinals, Hawkins stood back waiting for him to finish and put himself away before he struck the lad, as Gallagher turned around he saw Hawkins and said, "what's up Hawk?"

"What's up? Are you fucking kidding me, you got us fucked the other week and your acting like you don't give a fuck."

"But I said I was sorry dude, what else can I say? It won't happen again man," said Gallagher nervously.

"You're fucking right it won't," he clenched his huge fist and hit him hard in the chest knocking Gallagher to the ground, Hawkins jumped on top of him and repeatedly thumped him in the face until he stopped moving or putting up a fight. Hawkins stood up and looked down on his victim, he checked for a pulse, he was breathing but was knocked out cold and bleeding badly. He washed his hands in the sink behind him and then turned and walked out of the toilet as if nothing had happened. As he got back into the bar a couple of the lads had noticed that Gallagher had went in before him and hadn't come out again, they walked over to Hawkins and said, "So what's happened mate?"

"What do you mean?" he said innocently with a smirk on his face.

"Come on Hawk, where the fuck is Gallagher? I know he's a knob head but what the fuck have you done?"

"Taught him a fucking lesson, Welsh bastard!" and he walked back to the table where his drink sat and continued drinking his pint of larger.

The two guys went into the toilets and found Gallagher on the floor unconscious and quickly checked him for a pulse and started to get him up when some other recruits from another troop walked into the toilets. "What the fuck happened here?" asked one of them, "did you guys do this?"

"No man, he had a fall out with another lad in the troop."

"Oh so he wasn't jumped by a civi then?"

"No mate, we'll sort it, don't worry about it."

They helped get Gallagher to his feet and brought him round with some cold water on his face. As they were getting him out of the door one of the lads from the other troop asked, "So who is this guy and why did he get a kicking?"

"Did you hear about the guy who nicked someone's rifle?"

"Fuck yeah man we did. Is this him?"

"Yeah, this is him. He got what was due but still doesn't mean we don't care about what happens to him. He must have shit himself when he woke up and the rifle was gone."

"Yeah I suppose so. You never know what you'd do in the same situ until it happens to you."

A couple of the lads from his section decided to take him back to camp early, it was around 2130 hrs when they arrived back to the guard house to sign back in and the guys on guard duty were not happy when they saw the state of Gallagher. The Provo Sgt was called to the guard house; he was military police and didn't take any shit from anyone, the second most feared man at CTCRM after the RSM.

The lads were held there until he arrived; he got there in 3 minutes flat, he didn't fuck around, he always seemed to be on edge as if he was a coiled spring ready to go at a moment's notice.

"What happened son," he asked Gallagher

"I'm not entirely sure Sgt," came the response, "I was in the Nods Head and I popped to the toilet, and as I turned around from the urinal someone hit me in the face. I couldn't really see after that and he just kept punching me in the chest and face until.......well until I was out Sgt."

"Did you see anything that might help us?" asked the Sgt not buying the story at all.

"No Sgt, sorry, I wish I had," Gallagher responded.

"I don't fucking believe you son but it's your face. You lads get him to sick bay and I'll ring them and tell them you're coming. Who's your section Cpl?"

"Cpl Dunn of 501 Troop, Sgt."

The next morning Cpl Dunn and Sgt Mallaney turned up at the block and asked to see Gallagher in the office. They were in there with him for over an hour, they knew it had to be one of their own lads but Gallagher was giving nothing away, but he worried that the whole troop might be punished again. Monday morning Lt Wray did the inspection and then called the recruits to the landing for a de-brief.

"Gentlemen it appears we have a vigilante amongst us, and let me tell you that we do not have bullies in the Corps. If anyone is to be punished we will do it, is that understood?"

"Yes sir," everyone shouted

"Now I'm going to dismiss you all now and you have 30 minutes to get ready for drill practice. If anyone would like to come see me I'll be in the office, I think you all know what I'm asking."

The troops went back to their rooms and started getting ready and even though they all knew who did it they hoped he wouldn't go forward. One of the recruits quickly rallied around all of the rooms asking for a joint decision on whether Hawkins should own up or not and the recruits all said that he shouldn't and they would be prepared to take whatever punishment was coming. As this was being discussed Hawkins already in his parade gear walked over to the troop office and knocked on the door, Cpl Goode opened it, "yeah, what do you want Hawkins?"

"Cpl I need to talk to the boss."

"Do you now, I had a feeling you might," said Cpl Goode with a raised eyebrow.

Cpl Goode stepped aside and gestured for Hawkins to come in, he stood before Lt Wray, "Sir I am P99855U Recruit Hawkins of 501 Troop requesting permission to speak."

"Okay Hawkins, stand at ease. What have you got to tell me?"

"It was me sir. I assaulted Gallagher in the toilets in the nods head."

"Really?" asked the officer

"Yes sir, I don't want the others to get into bother for my actions sir. Nobody knew I was going to hit him, I just followed him and battered him."

"Why Hawkins, What the hell were you thinking lad?"

"I was furious at what he did sir and then we got thrashed for it. It was the worst beasting we've ever had sir and I know the line about if one fucks up then we all pay but it was just too much sir."

"Really?" questioned the officer, he wasn't happy with what he was hearing as he wasn't present on the exercise and it sounded like the instructors had maybe taken things a little too far themselves and this did not please the Lieutenant at all.

"Okay Hawkins you can go to your lesson now while we discuss what action to take."

"Yes sir," he saluted and about turned and left the office and fell in outside with the rest of the troop.

Both recruits ended up standing before the RSM to be dealt with, Gallagher was charged for taking a rifle without consent and was put on 7 days reduced privileges and Hawkins was given two days of constant inspections at the guard house. That was the end of the matter as far as everyone was concerned, the troop training team had obviously got a bollocking for the severity of their punishment too as they were a little more selective over the next few days leading up to the end of week 10.

Week 10 was their first weekend leave since starting the gruelling 30 week training programme but the instructors weren't going to let them go without something to remember them by, after all this was the Royal Marines Commandos.

The recruits knew something was amiss when the Cpl's told them that they would be staying on camp for a couple of days as the recruits knew that only Cpl Dunn lived on camp full time and the others wouldn't chose to unless there was something to be done with the troop.

It all started on the Tuesday afternoon when the recruits got back from there gym class pass out parade, they were all very giddy as they had all passed the PT test which meant no more of the boring ritual PT sessions and it was time to get into the commando type physical training. The Cpl's were waiting on the landing for the recruits to return to their rooms when Cpl Shaw called out, "landing," and the troop swarmed the landing and its stair wells.

"After scran lads we're going to play a few games so make sure you get plenty of nice hot scran down ya coz it's going to be a very long night," the training team laughed as they dismissed the remaining men of 501 troop.

The recruits were given admin duties to carry out first of all followed by several different types of inspection, at 0500 hrs on the Wednesday morning the men of 3 and 4 sections were asked to swap places and all equipment with the men of 1 and 2 sections on the floor below which all had to be done in under 30 minutes and then be ready for morning inspection by the Troop Commander, Lt Wray. Inspection came and went and the day went as normal, lectures on chemical warfare, first aid lessons, weapons training and then the fun began again on the Wednesday evening which ended at around 0300 hrs with all sections swapping back to their original places followed by one final inspection before grabbing one hours sleep and then onto a day with a difference. To celebrate making it this far the instructors took the recruits to a firing range in Exmouth to have a go on several different weapons, some of which they would never get to use, there was the new SA80A1, the HK MP3, Browning 9 mm hand gun, L96A1 snipers rifle and the GPMG.

John was most interested in the L96A1 snipers rifle and although a popular recruit with the instructors he hadn't mentioned his career aspirations to his peers. Cpl Goode noticed John pick up the rifle and as he was on range duty for this rifle he took an interest in showing John how it worked and gave him a few hints and tips on handling and shooting the weapon, John only got 2 shots with the rifle but boy was he on a high afterwards. After the weapons acquaint the recruits headed back to Lympstone to pack their bags for the weekend back home. Cpl Goode was still around at the end of the day and decided to stay on camp which made everyone feel uneasy after the last couple of nights and who could blame them, it wouldn't have been the first time the instructors had played a little trick or two on them.

Cpl Goode had no plans to disrupt the recruit's night before heading home; he knew how important the annual leave was to these guys, instead he went up the first floor where his section resided and sauntered into the room. John's bed was nearest the door, "room, room shun," called out John, everyone jumped to attention.

"As you were," replied the Cpl "so how did you find today on the range?" The four remaining members of the room all responded half heartedly with mumbles of, "yeah it was good Cpl."

"So Savage, I saw you admiring the L96A1."

"Yes Cpl," responded a slightly bewildered John.

"What was it about that rifle that got you hard?"

"Well Cpl I'm interested in becoming a sniper one day if I'm good enough that is."

"It's no fucking picnic I can tell you," said the Cpl with a smile on his face.

"Well it doesn't really matter yet does it Cpl, I'm just gonna focus on basic first before I get carried away thinking about what I'm going to do later"

Cpl Goode liked his response and smiled at John before saying, "that's right, none of you have passed yet."

The Cpl left his four men finishing off their leaving routine and popped into the room next door to see the other members of his section before heading off to his barracks for the night.

The train ride home was exciting for the men of 501 Troop, John and Mike chatted about what they planned to do for the weekend, catching up with their girlfriends, parents and possibly some friends.

Not for John though, it was home to see his mother for a few minutes before rushing off to see Amy, he couldn't wait to see his girl, to hold her close, to feel her skin and to kiss those lips. He had dreamed about that first kiss for the last 10 weeks and had worked hard to fight the feelings of home sickness that so many others in his troop seemed to be suffering, he loved Amy and his mother but this was what he had wanted for a long time and he wasn't about to jeopardise that for home sickness, he knew he'd get used to being away from home and he did enjoy the company of the other guys in his section.

John arrived home just after 2030 hrs and as he opened the door his mother was already there in the passage way waiting to greet him, she threw her arms around his neck and squeezed him hard. "Look at you; you're so different, all grown up."

"It's great to see you mum and I don't want to seem ungrateful but I'm going to pop out and see Amy. I'll bring her back here though so we can have a catch up tomorrow and maybe grab some lunch."

"Lunch, get you," she laughed at his new use of words, "what happened to breakfast, dinner and tea?"

"I dunno mam I guess when you live with 50 other blokes from every corner of the country your gonna pick up some new twangs."

She laughed at how grown up he sounded, it was hard to believe how much he had changed in just 10 weeks, "so do I have to wait until tomorrow to hear about your adventure?"

"Mam, come on I haven't seen Amy either and I've missed her too, don't make me feel bad please."

"Oh alright honey, I'm just playing with you. Are you bringing Amy back here tonight? Do I need to put some ear plugs in?" she laughed.

"Mam!" snapped John going red in the face with embarrassment.

John quickly threw his bag into the bedroom and rushed down stairs and gave his mother a kiss on the cheek before dashing out the front door and running the 1 km to Amy's house. She lived at the top of quite a steep bank which had previously been a mini challenge but not now, John didn't break sweat or even breath heavily, he hopped over the gate barely touching it with one hand.

He knocked at the door and stood to the side to hide his reflection through the frosted glass, Amy came to the door and as she opened it John was hiding to the side, "Boo" he shouted scaring her out of her wits and they both burst into fits of laughter. "You git, why you told me you weren't coming back until tomorrow afternoon."

"Yeah, I lied," he said laughing and he grabbed her and kissed her hard on the lips and lifted her off her feet.

"God I've missed you," she said looking into his eyes, "and get you, all muscular."

They spent the next 30 minutes catching up with Amy's parents and her brother before packing a small bag of things and walking back to John's mother's house, as they walked hand in hand Amy kept looking at John differently and he wondered what she was thinking.

"What's up babe?" John asked

"Nothing, I've just missed you and well............." she paused thinking carefully before speaking again, "well you seem different babe."

"What do you mean?" he asked feeling a little confused at the statement

"Erm well you just seem different, I don't mean it in a bad way, I just mean.......... well you seem very grown up, mature, different," she smiled and giggled.

"Well that's a good thing isn't it? I feel different to be honest, I feel stronger, fitter, more confident and happier and I've really looked forward to this weekend after 10 weeks away from the girl I love," he smiled.

"Aw babe's that's lovely, you really have grown up haven't you. You don't normally talk so openly and I think you look different too, I mean that in a nice way. The body is looking good, but your face is a little thin, I hope you don't mind me saying that?"

"No babe, I don't care so long as you still love me."

They got back to the house and sat for an hour chatting with Rebecca before heading off to bed for the night.

The next morning Amy woke up to an empty bed, she looked around wondering if John had just nipped to the toilet but she couldn't hear any movement outside the bedroom door, she got up and went down stairs to find Rebecca in the kitchen making a full English breakfast, bacon, sausage, eggs, beans and toast along with a pot of tea.

"Where's John?" Amy asked

"Out running, he said he would be back for 9 and he'd be ready for breakfast by half past but it's already quarter past and there's still no sign of him."

Amy wasn't happy about waking up alone and it showed on her face, Rebecca stood looking at her and said, "I'm sure he didn't mean to upset you Amy. He's just doing what he's trained to do now."

"I suppose so; I just figured he'd be able to go one weekend without training considering what he's been through over the last 10 weeks."

Just then the front door opened and in walked a very sweaty John and as soon as he saw Amy's face he knew she wasn't happy. "Morning babes," he said waiting for an angry response. She didn't respond she simply walked past him and upstairs, he looked at his mother and shrugged his shoulders and smiled, "I guess that's me in the dog house," then followed her upstairs.

A few minutes later Rebecca called them back down stairs for breakfast, "come and get it."

They ate breakfast together before going for a walk down to the beach just like old times, but it wasn't like old times at all, John was different, changing from boy to man rapidly without warning and Amy saw a slightly distant young man before her. They walked hand in hand the whole time and popped into the fish and chip shop to see his friend's mother and have a spot of lunch, good old fashioned fish and chips in paper.

The day went fast and Amy couldn't get enough of John's company, she wouldn't leave his side and as soon as he stood up she'd ask, "where you going?"

"Toilet babe, is that okay?" and he laughed at how sweet she was being, "you can come hold it for me if you want," he said with a smirk on his face.

She scrunched her face up with disgust but with a cheeky smile as she knew his sense of humour, she'd missed his silly behaviour and his enthusiasm.

The day and night went too quick and it was Sunday morning before they knew it and the mood was somewhat solemn, Amy was struggling with the fact that John seemed happy to be going back to CTCRM. She was already missing him and decided to make some idle chit chat to pass the time and to prevent herself from thinking about things too much.

"So what you got on over the next few weeks babe?"

"Just a load of prep work this week, then got the survival exercise in week 12 which I'm really looking forward to and then I have week 15 to look forward to."

"Why what's happening at week 15?" She asked.

John stopped what he was doing and looked Amy in the eyes, "what do you mean what's happening in week 15? Are you having me on?"

Amy looked at him and suddenly realised that she hadn't had the conversation with him that she had meant to, she didn't want to do it over the phone and had hoped to tell him during the weekend. "I meant to tell you, I have something going on at college that week, a couple of mock exams, so I won't be able to come to your half way pass out parade babe. Sorry."

John was gutted and couldn't hide it, "how long have you known about that?" he asked sharply

"Don't be angry John, it's not my fault. I don't choose when to have a mock exam do I?"

"You didn't answer the question," John snapped.

"A few weeks, but I didn't want to discuss it over the phone; I wanted to see your face so you wouldn't be upset with me."

"So instead you waited till 5 minutes before I left for camp, good move babe."

"I'm sorry John, please let's not leave things like this, I can't bear to think of you going back to camp angry at me. I'll see you when you get home for the weekend and then it's only a couple of weeks later when you get your summer leave. Three full weeks of just you and me babe, it'll be great." Her eyes welled up with tears.

"Yeah okay babe, you're right as usual. I'm sorry I snapped at you, I was just really looking forward to you seeing the camp and watching me doing drill and I already know which demonstration I'm doing."

"Really, what you doing babe?"

"I'm doing the assault course demo in full webbing and rifle; it would have been my time to show off to you," he said laughing.

"I'll be there for the most important one babe; I'll be there for your pass out parade when you get that Green Beret and when you march onto that parade ground in your dress blues."

"Yeah I guess so," he finished packing and carried his kit downstairs and awaited his taxi to the station.

"Do you want me to come to the station with you?" asked his mother

"Don't be daft mam; I'm not letting Amy come so you've got no chance."

His taxi arrived and he gave one last kiss to Amy and then pecked his mother on the cheek, "see you in a few weeks," he said as he climbed into the taxi and headed to Sunderland train station to meet Mike. When he arrived there Mike was just saying goodbye to his partner Sharon, she seemed to be having a really tough time of it.

John called out to his friend Mike, "hi mate, how's it going?"

Mike looked at him with sad eyes; he was obviously suffering too, "hi mate, I'm good, how was the weekend?"

"Good mate, glad to be heading back," John said smiling

"Yeah me to mate, looking forward to freezing my tit's off and starving myself for a few days," Mike said laughing

They climbed aboard the Newcastle train, as it pulled away Sharon waved to her man with tears in her eyes. Mike decided to tell John what was going on, "she's pregnant mate and she's not happy about me being away all the time, she wants me to wrap it all in and come back home."

"Fucking hell mate, I can't believe it. How far on is she? Do you want it? Are you thinking about wrapping?"

"Too many fucking questions man," he said laughing at John's bewildered expression

"Sorry mate, I mean congratulations dude. But you're not really thinking about wrapping are you?"

"No mate, that's what she's crying about. I told her I wasn't willing to give up my dreams this time and what kind of dad would I be if my kid knew that I gave up at the first hurdle? How do you think that kid would feel if I told them that I gave up my dreams coz they came along?"

"No mate, your right. He'll think you're the dog's bollocks if his first picture with his dad wearing a Green Beret."

"A he, eh? So you already know it's gonna be a boy do ya Jonny?"

"Yeah well it has to be doesn't it mate," he said laughing

The banter had relaxed Mike and he appreciated that, he enjoyed spending time with John; they had a good connection and had become good friends.

They chatted the whole way back to Lympstone about the weekend and about the coming weeks in training, Mike had only made it to week 8 the last time, even though he had told the guys on the PRC he'd left because of the amount of admin they had to do in training, he trusted John enough to tell him the real reason for leaving the Corps at week 8 last time around. He had failed Exercise Hunters Moon; a navigation exercise (navex) with time constraints and check points along the way culminating in a night navigation test which if failed meant an immediate back troop scenario for the failed recruits. Mike had failed the night navex and knew he would be back trooped as soon as they return to camp, so with this hanging over his head he decided to wrap before the exercise was over.

Mike was doing well in training and had passed all the exercises without any problem, he was a fit guy with a strong will, he had passed on his 8 weeks of previous experience to John and some of the other younger guys in the troop. They were glad to be in the same section and the fact that Cpl Goode had such a strong reputation they knew they were going to be the best when they eventually passed out of commando training.

Weeks 11 was a fairly dull week in comparison to the previous weeks and the troops were getting apprehensive about the survival exercise, Exercise Running man lasted 4 days and the weather was still quite chilly, the wind was strong and the rain was coming in from all angles. The Troop was split into their sections and were scattered across Dartmoor to learn how to fend for themselves, they were shown how to kill and skin a rabbit and a chicken. This exercise was not for the faint hearted or a vegetarian as the instructors seemed to take great pleasure in watching the recruits squirm as they came face to face with death, even if it was just a little animal.

John was given a chicken which he swung by its feet, the technique was to swing its a few times before laying its head down on the rock, then he placed a stick across its neck and pressed it down firmly before pulling at it hard by its feet ripping off the chickens head. He held on tight as they had seen the demonstration of the chicken running around without it's head on.

He plucked the feathers out of the body before plunging the knife into the end of the chicken and opening it up, pulling at the innards until the inside was clean, he cooked it over an open fire before ripping the chicken up and placing it in the pot with the root vegetables, the four man section enjoyed their chicken stew. It tasted like the best meal they had ever eaten. It was only day three of the four day exercise, the recruits were looking gaunt and feeling weary after the reduced calories. They normally functioned on around 3 – 4000 calories per day during basic training and now they had barely had 1500 calories in the last four days, they were tired and very much looking forward to returning to camp and feeding their faces until they could eat no more.

The next three weeks were filled with more drill than ever before and the final tests of phase one, the toughest being Exercise Baptist Run in week 13 where all of the infantry skills they had learnt so far were put to the test finishing with the 6 mile speed march in full kit which had to be completed in under 60 minutes to get a pass.

They did it, all 36 recruits of 501 Troop of which only 27 originals remained; they marched back into camp knowing this was the end of phase 1 of basic training and after which they no longer had to wear their blue beret's, after this they could wear the cap comfort worn by the old commandos of world war two. This showed everyone on camp that they were phase 2 recruits now and were about to enter commando training, advanced infantry skills, stalking the enemy, commando fitness, assault course, Tarzan course, advanced shooting skills to name but a few.

Week 15 was purely drill on the parade square and the families arrived on the Friday morning and John's mother was looking forward to seeing her son in his uniform marching to the sound of the band. When she arrived at Lympstone she was standing in the waiting area next to the main lecture hall.

A tall dark skinned lady and a pretty young girl were stood to the side of the entrance looking around as if they'd lost someone, the younger girl looked at Rebecca and walked towards her, "hi, sorry to be forward but are you Mrs Savage?"

"Yes I'm Miss Savage," she responded correcting her marital status.

"I'm Sharon, Mike Callahan's girlfriend and that is his mam, Maria. Do you want to sit with us?"

"Yeah that would be great; you never know who to speak to you when you come somewhere like this. Not that I'd know as I've never been anywhere like this before," she laughed nervously.

Sharon introduced the mothers and Rebecca noticed there was no mention of Mike's father and so didn't mention it or ask where he was, she knew how she hated answering questions about John's father and simply avoided it by saying quite sharply that he was dead, that always put an end to any questions.

All of the visitors were called into the lecture hall and sat down to await a briefing by Lt Wray. As he spoke about the recruits who were doing exceptionally well the parents glowed with pride. Lt Wray stood at the front of the hall and told them what they would be witnessing, starting with Cpl Wright's 1 section performing drill, Cpl Shaw's 2 section demonstrating the BST and the seal launch (a canoe being launched from the 10 foot diving board into the pool), very impressive, Cpl Goode's 3 section demonstrating bottom field including rope climbs in full kit and the assault course one item at a time before completing the whole course in under 5 minutes and finally Cpl Dunn's 4 section doing the gym demo. After which they would have a buffet lunch and speak to the instructors before regrouping back in the hall for the presentation and the pass out ceremony for the half way mark for 501 Troop.

It was a glorious day and the sun shone as the visitors walked onto the bottom field, the ground was dry for a change which was a relief to the ladies in their high heels and smart clothing being worn by all. Rebecca's face lit up as she saw her son standing there with his mates in full fighting order looking very manly, he looked like a Royal Marine Commando and she was so proud of him. Cpl Goode called his men to their positions and John jogged to the bottom of the ropes and awaited his command.

"As you can see ladies and gentlemen, we have recruit Savage on the ropes for starters, he is carrying full fighting order weighing 30 lbs plus his rifle, the new SA80 weighing a further 10 lbs, bearing in mind that young Savage only weighs 8 stone himself," he laughed with the crowd, "and his kits weighs 3 stone so needless to say he'll be lucky if he makes it to the top of the rope," everyone joined him in his laughter at Johns expense. John didn't mind he was used to the Corps banter now and he quite enjoyed the attention.

"Okay all joking aside folks Recruit Savage is going to demonstrate the 30 foot rope climb and decent under control before running the high obstacle course," he gave his orders, "Stand by, climb when ready."

John climbed the rope with great speed and ability; he made it look so easy even with full kit on his back, once at the top he put his hand in the loop at the top of the rope and called, "Savage Corporal."

"Under control, come down."

John came down; he made it look graceful and then went straight on to the bottom of the climbing bars which would lead him onto the high obstacle course.

"In your own time, go when ready," called the Cpl looking proud of his recruit

John shot off like a bat out of hell up the apparatus and across the high obstacle course and down the other side and then ran to the start of the assault course with his fellow recruits. He was to wait at the start line for the other recruits, Hawkins, Callahan and Smith to demonstrate how each obstacle should be completed and when they got to the end and Cpl Goode decided to throw them into the tank much to the amusement of the visitors.

Cpl Goode walked back to the start and asked the visitors to feel free to wander across the whole course so they could enjoy the spectacle. Rebecca stood near the monkey bars over the water in the hope of watching her son float over the course, and float he did. He shot off and was ahead of the other three recruits within seconds; he wasted no time on any of the apparatus and before they knew it he was sprinting uphill towards the tunnels; his mother had cut across the field to see him emerge out of the tunnels. He was breathing hard when he came out and powered up the wall and over the top and down the other side before running through the visitors and falling back in at the area next to the rope climbs to await the instructions of Cpl Goode. John's mother was beaming with pride and Sharon and Maria were ecstatic at seeing Mike Callahan going round the course and now standing by his best friend.

When they re-joined the group back in the hall the recruits were standing at ease in their drill uniform, they had only just had their Lovats and Blues uniform measure in week 14 so they wouldn't be ready yet. They were sat listening intently to Lt Wray as he described some of the exercise's the recruits had undertaken over the past 15 weeks and how well certain recruits had done.

"I would like you to join me in congratulating the following recruits for outstanding performance to date for their achievements. Recruit Hawkins for most improved recruit in phase 1, Recruit Savage for the PT prize for fittest recruit in phase 1, Recruit Steven's for best recruit in Drill and finally Recruit Halliday for best overall recruit in phase 1 training."

The crown applauded and cheered their sons, brothers, partners and fellow recruits who shared their experiences with their own families and the recruits stood proud at their achievements. Lt Wray called 501 troop to attention and then dismissed the recruits who would now be known as Phase 2 recruits and for those who made it would in 10 weeks time begin commando training.

They headed home for a long weekend with their loved ones, John enjoyed the eight hour train ride with his mother, and it gave them a chance to catch up properly just like they used to do. Mike's mother had driven down so they returned via the motorways and Mike enjoyed catching up with his mother and girlfriend as they discussed the baby, Sharon was very proud of her man.

"Mike I know I gave you a hard time last time you were home about coming out and going back to plumbing but after seeing you in your uniform today and looking as proud as you do I think you made the right decision to stay put. I'm glad you didn't give up your dreams for me."

"Thanks babe that means a lot. We're gonna be just fine babe, you'll see."

John had a great weekend with Amy and even managed to catch up with a couple of school friends, it made him realise just how much he had grown up and just how different he was from them. He was a soldier and they were civi's and they just didn't do the same things as each other or have the same interests and he knew that he wouldn't be spending much time with them in the future.

He lay in his bed on the last night of his leave and thought about what he had been through over the previous 15 weeks and realised that he was a very different person than the 16 year old boy who walked through those gates, he was a man now, a man who was sure he would make it through the 30 weeks of training and receive the coveted Green Beret at the end of it, he smiled as his heart rate picked up at the thought of becoming a fully fledged Royal Marine Commando. He was half way there and nothing was going to stop him now, he was sure of that.

The next 3 weeks were full on at CTCRM with another two field exercises and the fact that he had now entered the 'Operations of War Module' of training, this module ran from weeks 15-22 and exposed the recruits to many days on the range honing their weapons handling skills and practicing section attacks in the field, then came live firing, an all together different experience that got the heart pumping full of adrenaline.

At the end of week 18 the recruits had their 3 weeks summer leave, a couple of recruits were asked if they would be willing to come back a week early and do guard duty and when no-one volunteered a couple of local recruits were volunteered by their Section Cpl, they were gutted but they did get an extra weeks pay that month for their trouble so it wasn't all bad. The money wasn't a major issue for the recruits as despite their low wage they didn't really have anything to spend it on apart from going out on the piss every weekend and buying the odd bit of clothing.

Week 23 arrived and so began commando training, the last 8 weeks would be the toughest of the recruit's lives, a period none of them would ever forget. The majority of the first few weeks were spent in the field on exercise, as this would be the main role of a marine it was a vital part of the training and as the exercises got harder and the pressure to perform increased more recruits from the original 501 Troop fell by the way side, some through injury, some failed to make the grade and some just tried to quit. It wasn't easy to get out at this stage of training after all the government had spent over £80,000 training each recruit in CTCRM so there was only two voluntary opt out times for recruits and they were weeks 4 and 8 after which point it was pass or fail time and the choice was taken out of their hands, within reason.

In week 25 at the end of a horrendously tough exercise the recruits were given the first taste of commando training with the 12 mile load carry; this was 12 hilly miles mainly on road around Exmoor carrying approximately 85 lbs of kit on their backs. It was tough going and the heat didn't help things either, two recruits who had just joined the troop the previous week from 499 Troop collapsed with heat exhaustion and Callahan was also struggling as he had twisted his knee while on exercise.

There was no official time limit on this test but the pressure was on if they didn't make it to each check point within a reasonable time. Reasonable time, no-one ever did explain what reasonable meant in the mind of the commando instructors. By this stage of training there were just 21 of the original recruits from 501 Troop and another failed to finish the 12 miler so his dreams of passing first time was over, Smith was devastated, he was a fit lad from Liverpool who had a great sense of humour, a typical Scouse who always had something to say, when things were shit as they often were in basic training he could always make you laugh.

He wasn't laughing today as he reached the top of a long undulating hill at mile 8 when his ankle gave way under the weight of his kit, he buckled and fell to the ground gasping for air screaming with pain, it was purely coincidental that a medic in a land rover was driving past and stopped to help Scouse to his feet but it was no good, the medic reckoned it was tendon damage and no amount of pain killers would have got him through the next four miles, especially as the medic knew this route well and that three of them were as bad as the previous hill. He was nice enough not to mention that to the recruits still struggling on as he got Scouse into the back of the vehicle. Scouse was in tears as they drove away, he had made it to week 25 unscathed and now this.

If he had been asked if he wanted to leave at that moment I think he would have taken it, he was so distraught about not completing training with his original troop but he also knew that the guys from other troops who had joined 501 were never really treated the same as an original. John made it through the 12 miler with his buddy Mike by his side, Mike had tears in his eyes and was loaded up with pain killers to get him to the end but he made it. John made sure his mate wasn't left behind and he was there to keep him motivated no matter how much pain John was in himself, he wouldn't show it.

The instructors had been keeping an eye on John throughout his training and he had been promoted to Section Leader in week 16, a title most lost within a couple of weeks as they failed to make the grade of leader of their recruit section but not John, his section were more than happy to let John take this role on and he had the respect of the guys in his section, along with the respect of Cpl Goode although he rarely showed it.

Just before the troop set out for their 'Final Ex' on the Monday of week 26 they were informed that Scouse had to have surgery and would be out of training and in hospital for at least 8 weeks before being allowed to rejoin training and he would be sent back to week 24 and have to go through the 12 miler all over again. Scouse was gutted but at least the marines weren't giving up on him, they knew he was a good lad who would one day make an excellent marine. They operated successfully and he did make a full recovery and go on to pass out of basic training albeit some 20 weeks after his original troop passed out. John would see him again in the future, he was sure of that and they had both discussed which commando unit they wanted to go to and they had both put down 42 Commando as their first choice.

The final ex was horrendous, the recruits were pushed to their absolute limits, attack after attack, and defence after defence, shoot and scoot, sprinting from building to building, not a moment to rest. Seven days, six nights the exercise lasted and at the end of it they were exhausted and relieved it was over. It would be there last exercise in the 30 weeks of training and boy were they glad it was over, once again there was a load carry, only 8 miles this time over Dartmoor, and it was tougher than the full 12 miler the week before. Mike struggled again and was now worried that he might not be fit enough to pass the commando tests in the next 2 weeks.

Week 27 was trial time and they got a chance to get the Endurance Course out of the way in advance of the official commando tests, Cpl Goode stood at the start of the course on Woodbury Common and spoke to the recruits, "73 minutes is plenty of time to wander round this course and get back to the range. The Endurance course followed by a 4 mile speed march and then 10 rounds on the 25 metre range. It's a piece of piss!"

John wasn't with Mike on this test, he was put with Hastings another back trooped recruit form 500 Troop who had failed three of the commando tests, endurance being one of them, Tarzan assault and the 30 miler, so needless to say John wasn't very happy about being stuck with someone who might slow him down, Fentiman on the other hand was a good lad, fit as a fiddle so he hoped they could drag Hastings around if need be.

"Go!" screamed Sgt Mallaney and the endurance course had began at a very fast pace, John and the two guys were the first to set off so they were in the best position in the troop. If you went after this you ran the risk of catching up the group in front and getting shit kicked in your face inside the tunnels and nobody wanted to be behind someone else in a tunnel half filled with water struggling to catch their breath as the water ebbed over their faces.

They were going great guns by the time they hit the submerged tunnel and John knew they were making good time and started to wonder why Hastings had failed three of the eight commando tests in succession and on top of this he had failed the endurance course three times in two weeks. Hastings had been less than a minute out on all three occasions and the 30 milers was just bad luck as he was struck down with a tummy bug and ended up dangerously dehydrated after shitting no less than 10 times on the way round, he was pulled out at the 20 mile marker and had a drip shoved in his arm. Prior to this Hastings had gone through training without any problems so it was as much a surprise to him as it was to instructors that he suddenly started to struggle.

The three front runners, Savage, Hastings and Fentiman came charging out of the bushes and onto the road where they would start the 4 mile speed march back to camp, these guys weren't in the mood to march anywhere, they were hell bent on running the remainder of the course. Hastings didn't falter this time, he put in a sterling performance along with two of the fittest guys in 501 Troop.

They charged over the finish line onto the 25 metre range well within time, they had split up slightly in the last few hundred yards and Savage came in 65 minutes, Fentiman came in at 65 minutes 32 seconds and Hastings came 67 minutes. He was over the moon and by the time he landed on the range Savage had already cleaned his rifle and was in his firing position about to take his 10 shots, Fentiman was cleaning his rifle, "fire when ready," came the command from Cpl Shaw who was manning the range that afternoon.

The crack and thud of round after round rang out without much of a pause, thud, thud, thud they went, Savage stood up and waited for permission to advance to his target and check his score, the recruits must hit at least

7 out of 10 shots within the scoring area of the target. Savage got 10 out of 10, as did Fentiman and Hastings got 9 out of 10 so it was a pass for all three men and they didn't have to re-take the test the following week which meant one less thing to add to the pressure of test week.

The others came in thick and fast, there was only one fail on the endurance course which was an excellent result and the instructors were very happy with everyone's performance. The only fail was a shock to some but not to others as he had been struggling, Mike Callahan himself said he wasn't surprised when he failed by a staggering 3 minutes and only hit the minimum 7 out of 10 on the range. He was deflated and struggling with his injured ankle and was now getting stressed about the tests which wasn't helping him, Mike got quite upset when he was sent off to the hospital on camp again to get his ankle checked out. As soon as the troop were stood down for the day John asked if it was okay to go see his friend, Cpl Goode said it was fine and that he would go with him. Cpl Goode was also getting worried about Mike's ability to pass the tests this time round and he discussed it with Savage while they walked to the hospital.

"How do you think he's holding out Savage?" asked the Cpl

"He'll be gutted Cpl but he won't want to quit and I don't think it will have helped the fact that the other two guys left him on the run. I think that was a bit shit to be honest Cpl."

"Yeah I know what you mean but they only just made it inside the time, so I guess you can't blame them for wanting to pass first time. Would you have given up your time for your oppo?"

"Yes Cpl, I would have," he said without even hesitating and the Cpl believed him, he knew that Savage wasn't the kind of guy to leave a fallen comrade behind and he had proven to be an excellent section leader and was now quite rightly promoted to 'diamond' which was a senior recruit within the troop. Only three recruits in every troop could become a 'diamond' and those recruits would go before the King's Squad board and be assessed to see if they would receive one of the two prizes available. The Commando medal was awarded the recruit who had demonstrated the commando spirit which included Courage, Determination, Unselfishness and Cheerfulness in the face of adversity and then the most prestigious award was the King's Badge, a badge which was first given to the best recruit in training by King George 5th in 1918 and this tradition had been continued in the Royal Marines ever since.

"So how do you think he'd take it if he was back trooped?" asked the Cpl

"Not good Cpl, I know how much he wants it but I think it would really test his resolve if he was back trooped. Do you think it'll happen?"

"It's out of our hands, it's up to the medic's now. Let's hope not, it would be shame to lose him in week 27, I guess we'll see."

"Fingers crossed he'll be okay then Cpl."

The two men walked into the hospital and Cpl Goode went over to speak to the Medical Officer (MO) before going in to see Mike, John went on ahead to see his friend.

"Hey soft lad, how the fuck are ya?" asked John in a jovial voice in the hope of cheering his friend up.

"Hey skinny fella, good to see ya. I wasn't expecting to see anyone tonight." Mike said smiling at the sight of John

"I thought you'd be missing me ya big gay fucker! So what they said mate? How you feeling?"

"Not too bad Jonny boy, they've given me some more drugs to keep the swelling down but it looks like it's just me for the Endurance next week doesn't it?"

"Yeah I couldn't believe that everyone made it round to be honest. Fucking out of order for those two knob heads leaving you on your own though. I wasn't fucking happy when I heard they ditched you mate," said John passionately.

"No mate, I can't blame them. It was the difference between a pass or a fail wasn't it so I can't blame them for not wanting to do it again next week."

"Suppose so, but you know I wouldn't have left you. I'd rather do it twice than let my oppo down in his moment of need, what the fuck they gonna do when their out on operations in Ireland? Fuckoff and leave their oppo to the paddies?" John said angrily.

"Ha ha ya fucking nutter," laughed Mike, he was glad to see his mate and he knew he was telling the truth about not leaving him behind, "you make me laugh John and you're a fucking good mate. I know you wouldn't have left me but I would have been gutted if you failed coz of me, that's all I'm saying mate."

"So do they reckon you can carry on with the tests then?"

"Yeah for now anyway, I guess we'll see on Monday when I have to start the week with the 9 milers won't I?"

Cpl Goode arrived at the bedside, "so they reckon you're okay to carry on for now Callahan. How do you feel about that?"

"Over the moon Cpl, I knew I'd be okay, just a bad day at the office that's all," he said laughing

The Cpl was glad to see him in high spirits and knew Savage had a good affect on him, they were close and everyone in the troop knew it.

The Cpl left Savage to get him oppo back to the barracks, John made sure Mike was comfortable before leaving him for the night. The weekend seemed to go fast and before they knew it they were standing on the start line of the 9 mile speed march after which they would be marched back into camp with a Royal Marine Drummer and the whole camp would come to a standstill while the recruits of 501 Troop marched back into camp with honours.

Everyone made it round the 9 miler in the allotted timescale; in fact they came in at just under 88 minutes. Major Powers had joined the troop for the 9 miler as he regularly did, it was his way of showing them he wasn't just a desk officer and he still had what it took to be a commando, not that anyone doubted him. Major Powers started out as a recruit and received the King's Badge in basic training and 4 years later completed Officer training and received the Sword of Honour, the highest honour in officer training, he was also a Mountain Leader so was SF trained.

They felt extremely proud as they marched back into camp with everyone standing to attention and watching them, even the young officers in training stopped and watched as they marched past. They had never felt as tall and they were still 5 tests away from that Green Beret, it was later that afternoon when they did the BST in the pool, which everyone passed with ease, it hardly counted as a commando test in comparison to the rest.

Tuesday was Tarzan Course in the morning, to be completed in less than 5 minutes followed by the 30 foot rope climb in full kit, and before lunch there was no rest for the wicked as they were ready for the full Tarzan Assault Course which had to be completed in under 13 minutes, this was not an easy test.

Everyone passed the Tarzan Course in the allotted time but a few struggled on the Tarzan assault afterwards, once again the rope climb wasn't much of a test for these guys and everyone passed it with ease. John flew round the full course and completed it in 10 minutes 39 seconds, the second fasted time in the troop; Fentiman pissed John off by beating him by 3 seconds. He wasn't really pissed off with him; he just knew he would take a bit of abuse for coming second to another of his friend's from his own section, it did prove what was said in week 3 when these guys were told they had Cpl Goode for section commander, he produced only the best marines and his reputation was safe once again as his section destroyed the competition.

Callahan just made it round inside the time, 12 minutes 59 seconds as he climbed to the top of the 30 foot wall at the end of the course and boy was he relieved to have made it, his ankle was starting to play up a bit after a heavy day of tests and it was only lunch time. They had drill all afternoon to give them a break from the phys but this wasn't really a break at this stage of training as the drill was as important as the tests, especially to the Drill Leader.

At this stage Cpl Garver no longer had anything to do with the recruits, instead they were handed over to a DL1, the highest qualification in Drill Leader speak, his name was Colour Sgt Brown and was he mean, he took no prisoners on the parade ground and expected 100% at all times. Callahan had to do light duties of the drill as his ankle was already swollen quite badly and the instructors didn't want him missing out on the Endurance Course the next day, he only had another two attempts and he would be back trooped so it was vital that he made it around this time and inside the 73 minutes.

Wednesday was a catch up day for anyone who had failed any of the other tests so far, Mike got ready for the Endurance Course and Sgt Mallaney and Cpl Dunn were going to take him along with a PTI to keep an eye on things, for those not on tests it was an easy day of admin and catching on with their 'affair's folder', this was a huge folder of work that every recruit was expected to keep up to date, this was actually the one area where John struggled and his friend Fentiman used to help him out and make sure he was up to date in exchange for some ironing of his dress shirts.

It was a bit of a surprise when Savage turned up down stairs in full kit ready to accompany the Sgt, Cpl and Callahan to the endurance course, "what the fuck are you doing here?" asked the Sgt looking at John as if he was crazy.

"Support for Callahan Sgt," he responded with a big smile on his face. Mike just turned and looked at his friend, his smile stretched from ear to ear, he couldn't believe that he would do this.

"Okay ya fucking mad mackem bastard, you can come along. You don't need to actually do the course savage, you can run along the side lines and help at the tunnel, and then you can run the 4 miler with him, okay?" Sgt Mallaney was impressed by this show of commando spirit and he gave a wry smile to Savage as he got into the driver's seat of the Land Rover, Cpl Dunn got in the back with the two recruits and he too looked at Savage with respect, he knew he wasn't doing this to gain favour with the instructors, this was purely for his friend, his oppo.

Mike was going well until he emerged from the smarty tube and started limping, John wasn't about to let it slip away now, "Mike pick your fucking feet up and get on with it, I aint passing out without you so you better get a fucking grip!"

His attack startled the instructors but they knew what he was trying to achieve and surely enough Mike picked himself up again and his limp disappeared for a while, they came out of the submerged tunnel and Mike started to limp again, "not on my fucking watch you don't Callahan, move your arse," came another motivational attack from John.

They arrived at the roadside and began the 4 mile speed march, "what time we got Sgt?" asked John

"You've got 38 minute to do the 4 miler so you're gonna have to go some to get this. Can you do it Callahan?" asked Sgt Mallaney.

"Yes Sgt," came the weak response from Mike, he didn't look like man who believed he was going to make it.

"Mike, listen to me. We haven't got much fucking time and you're gonna have to dig out blind if you want to make this. I fucking believe in you man, I wouldn't waste my fucking time on just anyone now would I?"

"I know mate, I'm trying, I'm just in a lot of pain."

"Fuck the pain!" snapped John, "what you gonna do in the middle of the Arctic or in the field in Ireland? You got to get on with it and get this done, so get your head in gear and let's get it fucking passed!"

"Your right lets go," came the more positive response of a man who'd just received a wakeup call. He was right, John had chosen to do this to help his friend and what kind of friend would he be if he wrapped on his oppo when the going got tough.

They ran most of the way back to camp but as they reached the guard house at the entrance to the camp Mike slowed to a march and John hit the roof, he exploded at his friend, "400 fucking yards Mike, now get fucking running or you've fucking missed it!"

Mike started running again, the limp was getting pretty bad now and John was praying that his friend was going to be okay. He knew that in two days time they had the 30 mile Yomp, at the end of which they would get a pass or fail and receive their Green Beret's. Mike ran down to the range with tears in his eyes and as he passed the PTI he called out his name, "Callahan staff!"

"Well done lad, get your shit sorted, clean your weapon and get on the range."

"Did I pass staff," asked the exhausted Callahan

"Just get on the fucking range lad and we'll discuss the result when you've finished the full course. Now move your arse!"

Mike finished the range section with 9 out of 10 shots in the target and as he walked over to the PTI everyone had a solemn look on their face's including John who knew the result. The instructors had almost taken John in as one of their own after his show of friendship.

The PTI looked at Mike as he spoke in his usual matter of fact voice, "your time for the endurance course was 72 minutes 58 seconds. Well done lad, you passed."

Mike burst into tears as he heard the result and he grabbed hold of John and hugged him, "fucking hell Mike you know I'm taken mate," they both started laughing as did the instructors, they were happy that he had made it round on his second attempt but they also knew that he wouldn't have made it if it wasn't for his oppo.

Thursday was another day of admin and rest and for the few who had failed the Tarzan Assault course had their re-runs and for Mike it was extra rest and more tablets in an attempt to get him ready for the big day, Friday was the 30 miler carrying between 35 – 40 lbs.

It was a 0500 hrs start for the men of 501 Troop and with only 19 original recruits left out of the 28 strong they were ready to take on the ultimate commando test, this was the test which everyone recognised as "THE" commando test, the recruits have 8 hours and the 30 mile Yomp takes place on Dartmoor and would have 3 stops along the way, 10 miles, 20 miles and 25 miles before finishing and being presented with their Green Berets by Lt Colonel Moore.

It was tough going and many of the senior recruits from other troops before them had said it wasn't the hardest of the tests but these guys yomping across Dartmoor would disagree with that statement, at the 10 mile point the recruits were feeling the rubs and niggles of the webbing against their shoulders and lower back, 58 pattern webbing was not very forgiving to the skin, John had covered his lower back with plasters to prevent the rubbing and they were holding up at this point, by mile 20 they had all but rubbed off his back and they were beginning to chafe.

As they came into the final mile of the yomp the recruits had thinned out slightly, the final bridge was in sight, the instructors and support staff were lined up along both sides of the road immediately after the bridge. As the recruits came over the bridge everyone applauded the men who were about to receive their Green Berets. Once all of the men had made it across the finishing line they grabbed a pie and a mug of hot tea before falling into three ranks in open order, Lt Colonel Moore gave a compelling speech to the newly qualified commandos before walking between the ranks, speaking to each man before presenting them with their individual Green Berets, he spoke at length to the three recruits who were 'diamonds' and spoke about how proud they should be and what was expected of them once they arrived at a commando unit.

John felt overwhelmed with emotion as the Lt Colonel spoke to him, he felt 6 feet tall and couldn't believe it was over, the pain and pressure of the last 28 weeks was suddenly gone, every minute, every mile was worth it.

The troops stood to attention as Lt Colonel Moore handed each man their green beret, all except the three men who still had other commando tests to complete before they would earn the right to wear theirs. Afterwards Sgt Mallaney spoke to the troops, "Troop, stand at ease."

"Right men, congratulations to every one of you.....I know there are still three of you who need to re-take the

160

Tarzan Assault but I've every confidence that you'll do it tomorrow, well at least you better or that's your lot" he said with a smirk on his face.

The humour in the Royal Marines was unlike most others, they strongly believed in their commando value 'cheerfulness in the face of adversity' and boy did they like to take the piss when you're were all but beaten. All of Cpl Goode's section had passed and it was unfortunate that all three of the guys who needed to re-take the Tarzan Assault were from Cpl Wright's section and the other Cpl's were giving him a hard time about it but it was his first time teaching a recruit training course in his career so he had a lot to learn.

The troop climbed into the wagon and headed back to camp, they were buzzing from the excitement of having completed one of the toughest training courses in the world and were about to join the ranks in a commando unit and begin their lives alongside the other elite soldiers. On arrival back at camp the men carried on with their cleaning routine, every bit of kit had to be immaculate, dress blues, flat white cap, buckles polished so you could see your face in them, every item de-fluffed and buffed constantly as if to stop would mean failure. The next day drill began and the drill instructor put them through their paces, you would have thought they were new recruits again as he screamed and bollocked them constantly. The troop was doing well really but Colour Sgt Brown wasn't giving them any praise today, he wanted them to take this as serious as any of the commando tests and to put on a top quality performance at the pass out parade.

Colour Sgt Brown had served in the Royal Marines for 20 years and had been a Drill Leader for 12 of them so needless to say he was not in the habit of letting people just saunter through his classes, he was responsible for young officer training as well as the Kings Squad of every troop coming through CTCRM, he was at the top of his game and nobody messed with him in his world.

As Kings Squad the recruits got special privileges, they no longer had to wait in line for the Galley, they walked straight to the front and chose whatever they wanted. The other recruits looked at them with admiration as they entered week 29, there was something magical about the troops of 501 Troop. The end of week 29 marked a very big day for the Diamonds of 501 Troop as they were interviewed by the Kings Badge panel to decide who if anyone would be awarded the Kings Badge and with it came a 12 month promotion which meant a fast track to becoming a None Commissioned Officer (NCO), the rank of Lance Cpl could be attained in just 12 months with this behind them, they would also decide if anyone would achieve the Commando Medal as a bit of a runner up prize and the third Diamond would go away empty handed as if he had never counted in the first place, a bit of a slap in the face after all the hard work they had put in.

The interview took place on a Thursday morning and first in was Recruit Keith Fentiman of 3 section, followed some two hours later by Recruit Mark Stephens of 2 section and last but not least was Recruit John Savage also of 3 section.   Once again this showed the standards of Cpl Goode's training and he was very proud although he rarely showed any sign of emotion, he was a hard man who never seemed to tire of training the recruits.   He would put a lot into the training, he would push them beyond the other section commanders as he had a reputation to uphold and he had every intention of keeping that reputation.

He had spent his first 7 years with 40 commando before transferring to 42 commando for the next 7 years and then to Lympstone to train recruits and there he had stayed ever since.   He was an excellent Platoon Weapons Instructor and as well as training recruits and officers he also trained the snipers course of which he prided himself in being one of the best in the business. In his 14 years active service he had 26 confirmed kills to his name but was rumoured to have many more.

The interviews were over and Friday morning came and went, the nerves of the three recruits was now reaching fever pitch, after lunch the whole troop was called to the parade square for a double drill lesson before being allowed off camp.   The recruits were sternly warned about the consumption of alcohol as this would lethal on the parade ground were many a recruit had fainted with dehydration or heat exhaustion due to over doing it over the weekend.

"Kings Squad, attention!" came the voice of Colour Sgt Brown. As the troops stood there they could see their officer coming into view, Lt Wray marched onto the parade ground in his Lovats looking very smart indeed. He was serious for a change which worried them men slightly but once in front of them he gave his usual boyish smile and instructed the Drill Leader to stand the men at ease.

"Men I want to congratulate you in completing what are arguably the toughest recruit training in the world. I have served with the Corps for 5 years now and as my first troop I have to say I am very proud of the men standing before me. We are down to 27 men for the pass out parade of which 18 are the original 501 troop and I am proud to say that I have the results of the Kings Badge interview panel with me now. When I call out your name you will come to attention, march out to me and I will hand you your prize. First of all I would like to say commiserations to Recruit Fentiman as you were unsuccessful in achieving either award, so without further a due Recruit Stephens you are the winner of the Commando Medal for demonstrating the virtues of commando spirit and group values, congratulations Marine Stephens."

Stephens felt fantastic as he marched out to receive his Commando Medal while the whole troop applauded, only to have it taken off him by the DL for safe keeping and it was to be presented formally in front of family and friends at the passing out parade.

"Finally the kings Badge is awarded to a recruit, sorry a marine who needs no introduction to his colleagues and who has demonstrated the highest level of commando spirit all the way through basic training, he will make a great addition to 42 commando in a couple of weeks time, Marine Savage please come forward."

John felt on top of the world and to be honest he really wasn't sure about getting the award as the other two guys were top notch too. He grinned as he marched out to collect the cloth badge which would be sown on his left arm for the rest of his career in the Royal Marines.

The final week was upon them and the recruits of 501 troop were preparing for the presentation, family and friends had crowded into the hall to see their children, boyfriends, partners, husbands receive their green beret and begin their life on an ocean wave.

Rebecca and Amy had travelled down with Mike Callahan's mother and girlfriend who was heavily pregnant. They got the train from Newcastle to Exeter St David and then onto the little village of Lympstone to their B&B on the Thursday afternoon and met John and Mike in a little pub in the village. The men drank water as they knew what was coming on the Friday, the most important day in their lives, the official presentation of the Green Beret and any awards that may be given. They would then carry out their drill routine with pristine accuracy before being allowed to catch up with family, friends and the instructors in the bar. This would be the only day they would be allowed to wear their Green

Beret with their Blues uniform so a very special day indeed.

Friday morning was sunny and the temperature was close to 30 degrees, the families poured into the hall and sat waiting for the first sight of their boys. Major Powers did the opening ceremony by introducing the men of 501 troop, the curtains opened to reveal 27 Royal Marine Commandos in Lovats wearing their black beret for the last time.

Lt Wray then took the podium and went on to tell tales of how certain recruits had made them laugh and some had made them cry, with laughter of course and how some men had performed above and beyond the standards of even the Royal Marines. Awards were given to recruits for the following areas; the PT medal went to Marine Hands 40 Commando, Drill medal went to Marine Petty 45 Commando, Commando medal went to Marine Stephens 45 Commando and finally the Kings Badge went to Marine Savage of 42 Commando. The crowds went wild, they screamed and shouted support to the men, and afterwards the pass out parade took place without a hitch. Then they met up in Saville Hall for a few drinks and snacks.

Rebecca walked over to Cpl Goode and said, "Hello Cpl I understand you were my son's instructor?"

"Yes maam I was."

"Well I have to say that I am very proud of him and he has spoken very highly of you since the beginning. He was over the moon when he found out he had you."

"Really," he laughed, "there's not many would believe that maam."

"And why is that Cpl?" she asked feeling a little silly.

"Well let's just say that my reputation is not exactly fluffy, I'm regarded as the biggest bastard in recruit training if you'll pardon the language." He said proudly

"Well exactly Cpl, that's what he told us too but he knew that you would make him the best he could be." She said smiling at him

Cpl Goode was shocked and it was obvious to see that young John Savage had indeed welcomed the idea of having the biggest bastard in recruit training as he knew he'd get more respect for passing out with him than any other and pass he had, as best recruit.

Some of the new marines headed home for the weekend and others were given a week or two leave depending on their commando unit rota, while some had to stay at CTCRM for the next three weeks doing guard duty which they were not happy about. John and Mike were both heading to 42 Commando and were given one week off before coming back to CTCRM for one week of guard before heading to Plymouth to start their careers.

John was heading for K Coy (Kilo Company) and Mike was headed for L Coy (Lima Company) so they wouldn't exactly be working together. Mike had also secured a position in the Mortars section which he wasn't entirely happy about but he knew it would get him fit as they were renowned for carrying huge weights on their backs, where as John had secured GD, General Duties which basically meant he would be a normal fighting marine within his unit but he had also secured a place on a course, his parachute training was to begin just six weeks after joining K Coy.

Chapter 7

42 Commando

The following months passed by in a blur, Mike was suffering with his knee again as a result of carrying weights in excess of 100 lbs on exercises while John loved every minute of his life in the Corps. He had completed his parachute training and was now wearing his wings proudly on his right shoulder; it was only 6 months before John was noticed for a very unique skill.

He was totally at home when in the field, camouflage and concealment were his forte but also his marksmanship was second to none so after just 6 months in the Corps he was moved to 42 Reconnaissance (Recce) troops where he began to learn more field skills that would make him a formidable soldier should he ever go to war. John made Lance Cpl after just 13 months in the Corps and was already building quite a reputation for his soldiering skills within the unit.

After spending 3 months in Norway on his first draft and learning the skills of mountain and arctic warfare he returned to the UK to some welcome leave. He had just received his first stripe and sown it on his uniform before he headed home to his mothers. Amy was waiting at the house with Rebecca and John had told them he had some news and so they were both very excited. He walked in and hugged them both before sitting down to have a cup of tea and his mother said, "well come on then, let's be having it. What's this great news?"

"Yeah come on Mr secretive," said Amy getting quite giddy now.

"Okay, well as you know I've been putting in a lot of effort over the last 13 months and........well I've been promoted."

Both of the girls shrieked, "Well done son," called his mother, "well done darling, you really deserve it babe," said Amy.

"Well that's not all the good news to be honest, I've also been selected for sniper training and if I pass I'll be the youngest person to do so in the history of the Corps," he said getting very excited about this fantastic news he had just received on the morning he left.

"Well that's great son," said Rebecca not really knowing what a sniper was or did. "I'm sure you'll pass with flying colours and do us very proud as always son."

Amy wasn't so happy about this news, yes she knew this was his dream but John was 18 years old and she knew exactly what a sniper did as John had told her about it over and over again. It showed on her face but she tried to play it down, "wow that is great news John but I thought you needed four years experience for that?"

"Yeah you're supposed to but they said I'm so good in the field and such a good shot that it would be a natural progression for me so I'm back at Lympstone in 6 weeks time for the 8 week training course. I am so psyched! Are you okay hun?" he asked Amy wondering why she seemed unhappy. She brushed it off and he figured they would no doubt discuss it later.

Rebecca broke the tension, "so how's Mike getting on? I see little David is doing great and his mam is so chuffed to be a nana even though she wasn't looking forward to it originally."

"Erm I'm not too sure to be honest, he's struggling with his knee again in Mortars coz those guys carry some serious weight around. I mean in Norway we're carrying like 100 – 120 lbs and those guys were carrying an extra 30 lb of kit compared to us."

"Don't you see him anymore?" asked his mother, disappointed at her sons comments.

"Every now and then but we're in different sections so he's got his mates and I've got mine. We still have a pint every now and again but we really don't have a lot of time to socialise outside of our own sections to be honest. That's just life I guess, mind you I do miss him and our banter, I thought we could travel up this week together but he's off to Ireland next week doing GD with L Coy so at least he won't have to carry the weight for the next six months."

"Six months," cried his mother, "bloody hell that's a long time to be over there isn't it?"

"No mam that's how long our draft is, it's a bit rough at the minute as well with all the riots and stuff kicking off in Belfast so he'll probably get to see some action too."

"Oh his poor mum and Sharon, I bet they're terrified bless them."

"Why, that's what we're trained for. We're over there to keep the peace as best we can but it's inevitable that it's going to kick off at some stage and we'll be in the thick of it when it does. That's what we do!" As he spoke he realised that he was getting quite passionate about going to war while his mother and Amy were obviously worried about what would happen if he had to go over.

His mother decided to try change the subject a little, "have you heard about all this bother over those Argentine Irelands or summit like that? The Malvinas of summit silly." She said sniggering at her lack of knowledge.

"Yeah they reckon it might kick off, but although they're over there they belong to us, you do realise that? It's got British inhabitants and a small deployment of Marines on there."

"So do you think they might go to war over them?"

"No I doubt it mam, the boss reckons not but he says we'll probably be put on standby soon just in case it does. They reckon it will be commanded by General Moore, that's the bloke he gave me my Green lid you know."

The week was a bit tense with Amy as she wasn't happy about John being put through the snipers course so soon but especially now he could be put on standby for the Falklands Irelands should the Argentineans declare war on British soil. She had voiced her concerns several times over the week and John was growing tired of it. He wasn't due back to Plymouth till the Sunday but decided to go back a day early. Amy was not happy!

"Why are you leaving early babe?" she asked angrily

"Coz I need to get my stuff together for a field exercise next week and there's all sorts of stuff to do before hand."

Amy wasn't convinced and decided to push again, only this time John was getting really pissed off with her constant nagging and he snapped at her.

"Hey knock the fuck off will ya! I'm fucking sick of you moaning and bitching at me this week okay, that's why I'm gannin back tomorrow instead of Sunday and you don't have to stay tonight if you don't want to either."

His words struck her hard and she burst into tears, he learned over immediately regretting what he had said.

"I'm sorry hun but you've really given me a hard time this week, you haven't let up once, you've bitched at me every fucking day and I've had enough babes. Do you understand? Do you even know you're doing it?"

"Yes I know babe but I can't help the way I feel about this. I mean what if you pass this course and then the Falklands kick off? What are you going to be doing over there?"

John held her in his arms and decided to stay for the rest of the weekend to comfort her. She was right, what if he did have to go to war, was this how he wanted to spend his last week with Amy? Fighting over something out of both of their controls.

John spent the next few weeks gaining as much experience as he could in the field, working with other trained snipers to gain hints and tips before the course. Christmas was tough as he had been selected to do guard duty for the whole period including New Year 1981. The sniper course started at the end of January 1982 and lasted 8 weeks, it was tougher than he had expected. The first weeks of trying to spot as many items as possible as they were laid out across the field in front of them was a giggle to start with but got very serious when most of the attendee's only managed to get between 4 and 8 items out of the 16 laid out.

Then as expected there was lots of field work along with days at a time on the range, mostly field ranges so it had undulating ground and a more realistic feel to it, John was doing well.

This was his forte, being in the field was where he was most comfortable and his marksmanship skills were already getting people's attention in the unit. The shortest distance they shot at was 200 metres as this was the closest a sniper should get to his target, any closer and it would be considered suicide as he would need an escape route for after he had taken out the target.

There was a strange attitude in sniper school as everyone talked about killing as if they were brushing their teeth, as if it was nothing. Strangely this actually appealed to John's nature. It wasn't that he didn't appreciate life or care about taking another human's life; it was just the way you had to be in order to be successful at this trade. The sniper is without a doubt the most feared man on the battlefield and one of the most respected men in any force around the world.

This snipers course didn't just have the usual Royal Marine's attending; there were three men from the SAS taking the course. The SAS agreed that the Royal Marine sniper course was the best in the world and so if a new trooper passed selection who was not already sniper trained by the army then they would usually send them to CTCRM to be trained by the marines. This was great for John as he was intrigued by the idea of the Special Forces and wasn't sure if he'd be good enough in the water to pass SBS training due to the intense nature of their amphibious role, they didn't dive in the crystal clear oceans of the Caribbean, well not usually, they dived in the North Sea where you couldn't see a hand if it was in front of your face and this scared John a lot.

The training intensified very quickly on the S3 snipers course, more field work, and stalking trained sniper spotters was no mean feat, it required perfect camouflage and concealment skills. You had to get anywhere between 200 – 400 metres of the target and take a shot, then the walker would go to the sniper and put his hand on their head and if the spotter still couldn't see him then he would take one more shot while they looked straight at him and if they still couldn't see his position he passed the stalk. Only two men passed first time, John and a Scotsman from the SAS called Brin, he was a slight man who looked as if a gust of wind would knock him over, but then again so did John. They both weighed around 9 stone dripping wet but were extremely fit and capable of taking care of themselves.

The field training was relentless and the trainees were expected to make a head shot at 600 metres and a body shot at 1000 metres with their L96A1 snipers rifle. John passed the course with a superior pass and was badged top sniper after making a head shot at 1000 metres in medium winds which was no fluke as he was asked to perform the same shot three times and hit all three targets in the head. This was a very proud moment for John and one of the SAS guys, Major Stephen Harris had took a real liking to him.

"Lance Cpl Savage, I have to say that was some very impressive shooting.   I'm sure they'll be looking at advancing your skills very soon, hopefully after you get your next stripe on your arm.   Maybe one day you should consider turning over to the dark side." He said laughing, "The SAS are always looking for good men regardless what regiment or Corps they come from. Think about it, here is my card if you'd like to speak with me further once you have a couple of year's service under your belt."

"Thank you sir," said John feeling like his head would explode with excitement at the prospect of being poached by the SAS at the tender age of 18 years old.

John kept hold of that card in his personal belongings in the hope that maybe one day he would move over to the dark side if his career became stale in the marines, but right now he doubted that as he was about to start the adventure of a lifetime as a Royal Marine Sniper in 42 Commando Recce Troops.

Chapter 8

The South Atlantic

The news was gathering momentum and Margaret Thatcher was in no mood to take threats from the Argentine Government over who the Falkland Islands belonged too. Rumours were also gathering pace throughout the British armed forces as to who would be going should it kick off. It was said that two of the militaries biggest rivals would be expected to work together, the Royal Marines and the Parachute Regiment. There would be many others sent should the need arise, Scotch Guards, Black Watch, Light Infantry, Royal Navy and RAF to name a few. But in truth no-one really expected it to come and then one day all weekend leave was cancelled, the officers on camp called emergency meetings with all NCO's from the rank of Cpl upwards which unfortunately didn't include John. The rest of 42 Commando had been pulled out of Northern Ireland early and 40 Commando sent in their place as the task force was established.

The Regimental Sergeant Major (RSM) WO1 Savage who John had met years earlier on his PRC was now standing before the men of 42 Commando ready to give them the words they had all been waiting for. "Amphibious Operations are go gentlemen and we're off to the Falkland Islands in nine days time. A rota will be set up for weekend leave etc but stay off the piss. It will probably be cancelled by the time we get there but just in case Maggie grows a huge set of hairy bollocks you had better be ready men."

The room was silent for a minute and then as usual someone made a joke about killing the Argie bastards and everyone laughed along even though John sat there thinking, "Shit, this is it! I'm going to war."

John was given weekend leave to go home and see his family since he had missed out on Christmas and New Year. Mike was at the train station when John arrived and they caught each other's eye at the same time.

"Hay big man. How ya doing ya fat bastard!" called John across the station much to the disgust of some elderly ladies waiting for their train.

"Skinny twat! I've missed ya me old mucker" came the response from Mike as he grabbed his old friend and gave him a huge hug. Mike had put on around 2 stone in weight since the last time John had seen him.

"Fucking hell mate, who swallowed my old mate Mike then?" John said laughing

"Yeah I know mate, all that yomping with huge Bergen on ya back, plus the guys told me I'd have to bulk up on the weights if I wanted to be a good Mortar man so that's exactly what I did mate. Heavy weight lifting and loads of yomping which has done my knee the world of good I've got to say. Plus I'm finally going on my AE (Assault Engineer) course in September mate so that's good news."

"No more problems eh mate, that's great news but I still can't believe the size of ya man. Are you on steroids or summit?"

"No mate, just loads of heavy weights and loads of scran."

Mike didn't want to get into that subject because the truth wa, like many of the other guys in Mortar Section he was indeed taking steroids now and was looking quite formidable with his new physique. John has also gained a little weight since joining up, but then he was just 8 stone when he started basic training and was now 9 stone but yet he was renowned for his yomping ability and ultra fitness even by Royal Marine standards.

The two men chatted all the way back home and the girls didn't know why they were coming back so soon but Amy didn't feel comfortable about it at all. Although she knew he was owed some leave she wasn't expecting to see him for some months due to his training commitments and new found skills as a sniper. They tended to send them on several long exercises in preparation for the real role before sending them out into the wild so to speak.

The two men were excited about the prospect of going to war but anxious as well which was to be expected considering they would be on ships for a couple of weeks leading up to the assault which they really didn't believe would actually happen. The officers and NCO's were all convinced this was going to be a very expensive exercise and a nice trip abroad all expenses paid, catch a bit of sun and be back in time for summer leave.

Once home John acted as if he was just on leave and on the third day he came home from a run to find Rebecca and Amy sitting watching the news with tears in their eyes. They turned and looked at him as he entered the room.

"How could you not tell me!" screamed Amy, "you fucking knew didn't you?"

"Amy stop, please." But it was too late, she was furious that he hadn't told them he was on standby and he didn't quite understand how they knew he was going by the news clip. "What's going on?" John questioned trying to control his own emotion.

Rebecca spoke slowly, her voice breaking at what she had to say, "Your camp has called John. A guy called Colour Sgt Rothwell, he said your leave is cancelled and they want you back down there by 2200 hours tomorrow."

"Oh, Amy I'm sorry hun. I was going to tell you both but I thought I had a full week to prepare and there was no point upsetting you the minute I got home. Look at the grief I got last time I was home." John said trying to justify his actions.

"So what's going to happen John? Now that it's out in the open." Asked Amy with tears flooding down her face.

"We're heading out by ship from Southampton. It will take about two or three weeks to get there and then it will probably get called off. No-one expects to go to war and the boss reckons it will be a very expensive exercise. I'm sorry babe, but this is what I do. I'm a soldier....." but he was cut off by the next barrage of anger from Amy.

"No John, you're not just a fucking soldier though are you? You're a Royal Marine Sniper trained to kill people at long range and gather intelligence from behind enemy lines aren't you!"

Rebecca was shocked at this outburst, she had no idea who her son was. "Is that true Jonny? Is that what all this training has been for?"

John felt a knot in his stomach as if his intestines were being twisted around inside of him, "yes mam, I am trained for all the things Amy just said but that doesn't mean I will have to do them this time."

Rebecca cut in, "oh well excuse me if you don't have to do it this time. Well that makes it all right then doesn't it?"

John had had enough of this now and exploded, shouting at them both. "Yes this is what I fucking do, what the hell did you think I was training to do for Christ's sake? I'm a fucking Royal Marine; I'm not in the bloody Salvation Army am I? This is what I do, it's who I am and if you don't like it then I'll fuck off now and won't come back. Will that make you both happy? Is that what you want? To disown me and act like I'm some kind of animal!"

John had never sworn in front of his mother let alone at her before and the shock had frozen both Rebecca and Amy rigid in their seats. He was pacing the floor in the living room before ranting again.

"I've got to go upstairs now and pack my fucking bags and then I leave to go to war for fucks sake. What a way to leave! What if I don't come back? How will you both feel then after the way you've just treated me?"

Amy leapt out of the chair and threw her arms around his neck and kissed him on the mouth, she broke down sobbing as she clung to him like she would never let go again. His mother stood up and walked over to him too; she put her arms around them both and hugged them.

"I'm sorry son," said Rebecca softly, "I guess I never really thought about you as a soldier or even a man for that matter. You'll always be my baby Jonny and I love you with all my heart. I'm just scared, I don't want to lose you, your only 18," she broke down in tears sobbing alongside Amy. They couldn't believe they had just put John through this when he had to leave and go to war. They both prayed that he was right and that it wouldn't happen.

"Can I come to Southampton and see you off?" asked Amy swiftly followed by his mothers request to join her.

John looked at them both with tears in his eyes before answering softly, "No. I can't take it if your both there crying and waving me off as if I'm never going to return. I have to stay strong and I will be coming back so I'll see you when I get back in a few weeks. Okay?" he said firmly.

They were both upset but John went upstairs to get showered and get his kit together, Rebecca rallied round helping to get the washing dry and do some ironing to give him some time with Amy. He spent the day visiting Amy's family and a couple of his friends before heading home for the night. Rebecca cooked and the three of them sat together eating and chatting about what they would do when he got back.

"Maybe we could have a holiday when you back hun?" asked Amy trying to stay positive.

"Yeah a holiday sounds great babe. I'll have to get it approved of course but it should be okay once we get back. I'm owed a bunch of leave so they got to let me have it eventually." He said with a relaxed smile across his face, but inside he was starting to think about the trip ahead and wondered if he would ever see them again. But he couldn't afford to start thinking like that; he was a Royal Marine Sniper and it's the enemy who should be afraid. He was a force to be reckoned with, a sniper who was about to enter a world he'd longed for his whole life, to fight the enemy and prove his superior fighting skills to himself and to those around him. This would silence the doubters once and for all, his friends he visited had a lapse attitude to him going to war, and they laughed at him as if he was some pathetic school boy again, this angered him but he thought better of showing them by thumping them. He had bigger fish to fry than these civvies.

They left the docks in Southampton to a hero's send off with thousands of friends and family all ascending to say their goodbyes to their husbands, sons, partners and boyfriends. It was an emotional send off with many tears being shed as young children said goodbye to their fathers, for some they would never see again.

The war did go ahead, the order to return home never came and the news came on board the Canberra that on 2nd April the small number of Royal Marines based on the island had put up a gallant fight and had now been taken captive.

The Argentine government had declared war on British soil and Margret Thatcher was not about to let this go without a fight. Thousands of Army, Navy, Royal Marines and RAF, soldiers and sailors were heading to the Falkland Islands in the South Atlantic. Each day on the ship was used for training, daily circuit training and running around the decks of the huge cruise liner that were formally used for cruises for the middle and upper classes.

Shooting practice as drums were thrown into the sea and used as targets, inter forces challenges were set up in an attempt to bury the hatchet between the Royal

Marines and the Paras as these two were arch rivals who hated each other with a passion, they both believed they were the best and toughest fighting force in the world. They behaved themselves the majority of the time and the fact that the war would be lead by Brigadier Moore of the Royal Marines was a real slap in the face of the Army.

It was 22nd April 1982 and news had come in that 18 members of the SAS had died in a helicopter crash the previous evening trying to land on the Fortuna Glacier and the Royal Marines took a whaling station in South Georgia in preparation for the actual landings on the Falkland Islands. May 1st the SAS and SBS landed on the islands and begin to recce the islands in preparation for the beach landings.

This was to be a Naval and Air war and if the troops didn't have to hit the beaches then Maggie would have been happy to have got away without any soldiers losing their lives, but this was not to be and the troops would be landing in LCVP's (Landing Craft Vehicle Personnel) as they hit the beaches just like D-Day in 1944. Even the marines were a little anxious at hitting the beach and having a heavily armoured enemy waiting for them with machines guns ready to pump thousands of rounds of 7.62 ammunition into every man as the tail gates fell and a massacre of hundreds of elite soldiers.

The Paras were uneasy about landing via the sea as this was alien to them and as the LCVP containing them hit the beach the Paras stood still for a minute as they weren't sure what to do next, then one switched on marines screamed form the back of the LCVP, "Green on, Go, Go, Go!!!!" and they came running out as if they were exiting a plane at full speed. They were professional troops and even if the marines didn't like to admit it they were quite glad that the Paras were going into action with them, after all they were the second best unit in the British forces.

It was May 14th when the SAS attacked Pebble Island and destroyed aircraft and fuel supplies, a devastating blow to the moral of the Argentine forces. It was also the day of the beach landings, which went without a glitch. The weather was horrendous and the cold was crippling, this was winter time on the islands unlike the spring weather being enjoyed back in the UK at that time. By 30th May 42 Commando was approaching Mount Kent and Mount Challenger and after some stiff opposition the marines took both mountains on 31st May.

It was on Mount Kent that John had his first experience of war, he was charging up the mountain with the other men of K Coy when he saw a section of men being pinned down by sniper fire, he immediately broke off from his own company and crawled across the open plain to get a better view of the situation, his commanding officer (CO) noticed John's move and laid down covering fire to distract the sniper hiding on top of the mountain.

John took out his sniper rifle from the bag on his back and loaded it with the ten round magazine of 7.62 ammo and zeroed in on a shape that kept popping up along the ridge, he could see other marines from his company now approaching the summit and knew they would face being shot if he didn't take out his target.

His heart was racing and he had to calm his breathing in order to take aim, he had the object in his sights, 400 metres uphill, not an easy shot, wind speed 20 knots and the noise of battle filled the air. The ground shook as mortars and artillery came down on the marines as they made their way up the mountain side. John took a breath and released it, he took another breath just as the figure popped up again, he held his breath and squeezed the trigger, heard the crack and thud of the round go down and watched as the figure lay still, just then the other men of K Coy took the summit, there was an exchange of gun fire and a couple of marines were injured but not before they threw in a couple of grenades and took Mount Kent. It was his first kill and he felt good, strong and professional as he had done what he was trained to do.

As a result of his shooting skills John was selected to go with the Mountain & Arctic Warfare Cadre to take Top Malo House which was being held by Argentine Special Forces, he was to stay back and watch the action from a distance of 800 metres and give them covering fire should they get into trouble. The fire fight erupted and these weren't the conscript soldiers they had come across earlier, they were Argentine Special Forces soldiers but they were no match for the ML's (Mountain Leaders) and John took out two more enemy soldiers as they became visible in the windows of the farm house.

Three kills in one day, after the battle was over he entered the house to see the dead, this left a strange feeling in his stomach, now he was face to face with the people he had shot and killed. ML1 Sgt Green came up behind him and spoke loudly and with pride, "well done son, fucking good shot. Two head shots at what was it 800 metres? You're a fucking star." He left laughing at the dead, John laughed too but it was a nervous laughter that he felt he had to do to keep face with the others, he was supposed to be hard, that's what snipers do, they kill and move on.

The men of 42 Commando dug in below Mount Harriet and was taking heavy fire for several days before they made the move to take the mountain. It was a night assault on 12th June when they took Mount Harriet; once again John was utilised as a sniper rather than a foot soldier, this time he took one confirmed kill but possibly another three which remained unconfirmed. Part of him wanted the clarity but another part was glad he didn't have to face these young men lying there pale, dirty, starved and with part of their heads missing.

On June 14th the Paras took Port Stanley and the yomp into the port began, it was a bit of an anti-climax after all the fighting the marines had done to be beaten to the post by the Paras but someone had to be first into the town and at least the war was over. The senior officers flew into Port Stanley on 15th June to accept the full written surrender of the Argentine forces.

The men took part in the clean up and helped the British civilians to rebuild their homes a little before heading back to the Canberra and the return trip back home to Southampton to a hero's welcome.

This time Amy and Rebecca where waiting for him to return and as he hadn't spoken to them since the morning he left on 9th April they were bursting with excitement. They knew he was okay as they had got a letter from him sent on the 1st June just saying that he was okay and what a place to spend your birthday.

It was 11th July when he returned home and he was a very different man. He knew he had four confirmed kills but possibly seven, he felt different to before, he had stared death in the face and won, he had fought the enemy at close range and used his sniper skills to take out enemy soldiers and contributed in winning the war. He had been baptised into the world in which he was destined to spend the rest of his life......at war!

After the debrief in Plymouth John was given three weeks summer leave but as he was owed some they gave him an extra week, four full weeks. He didn't know how he was going to manage it; he'd never been away from the Corps for this long. He had promised Amy they would go on holiday and so he did exactly that, after a week at home they went to Tenerife for two weeks of sun, sand, sea and sex and plenty of it. It was a great trip but Amy still couldn't understand why he felt the need to train every other day. John on the other hand thought this was a great achievement as he wasn't training every day. On their return they enjoyed another week together before he headed back to Plymouth to rejoin his unit and his troop.

Chapter 9

The 1980's

After the Falkland's conflict things were a little strange, some men were deeply affected by the trauma of what they had seen or indeed done. There wasn't a lot of war going on around that time other that the conflict in Northern Ireland (NI). Although things were seriously heating up in NI with several riots getting out of hand, soldiers were being targeted by IRA snipers and bombs going off regularly wounding and killing civilians who supported the British.

In 1983 John gained more field experience on numerous exercises within Recce Troop and later that year was sent on exercise with the rest of 42 Commando to Canada. It was a two week exercise with Canadian Special Forces and Mountain Troops and as usual the Royal Marines kicked ass then took the piss out of the host nation's soldiers. It was all done in good humour and as usual the Canadian's like many other forces around the world who served with the marines gained a respect for the level of professionalism and fitness these guys had.

In 84' John was sent on a medic's course which he wasn't really happy about as he didn't want to get lumbered doing the role of a medic when they went out into the field as he was a sniper and was far too important to the unit to be slapping bandages on people. He did it all the same and passed as usual with a superior pass, he couldn't understand why others didn't get the same grades as him as he found anything military fairly straight forward and interesting. At the time John couldn't see the full picture of what his CO was trying to achieve by sending him on these courses, especially when later that year he was sent on a signaller's course.

His relationship with Amy was blossoming after those tough early days in the Corps, she decided to simply accept what he did and although he never spoke of what happened on the Falkland Islands she knew that he must have taken life, he occasionally woke up suddenly in the night sweating and alert as if he was ready to fight and although this worried her she accepted that even he could have bad dreams from time to time.

John continued to improve his sniping skills and had the privilege of taking part in several exercises with the Special Forces. As a sniper John had all the skills necessary to slot right into the team of SF soldiers and so took part in no less than six SF exercises, sometimes as an observer to the training team who were running the exercise or as a support function as part of a four man section. This was the time when he was thankful for being sent on the training courses his CO had insisted on him doing and suddenly it was becoming apparent that he was being groomed for a future in the SF.

He was regularly used as a medic or signaller on these exercises as well as utilising his skills as a sniper to get close to the enemy undetected and gather vital intelligence to feedback to his section commander and complete the exercise. He was very popular with the SF teams for his zest for life and his ability to always be positive and optimistic.

It was the summer of 85' when John attended his Junior Command Course and was promoted to the rank of Cpl.

In 86' John was sent on exercise with the remainder of 42 Cmdo to Portugal. The trip was fun but didn't really challenge him or utilise his skills and he was quickly realising that the normal duties of a commando unit wasn't going to do it for him for much longer.

John did two tours of NI during the 1980's. His first was in 84' and was a six month tour with K Coy as a foot soldier and he wasn't used as a sniper at all which he was a little disappointed about, his CO explained that he needed experience in general soldiering skills as well as his SQ (specialist qualification) and that he should take every opportunity to gain a wide array of experience whenever the chance came along. The time spent in Belfast was not without action, two explosions, several attacks on Royal Marine check points and three riots to contend with so John was happy for the experience and was learning to listen to his CO. John's CO was an ex SBS officer with many years experience; he had chosen to go back to his original unit for a while to take a rest from special operations (SOP's). He had spent 10 years with the SBS taking part in SOP's and they were starting to take their toll on him. He had been told to RTU (return to unit) voluntarily for a two year draft to pass his expertise on and take a well earned rest from SOP's and then he could return to the SBS and continue with his career there.

In one riot in 84' John's section was petrol bombed which set fire to his left arm and back, he didn't notice at first as he was trying to push back the crowd, then suddenly he heard the fire extinguisher behind him and was surrounded in a fog of white dust as a powder extinguisher was released over him.   John's reaction was hilarious, "what the fuck you trying to do to me?" he shouted laughing at the guy behind him, "If the fire doesn't kill me you will, you're choking me to death."

The riot was tough as the IRA had strategically placed women at the front as a propaganda trick so when the marines pushed forward it would look like women civilians were being injured which of course would hit the headlines in both NI and mainland Britton as part of a plan to gain more support for the IRA, or at least that is what they hoped for.

The IRA was still viewed as terrorists in the eyes of the majority but these staged riots didn't do the British forces any good either. Several women were injured as the riot progressed and John was caught on camera as were other marines in full flow crashing into the crowd as they'd had enough and received the order to take charge and push the riot back into retreat and get it ended as fast as possible.

The marines did exactly that, they went in hard and fast making dozens of arrests, mainly women who had been smashing bricks into the face visors of the advancing soldiers. John was standing side by side with his old friend Keith Fentiman and after the fire some 15 minutes earlier they were in no mood to take any more shit from these Irish bastard's.

K Coy went crashing in hard and smashed the crowd back with real force, an act of violence that would be recorded and broadcast across the UK on every TV channel. John was hit in the face with a breeze block by a large woman standing at least six feet tall and weighing around 18 stone, he felt his head jolt back and the pain shoot through his head and neck with the force of the impact, "Fuck!" screamed John as the front of his visor split down the middle, he erupted into a frenzy of controlled aggression punching the woman in the throat with his left fist, it was a sharp powerful jab and then followed it up with his riot stick in his right hand as he hit her across the knees. She fell to the ground holding her throat and trying to shout for help but John dropped his right knee down into her solar plexus winding her further, another woman hit him over the head with a piece of broken pallet as Fentiman struck her across the face full force with his riot stick breaking her jaw.

The remainder of the riot quickly dispersed as the marines charged forward with force and dozens of arrests were made along with several severely injured civilians and soldiers alike.

When John arrived home from NI a few weeks later he had a week off so headed back up North to see Amy and his mother, when he arrived home his mother was sitting quietly in her chair just staring at the TV screen which was switched off. "Mam, are you okay?" asked John as he entered the room.

She sat there with tears in her eyes for a moment before speaking, it was the longest 10 seconds and John was really worried about her.

"How was the tour?" she asked

"It was okay I suppose a bit rough in places but hey that's just the way it is out there. What's up?"

"Amy will be down at 6 o clock John; she's just helping her mum do some bits and bobs first."

"Okay, so are you gonna tell me what's wrong then? Why are you sitting looking at a blank screen?"

"Amy rang me a couple of weeks back and told me the marines were on the news, something about a riot that 42 Commando were involved in."

"Oh," was all John could say right then, he wasn't sure how it had been portrayed but he knew there was an investigation into the exact orders received by the CO and the level of violence used to bring it to an end.

Rebecca continued in a slow and slightly shaky voice, she was clearly struggling to hold back the tears. "So I thought I'd stick a video in as I was heading out to work and didn't have time to watch it when it was on. When I got home that night I watched the news back and I was so shocked and disgusted at what I saw that I was physically sick."

"Wow, just stop right there mum," said John seeing where this was going and it was pretty obvious that he was looking like the bad guy in all of this. "You don't know the half of it and I don't think we should be discussing this if you're gonna get upset every time you hear something bad on the news. It's paddy propaganda that's all part of the plan."

"Don't understand!" she yelled as she leapt up and switched on the TV and video, "I'll show you what the world saw should I son. If I can still call you that anymore! What all our friends and family saw should I John? Just sit down and watch the news I recorded. I rang Amy the next day and she had to take the day off work she was so upset."

"Okay if that's how you want to play things then play the bloody thing and let's get it out of the way and then we can talk about it. Or would you rather wait until Amy's here as well so we can have it out again, just like every other bloody time I had to do my job."

Rebecca pressed play on the top loading VHS video player which John had bought her with one of his first wages as a fully trained marine. The news began to play and he saw for the first time what everyone else had seen, a brutal attack by the marines of K Coy attacking unarmed civilians and he was furious at how they had edited out the real picture of what was going on over there in NI. They failed to show the real horror these troops were facing on a daily basis and what they had experienced over the 6 month tour.

He watched as the footage showed him and Fentiman ploughing into the crown of women with teeth gritted and demonstrating what could only be described as their war face as they swung their riot sticks into seemingly unarmed women, they had even managed to cut out the part where John was hit in the face and over the head and instead showed John drop the large lady and then drop onto her as Fentiman broke the jaw of another woman. It was horrific and he understood why she was so upset. But why hadn't Amy mentioned anything when they spoke on the phone or in a letter, he just couldn't understand how she could have kept it all locked up inside without mentioning a thing

The news finished and Rebecca switched the TV off as she sat back in her chair and stared at her son with disbelief at who he had become. "So what have you got to say about it now son?" she asked with venom in her tone.

John sat in the chair opposite his mother for a moment before starting, "well what can I say, if it's on the news then it must be true eh mum. How could you be so stupid to believe that this is anything more than clever Irish propaganda?"

Just then Amy arrived and as she walked into the living room she could see that it had already begun. She walked over to John and gave him a big hug, "Oh baby, I've missed you so much." She said with a smile across her face, she looked at the man she loved with sadness in her eyes and it was obvious that she was trying to put on a brave face in order to make him feel welcome back home but she knew it had already begun and this was a very tense situation she had walked into.

"Your just in time babe," said John, "My mam has just showed me the news clip that upset you both and I can't blame you for thinking the worst but I think we need to discuss the truth behind all this Irish shit before you judge me again."

"Okay babe, but you know we love you regardless," she said holding back the tears and her voice starting to break.

"I don't know if I still love him yet," snapped his mother.

John was furious at this and reacted badly to this slur, "Right then, and if you don't fucking like it I'll fucking go. I'm fucking sick of every time I come home being bashed coz of your fucking ignorance!" he shouted before continuing, "Let's take a look at the footage again should we?" and he switched the TV back on and rewound the tape slightly, pressed play and then paused the footage. "Do you see what I'm wearing?"

"Yes babe," responded Amy trying to calm him down as he was visibly shaking with anger now.

"What colour is my left arm and shoulder?" he snapped.

"Black," came the response from Amy as his mother sat up and stared at the screen intently wondering where he was going with his story.

"Well what colour is the rest of my uniform?"

"Green," whispered Amy starting to regret this whole event.

"Yeah fucking green, well done. The arm and shoulder are black coz that's where 10 minutes earlier I was on fire after being petrol bombed and all the white shit I'm covered in is the powder from the extinguisher they used to put me out. Now can you see the front of my face visor?"

This time Rebecca spoke up as she could see that Amy seemed to be taking the brunt of his questioning, "Yes, I do."

"What do you see mam? Come on tell me what exactly can you see?"

"I don't know, it looks like a crack or something."

"Yes, a fucking crack down the full length of my reinforced riot gear, where seconds earlier that fat bitch smashed a breeze block into my face nearly breaking my fucking neck. So yes I fucking thumped her in the neck and then dropped her using a legitimate riot technique taking her knees out before dropping onto her to carry out the arrest. I wasn't taking any more chances with that big bitch and then that other bitch that Fentiman just dropped and yes broke her jaw had just hit me over the head with a plank of wood."

"Oh babe, I'm sorry. It was just such a shock when we saw the news. I was hoping to catch a glance of my fella in uniform walking around the streets of Belfast. I wasn't expecting to see him laying women out cold in a riot," said Amy crying and looking at Rebecca, waiting for a response from her to support her.

"I just can't believe that this is who you've become son," said Rebecca. "I always knew you wanted to be a soldier, I was proud of you and what you've achieved but this is just too much. I don't think I can handle seeing you like this. You've changed John and I don't like what I'm seeing," she stopped for a moment and then looked John full in the face, staring him in the eye as she continued, "I don't want you here anymore John."

"What!" came the shocked response from Amy, John just stood there staring back at his mother not quite sure what to say. His eyes filled with tears as he stood in silence.

"I want you to leave this house now. I'll arrange with Amy to collect your things over the next few weeks. You're no son of mine!"

"Rebecca, don't do this please." Begged Amy seeing how distressing this was for everyone involved.

John interrupted speaking softly and deliberately, "its okay hun, its fine. If she wants me to go then I'll go. But know this mam, once I walk out that door I'll never walk back through it again and you'll grow old and lonely, bitter and corrupted by the media whose job it is to grab people's attention and boy did they do a good job on you. If you can do this to your own flesh and blood then you're no mother of mine."

The pain of those words struck Rebecca as much as hers had struck John as they left her mouth. They were both gutted by what each other had said but it was too late now, John turned and walked out the door with his burgan still over one shoulder. He was devastated but the skills he had acquired as a marine came into play and he showed no emotion as he walked away.

Amy couldn't believe what she was seeing or hearing, she followed John out of the house and closed the door behind her. They walked the one kilometre to Amy's parent's house without speaking, Amy just linked John's right arm and gave him a gentle squeeze to let him know that she loved him. They didn't need words, he knew she loved him and would stand by him no matter what he did in his chosen career.

As soon as they entered the house John walked straight upstairs and lay down on the bed while Amy explained the situation to her parent's. They couldn't believe how

Rebecca had reacted to this and they said he could stay there for the week with Amy. Amy's parent's Liz and George were easy going people who liked John and knew how happy he made their daughter. They often wondered how long it would be before John took the initiative and would propose to his darling Amy. His love for her was obvious and they both said they wanted children so everyone was quite surprised that it hadn't happened already. But at 21 years old he was still focusing on his career in order to secure their future together. She had made no secret of the fact that she wanted to go wherever he was posted as his wife so there wasn't any obvious reason for the delay.

John did however have a plan in his own head and he wanted to make Sergeant before applying for married quarters as this was of a much better standard and they would be more likely to get a long term post, but this was also one of the reasons for his apprehension as he didn't want to be restricted because he was married.

That was the last time John saw his mother until 5 years later at a close friends funeral back in the North East

John's second tour of NI came in 89' and this time he was sent in for three months with the 42 Recce Troop as a sniper, this was to be a very busy tour for John. He had been working in numerous regions across Ireland; he served in South Armagh, Belfast, Fermanagh and Enniskillen as well as along the border separating North and Southern Ireland. He would work with the SF patrols waiting for the newly recruited, newly trained members of the Provisional IRA (PIRA) to try and sneak across the border under the cover of darkness to join their comrades in the war against the British.

It was May 25th 1989 when John was due to leave the base in South Armagh with an experienced S1 sniper named Colour Sgt William McLean, nick named Mac. He had been in the Royal Marines for 20 years, 16 of which he had been a sniper in various commando units but on this evening he wasn't feeling well and had a dodgy stomach, he'd been shitting all day and wasn't looking forward to going out on patrol tonight feeling like this but he knew there were no other lead snipers available for the four day OP (observation post) they were headed to. It overlooked miles of open countryside set back 800 metres from the Southern border and also overlooked some country roads that the marines planned some random road blocks over the next couple of days. Random to the public but strategically planned in the hope to catch a couple of PIRA suspects smuggling guns across country.

It was 2000 hrs when they set off; they were dropped by a Sea King helicopter out in the countryside some 6km away from the OP. The OP had been set up some 5 days earlier by a two man SBS recce team watching the border and gathering intelligence about familiar vehicle movements in the area by known PIRA members so the sniper team were sure it would be a top quality hide from which they could do their own observations.

They had only been going for just over 2 km when Mac said he wasn't feeling too good, he decided to leave John to go it alone and head back to a planned road block being manned by 42 commando so would arrange a collection from there. He got on the radio and spoke to HQ and got the all clear to brief Cpl Savage on what was expected of the 4 day OP and then they arranged the pickup of Mac from the road block in an hour's time. He was shitting badly and needed to get back to camp and re-hydrate.

Mac briefed John and they went their separate ways, John arrived at the location at 0200 hrs and setup the OP and started watching and making records of the goings on he witnessed. There wasn't a lot really, but between 0500 and 0600 he noticed the same car drive up and down 3 times. It was a Ford Escort and the suspension seemed to be very low on the second trip which could have meant they had been to a weapons collection and the third run could have been returning for a second run. So he radioed HQ and passed the info on to 14th Intelligence Unit (14 Int) and they said they would be setting up a road block during the day and he was to keep a watch over the men putting up the road block.

John wasn't too worried about any of this as he had done this sort of thing a hundred times before, keeping watch over the Royal Marines and other British forces just in case of a contact in which he may be the difference between no casualties and a whole section being wiped out by the enemy.

John was getting tired but as he was a lone sniper wouldn't be able to get much sleep over the course of the 4 day OP, he started to nod off when something made him jump and he suddenly felt very exposed as he heard what sounded like a tractor engine coming towards the OP. It wasn't unusual for a farmer to notice a slight difference in his own land, on his own fields where he had probably spent his whole life living and working, this sometimes exposed a hide.

The tractor came within about 200 metres of the OP and John made his rifle ready but knew if he was confronted and shot the farmer there would be hell to pay when he got back to camp. Instead he would hope to get away unnoticed and sneak out under the cover of darkness, unfortunately it was 0700 hrs and the sun was up and it wouldn't be dark for another 14 hours. This was not a good situation to be in, just then he also noticed the first road block go up on a road some 500 metres to his left, not at all where he'd expected it to be and this would also highlight this piece of land as a perfect OP. The IRA weren't stupid and they knew the land marks as well as any of the British intelligence so would know the best locations for an OP if a fixed check point was set up, fortunately this was an adhoc check point so they wouldn't have time to search the land for an OP without arousing suspicion.

The farmer started walking around the hedges 100 metres away from John's position with his shotgun snapped open over his right arm, he was looking very suspicious and locked the shotgun into position and started firing randomly into the base of the hedges, John's heart was thumping as this would have been the normal place to build a hide and if that was the case the farmer would have had to be killed, with his own shotgun to make it look like another farmer suicide of which there were many at this period of the 80's. He loaded up again and again and let off eight rounds in total before heading back to his tractor and drove back to the farm some 2 km away.

John settled back down and began to watch the road block check point as the soldiers carried out car to car searches, he couldn't make out the regiment that had set up the check point but he knew it was Army by the way they handled themselves. He was very alert after the farmer incident and prayed he didn't return. John put in another call to HQ once the road block was lifted and the Ford Escort hadn't returned during the day. He managed to grab a couple of hours sleep before he had to check in with HQ again, it was important to keep contact in case he had to move to another location under the cover of darkness to carry out any close range reconnaissance elsewhere.

It was 1800 hrs when he noticed the Ford Escort moving at speed along the road 800 metres away right on the border, it looked light and the suspension wasn't weighed down. Ten minutes later another unit arrived directly below his position and set up a temporary road block check point. It was a bootneck unit, he could tell straight away and at closer inspection through his scope he noticed a couple of the guys by their stances and body language. It was L Coy 42 Cmdo and it was an 8 man section, 4 in a temporary shelter with GMPG and 4 sentries stopping and checking the cars, their occupants and whatever they had in the boot.

John had just started to relax when he saw the Ford escort approaching from the right of the road and was heading straight for the check point only this time it was slower and the back end was very low. He spoke to himself in his head, "Right lads, look alive and be prepared."

The car didn't see the check point until it was literally 30 metres away as it came around a bend and as there was another car behind it, it couldn't have turned and made a getaway. Plus with whatever was weighing it down the GPMG gunners would have made mince meat out of it and anyone in it from that range. The car was third in line and it crept forward at a speed of around 3 mph until it came to a halt, a marine came to the window of each car to check documents before waving them onto the next marine who would ask them to get out of the car while two others searched it inside and then the boot. John knew the routine as he had done it many times himself. John was now very alert and watching not only this car but the others in front and behind in case they had back up, he knew the car was an unregistered car to the PIRA but as it couldn't be found during the day it was obviously being hidden out of sight and they would only do that if they had something to hide.

The marine took their documents and looked at them, he seemed happy with them and as they crept forward to the next point John's heart started to thump hard in his chest as he watched the two men in the front seats of the car. He had a bad feeling in his gut, he didn't like it one bit and was totally focussed on the car now, he got his sniper rifle ready and checked his range was at 800 metres and began to take his preparation breaths as if he knew he was about to take a shot. He watched the car come to a halt and as the driver applied the handbrake he didn't retrieve his hand straight away which immediately made John suspicious, he breathed again and let it out as he watched the cross hairs rise and fall over the passengers head and then slowly to the drivers head.

He watched as the passenger got out of the car on the side nearest him but he knew if he had to make the shot it would block his view of the driver, he had no choice it would go down however the chips fell now. There was no more time to prepare and the whole thing seemed to take minutes when in fact the whole incident lasted only a few short seconds, as the passenger climbed out of the car John noticed the small arms in his left hand and as he stood up and started to raise his hand...BANG!

The round rang out across the fields and down 800 metres before making contact with the blokes head, the blood exploded across the top of the cars roof splattering the face of the marine who took a step back blinking as the blood covered his face. He started to raise his rifle but it was too late, the driver brought up an Ingram 9mm Sub Machine Gun on rapid fire and sprayed the marine across his body with 9mm rounds. As the passenger fell away from the car John took another breath and saw the drivers head just come into the top of his scope, BANG!

The round went down again and once again made contact with the head of the driver, blood exploded filling the inside of the windscreen of the car and the other marines had already sprung into action and were holding all other vehicles in position and rallying around the car as well as looking around to see if the sniper was aiming for them or the enemy, they quickly realised it was a friendly sniper that had taken out both men in the car. One marine was on the ground taking care of the wounded soldier who must have taken at least 10 rounds in the chest. Once the dust had settled and the boot of the car was opening it was found to contain 100 kg's of high explosive and raw materials that could have been used to make dozens of bombs and killed countless numbers of soldiers and civilians.

It was a good catch and the two dead men were confirmed to be active members of the PIRA. John sat back in the OP to gather his thoughts and calmed down after the action that had unfolded, this was the first time he had been totally on his own and he still couldn't make a move out of the OP until it was dark and of course by that time the news would have hit the IRA HQ and they would be suspicious of a hide in that particular location.

By the time the area had been secured and cleared it was 2200 hrs, John knew he would have to make a move soon, but he couldn't make contact with HQ for some reason which made him suspicious that the IRA might have set up some kind of jamming device in the area to leave any snipers exposed and alone in no mans territory. John was a good sniper and decided that the risk was too great to make a move on this night so stayed put for another 24 hours. Once again the farmer came out at the same time the next morning and shot some more rounds into hedges and rocky outcrops in the hope of hitting a hide and once again John was ready to do what he had to do if he came too close.

It was 2200 hrs when John was ready to move out of the OP and back to his planned RV some 4 km away, he knew he only had 2 hrs to make it which would be a push if he had to crawl slowly to avoid being spotted. Just as he was about to break cover he heard twigs breaking not more than 6 feet away to the right of the OP. He moved to the right of the OP quickly hoping to avoid being seen and as he did so he saw a familiar face, it was the bloody farmer again nosing around. He was stalking across his farm land and was suspicious of the location of the hide but it had taken him 3 days to realise there was something different about it.

The farmer stood 2 feet away from the OP now and spoke in a gruff broad Irish accent, "You better fecking step out of there now boys before I unload both rounds into ya."

There was no movement inside and so the farmer made the mistake of getting down on all fours. Taking the end of his barrel he slowly started to peel back the entrance to the hide. At that second John launched his right hand through the entrance of the hide holding his commando dagger tightly in his fist thrusting it into the hollow point just below the farmer's Adam's apple, the gurgling sound was quiet and he couldn't call for help as the sniper pulled him into the hide and took the shotgun from his hands. John looked the man in the eyes as he removed the dagger from the throat, he turned the shotgun around and shot the farmer in the throat at the exact same point he had stabbed him. He quickly dragged the body out of the hide and collapsed it, it made no difference if the IRA knew about it now, it would never be used again and nor would this farmers land.

He left the farmer on the ground dead and started off at a brisk pace yomping across country knowing that he didn't have much time to make the RV and if he failed to meet this RV it was another 24 hours to the next one and that was another 20 km west heading towards the coastline.

It was midnight when he saw the lights of the chopper in the distance; it was taking off without him. It couldn't have been more than 500 metres away but he knew if he jumped around there was a risk that he would become a target should any IRA snipers be on the lookout. He accepted his fate and lay low for a few minutes until the helicopter was out of sight, he took a different route south to confuse any possible observers before heading towards the West coast again. He arrived at a disused farm house 1 km away from his secondary RV and made his way under the floorboards of the house before first light, it had been a tough night with a lot of yomping and a strange 48 hours behind him. He lay there pondering on the previous days occurrences as he drifted off asleep.

He slept on and off for most of the day, no-one came close to his location so he was relaxed and comfortable as he awaited his pick up. It was 2355 when he heard the huge beast heading in low for a quick landing, he flashed his red torch signal to the pilot who then came in quickly for the pickup, it didn't actually touch the ground, it kind of hovered around 4 feet above as a giant hand came out and grabbed John's and pulled him into the Chinook Helicopter. As it shot off into the sky and over the fields John looked up to see the man who had pulled him aboard was none other than Colour Sgt Mac McLean with a big cheesy grin across his face, Mac leaned forward and shouted under the noise of the aircraft, "We'll talk back at the debrief, you just sit back and relax sunshine."

John simply nodded and sat back and enjoyed the ride. It was the first time he'd felt relaxed in a few days so was quite happy not to have to talk right now, he just went over the week's events in his mind in preparation for the debrief. It was going to be an interesting one that was for sure.

When they arrived back at base John was allowed time for a shower and Mac brought him a huge beef sandwich dripping with onions and gravy while he got ready and into some clean fatigues. He ate it as if he'd never eaten beef before, his face contorted at just how delicious it was, making sounds like he was having the best sex ever, Mac laughed at him. As they walked to the debrief Mac said there was some good news and some bad news so to be prepared at the briefing so John felt a little uneasy and wondered if this was about the farmer he'd had to kill.

They knocked and entered the room; it was bright with white washed walls and a huge table with a map on it. There were seven men in the room after John and Mac; he recognised his CO and a RM Captain from HQ, two SAS soldiers, one SBS Officer and three people dressed in civvies. He figured they were 14 Int and as he was introduced to everyone he had been right in all cases.

The SBS officer Major Grant was running things and asked for a step by step debrief of everything that had happened from leaving Mac on the Monday night. John went through the events leading up to the point of the execution of the passenger before an SAS Sgt interrupted, "So has anyone told him yet?"

"No not yet Sgt, I was getting to that in a moment" replied Major Grant. John looked at him curiously but showed no emotion as he was trained not to react to such things.

John decided to just come out and ask, "What is it boss? Where they not PIRA as I suspected? Or is this about the farmer?"

"No Cpl Savage, you were spot on with the two in the car and we'll deal with the farmer instance separately but you've nothing to worry about, you did a good job at making it look like a suicide. Although he is a known IRA supporter so they suspect foul play regardless of what we say, especially after two PIRA members being taken out by a sniper at 800 metres. Bloody good shooting by the way." He said smiling.

"Thank you sir," John replied with a wry smile on his face, Mac put his hand on his back before speaking.

"Boss, if I may?" said Mac

"Certainly Colours, go ahead. He's your boy."

Mac spoke deliberately and very factually as he continued, "John you know there was a marine caught up in the fire fight?" he continued without a pause, "well he didn't make it son."

"Oh okay, that's bad news but I accept that these things happen. So, why the big deal about it? No offence intended sir."

"John," Mac continued. "The marine was Lance Cpl Mike Callahan from L Coy."

John struggled not to react to this news that one of his closest friends in the Royal Marines was dead but not only that, John suddenly felt responsible that if he'd taken out the driver first maybe Mike would still be alive and Mac had pre-empted these thoughts before John had heard the news.

John looked around the room at the others not sure what to say next, "Okay sir, shall we finish the brief and then we can worry about the other details later. I need some scran and a good kip sir."

"Very well Cpl," replied the Major and he continued with the de-brief, it was all in all a very successful operation which had unintentionally unfolded and lead to Cpl John Savage killing two members of the PIRA and a civilian farmer. Killing someone at close range was a totally different kettle of fish than taking a shot at 800 metres; you could see the whites of the man's eyes and hear the gargle of blood in his throat as he tried desperately to gasp for breath as his last breaths were taken away by the hands of a Royal Marine Sniper whose only goal was to survive and return back to base safely.

John served the remaining 6 weeks in NI without seeing any action and was sent out on foot patrol with the remaining men of L Coy 42 Cmdo. Some of the other's talked about that night in front of John deliberately to see if they'd get a reaction as they all knew he was a sniper from Recce Troops but most of Recce were spread across the company as there was no operations to take part in, in those last few weeks.

42 Cmdo returned back to the UK having lost 4 men in NI during their 6 moth draft, it was not a good trip for the men of L Coy, the other three men were hit by a roadside bomb and the 5 men in their section only survived because the device went off early and they were still around the corner of a building.

John came home and as he was not in the same company as Mike he would not be asked to be a pall bearer at the funeral which was to be held in Sunderland at the crematorium near the town centre. Mike was 34 years old with a wife and two children. They were devastated and Sharon looked to John for comfort as she broke down during the service, he was sat half way back in the congregation as he didn't want to step on the toes of Mike's own company.

As they sent him through the curtains to the tune of a trumpet playing "The Last Post" every civilian present broke down into tears and it seemed to get louder as he played "Revile" in memory of the dead rising again. Military funerals were tough on everyone, marines included and some of his oppo's broke down too. It was sad to see his mother and wife and his two children break down, John had to blank his mind of emotion for his fallen friend in order to be strong for Mike's family.

Amy was in bits too, she sobbed and looked at John for any sign of emotion, there was none. But not in a sense that he didn't care because she knew he did and she knew that he knew what had happened to Mike but that he wouldn't talk about it with anyone. As they left the congregation Mike's brother who John had never met spoke out loud and invited all to join his family at "The Barnes Pub" for drinks and a bite to eat to mourn his fallen brother.

As Amy and John entered the bar Rebecca was stood at the bar looking around in the hope of spotting her son. The son she had cast aside 5 years previous and on a day like this missed him more than ever before. Rebecca looked old as her face searched the room as it filled with marines, Amy squeezed John's arm and started to say, "You're......" but she was cut short by John, "I know, I see her."

John wasn't sure what to do or how to feel about seeing his mother after all these years, he felt no malice towards her, he didn't actually feel anything towards her anymore.

Sharon saw John and Amy and went over throwing her arms around John's neck and holding him tightly as she broke down sobbing uncontrollably. John stood there and held her for a moment as he knew that was what she needed, the kids came running over to Amy and she held them both as she spoke to them.

"Wow look at how big you boys are getting. You're almost as tall as me." She said laughing with them trying to distract them from their mother's grief.

"Tell me John," said Sharon in sobs, "tell me what really happened. I have to know!"

John held her close to his chest again hoping that she was stop asking him the question but she wasn't about to give up that easily.

"Please John, I'm his wife I deserve to know, please tell me."

"I only know what you were told Shaz sweetheart. I don't know any more than you. I'm not in Mike's unit so I wasn't even in the area when it happened."

Sharon glared at him. Meanwhile Rebecca had walked over to Amy and started talking to her.

"Hello Amy hun. How are you both?"

"Hi, I don't know what to say to you Rebecca. I really don't and I'm not sure this is the time or the place to start." Said Amy.

"I'm not starting anything Amy; I just wanted to see my son. I couldn't believe the news when I heard about Mike. I'm devastated and just kept thinking that it could have been my John. I really would like to speak to you both, do you think he will? After this I mean?"

"I don't know Rebecca; you'll have to speak to John. I'm not doing it for you. You really hurt him; you have no idea how different he was after that day. Five years Rebecca, five bloody years and nothing and now suddenly someone dies and you want to make amends. I just don't know, I'd love to have you back in our lives but I'm not sure John will."

John was still trying to console Sharon but she wouldn't let up with all the questions, "John, why are you lying to me!" she shouted and the whole pub stopped and looked at them.

"I know you were out there the same time as him and I know what you do out there, Mike used to tell me all about how much you'd changed since joining Recce Troop but I never thought you'd do this. You stand before a grieving widow and fucking lie to me!"

"Sharon stop, please. I'm not in Mike's unit and I wasn't there when he died so I don't know what to tell you. All I know is he was shot by the Provo, what else do you want me to say? Don't try lay this at my door, I didn't bloody shoot him."

His words shocked the room; even the other marines couldn't believe he just said that to a grieving widow. He didn't care; he had also lost a dear friend and was just as upset as everyone else and he just didn't know what else to say.

Mike's brother got up at the front of the bar and started to speak loudly so the room could hear him.

"I would like to say a big thank you to all you guys from the Royal Marines for being here today. You're all heroes in my eyes and the eyes of our family and we thank each and every one of you for trying to save my baby brothers life. I want you to join in mourning my brother."

Right then John had had enough of this drunken shit who actually hadn't spoken to Mike for over ten years and now wanted to be centre of attention on Mike's day. He stormed to the front of the bar and started to raised his voice.

"How fucking dare you! How dare you stand here before us, his family and real friends and talk all this shit. You didn't give a damn about Mike, you haven't spoken to him for over ten years and what's all the hero talk about you muppet. You have no idea what you're talking about. This is his fucking day, not yours so drop the fucking act!"

Sharon had followed John over to the bar and was hanging onto his every word hoping and praying that this outburst would give her some clarity. Give her a clue as to the truth; the fact was she already knew the truth. There was nothing to hide in this case, Mike had been a casualty of the NI conflict and was just in the wrong place at the wrong time. John continued with his own unprepared speech.

"I've known Mike for the last 10 years, we were on the PRC together right at the beginning, we did basic training together and we chose 42 Commando together. He chose his path and I chose mine, we didn't stop being friend's coz we served in a different company. We were like brothers and yes I was in Ireland when he died and yes I know exactly what happened. It's exactly what you've been told happened; the Corps isn't lying to you all. He was bloody unlucky that's all. It comes with the job; some of us die fighting hand to hand combat in some far away countries, some of us get killed in a car crash on our way home to see our loved ones and others are in the wrong place at the wrong time."

"Do you really think that if those guys had known those Provo's were there with a boot full of explosives they would have just wandered up to the car as they do with every check point. Shit happens and Mike accepted that as part of his job, it wasn't just a job to Mike, he fucking loved his life and being a part of the Corps. Just like most of us do, we do what we do for the man standing by our side, not for Queen and Country. He died doing what he loved doing; he died a Royal Marine Commando, he died proud. I'm not here to mourn him; I'm here to celebrate his life and what he stood for. So bollocks to you and anyone else who thinks any different."

John turned and walked out of the pub and headed back to the car, Amy ran after him and the room stood in silence. Then Mike's Company let out a roar, "three cheers for Mike Callahan and all that he stood for!" The room joined in cheering for him and the party went into full swing with drinks flowing and friends and family talking to the other marines Mike had served with.

Outside John sat in the car next to Amy in silence, "they're cheering for him now babe. Should we go back in and rejoin the party?"

"No, I can't go back in there. I don't want the attention; I've said what I had to say hun. Let's go back to the hotel."

Rebecca came walking over to the car as he started the engine. She stopped as she heard it roar into action and stood in the middle of the car park looking at her son through the window. John turned and saw her, he paused and wasn't sure what to do. He applied the handbrake and got out of the car, "Hey," was all he could summon.

"Hi son, how would you feel about spending a bit of time with your old mam?"

John walked over to her and held her tightly, he could feel her shaking as she broke down and held onto her son for the first time in 5 years. He walked her back to his car and put her in the back, Amy just smiled at her as she got in and her eyes filled up with emotion. She was so happy he had reacted the way he did. They drove to Seaburn to the Swallow Hotel on the sea front and sat in the bar, John was still in his Blues uniform as he sat talking and listening to his mother. It was as if he had just been away on leave and both Rebecca and Amy were so happy to see each other again. Rebecca realised what she had done and given up and now after hearing the news on TV about Mike's death it hit her that this was what her son was out there to do. To look after his oppo's and protect the British public from terrorism. It was a great day considering it was Mike's funeral and all, but Mike wouldn't have wanted it any other way, he was a good guy and he would often tell John to go home and speak to his mother and make things right between them but he was a stubborn sod and would never have made the first move but he was man enough to accept her apology and to move past the whole situation. It was history now and that's where it would stay.

John had managed to get a an additional three day pass via the recruitment office, it was interesting when he rang the bell on the door and the same nasty little shit came to the door. Chief Petty Officer Stone stood there and he recognised John immediately. They chatted about his time in the Corps and the Chief enjoyed catching up with the young man who had walked through his doors ten years earlier although he was sorry to hear about Mike's death. They chatted for a couple of hours and the Chief managed to get him his three day pass so he could spend some time with Amy and his mother. It was a good three days and they all felt very happy to have each other back together again.

Chapter 10

The 1990's

February 1990 was the start of John's Senior Command Course to become a Sgt and once again received a superior pass as he had on his Junior NCO's course winning the 'Leather Neck Trophy'. It was also the year he decided he wasn't getting the challenge he needed from the Royal Marines anymore. He passed the Senior NCO's course and received his third stripe in the August just in time for his three weeks summer leave.

John and Amy had bought a house in Washington just a few miles away from Sunderland so Amy could still be within travelling distance of her family and Rebecca. She never did achieve her goal of becoming a Doctor but instead became a Pharmacist and had landed a good job working for Boots in the Washington Galleries; she loved her job and her work colleagues. They never understood Amy much, they couldn't believe that John and Amy lived such separate lives but they were happy and this way John could concentrate on his career without having too much impact on Amy's.

He wanted her to be her own person and not have to depend on him. He told Amy this was for her own growth but really he was thinking of what would happen if he was killed in action (KIA) and then she had to rebuild a life up North after leaving all of her friends and family behind.

Amy suspected as much, she was an intelligent lady and loved John very much, she figured he knew what was best for them in the long term. She knew he would have a plan and even though he had planned out in advance his promotion chart prior to going in the marines she would sometimes tease him about it taking him so long to climb the ladder. He had indeed made Lance Cpl in just one year instead of two but took five years to make full Cpl instead of four and he had only just made Sgt after almost eleven years instead of the planned seven. But he was a career marine with bags of combat experience under his belt now and one day while he was cleaning out an old kit bag he found the business card of the SAS officer he had met on his sniper course all those years before and wondered if he was still serving or even alive for that matter.

He came home on a Friday night on this occasion instead of waiting for the less busy traffic of the Saturday morning. Amy thought this was a bit strange but knew he had promised to be with her for the full three weeks without being called away so she was just looking forward to having him home one extra night. On the Saturday evening he had taken Amy out for a meal in their favourite Italian restaurant named Gabrielle's which was situated on the sea front of Seaburn in Sunderland. They enjoyed a beautiful three course meal and a bottle of wine between them and John suggested a walk along the sea front before the headed home, just like old times.

It was a beautiful still night on the 23rd August 1990 when John stopped and sat Amy down on a wooden bench looking out over the ocean, the moon was almost full and the sky was so clear you could see the reflection of the moon on the still water below. Amy was enjoying the closeness of being with the man she loved when he suddenly stood up, "Oh are we going hun, I was enjoying that?" she asked.

John knelt down on one knee and Amy's eyes almost popped out of her head, "Amy, you are the love of my life and I can't imagine life without you by my side. So would you do me the great honour of being my wife?" He popped open a box and inside sat a beautiful white gold 1 carat diamond ring.

Amy started to cry with happiness and was stunned for a moment before answering, "Oh my God yes John I would love to be your wife and I'm not going anywhere my love. I will always be right by your side no matter what the world throws at us."

He placed the ring on her finger and it fit perfectly, he pressed his lips against hers and they sank into each other as if they were the only two people in the world. It was the happiest day of Amy's life and she couldn't wait to tell everyone about it, so much so that on the way home she tried to convince John to pop into his and her mum's to tell them the news but he was having none of it. This night was theirs and theirs alone, they could share the news tomorrow when they went for Sunday lunch. They spent the night making love and fell asleep holding each other and never wanted to let go.

The next day they discussed wedding plans which shocked Amy as this showed her just how much effort and thought John had put into planning everything from the engagement down to the wedding dates to ensure minimum disruption to their plans and honeymoon. They agreed on a date John had already agreed with his CO back at base prior to proposing, the date was to be Saturday 14th July 1991 and they would go for a honeymoon to St Lucia for two weeks all inclusive. He left Amy to organise the rest of the details as he had taken charge of the major points that most couples haggle about.

A couple of days before he was due to return to camp he sat Amy down and started to talk to her quite seriously.

"Amy, you know how we're doing all this stuff for us?"

"Yeah, don't tell me you're having second thoughts already buster, you only just bloody proposed to me," she laughed nervously because she knew that when John sat down to say something serious then it had to be serious and it meant it could have an impact on both of them. She was a little worried because she thought the proposal was all the surprises he had planned for one year.

"No daft arse, I'm not having doubts. You know I love you to bits and I'm never going to lose you. But you also know how important my career is to me."

"Yeah I know babe and I support you no matter what," she paused now thinking that she might be saying something she might regret.

"Well lately I haven't been feeling very challenged in my role."

"What? How can you not be challenged John? You're a bloody sniper for crying out loud. Is that not action packed enough for you or something?" she said once again with a jovial voice as she started to realise where this was leading.

"Well darling, actually no it isn't and I've decided to go for Special Forces selection next month." John sat and waited for a reaction but by now Amy had realised this was coming.

She spoke quietly now trying to hold back her emotion, "So what does this mean to us?"

"Well it means that in 3 weeks time I'll be starting joint selection at Hereford and I'll be gone for the next 16 weeks before I get any leave and then I'll be gone for another 13 weeks before I have to decide whether to go for SBS or SAS."

"But aren't you a Royal Marine first and foremost John? Why would you transfer to the Army?" Amy was confused by this turn of events, she knew he would end up in the SF eventually but she never thought she'd see the day when he considered transferring to the Army just to be in the thick of it.

"Yes I am babe and I always will be. But it just depends who can offer me the best career prospects and you know my concerns about the diving phase."

Amy cut in and interrupted him sharply, "you mean who can promise you the most action."

"No necessarily babe. I'm a career soldier and I don't want to be stuck behind a desk in 10 years time as a bloody Quarter Master in the stores. I can't do that, I'd rather be in a training position and make a difference to the men we send to war."

"John, you'll do what you want to anyway, you always do. I don't mean that to be stroppy, but you will. I've never had a say in anything you ever did so why is this any different?"

"Because I'm asking you if you're okay with this. If you're not then I won't do it hun, I promise I'll find something else. I'm not quite sure what but I will if it makes you happy. You're gonna be my wife and I do care what you think."

Amy had never been consulted on anything John had done since the day she had met him and she was flattered and she believed him when he said he wouldn't do it if she didn't want him to, but she also knew that she couldn't live with herself if he ended up working in the stores at CTCRM or ended up on secondment to the RMR in Newcastle for a couple of years training wannabe marine reservists.

"I want you to do it babe. I know you'll not be happy unless you give it a go and who knows you might bloody fail Mr Smart Arse," and she laughed knowing his track record for training courses and always getting the highest pass rate possible. She knew he wouldn't fail but she also knew he wasn't crazy about the diving phase of the SBS which meant that he was seriously considering leaving the Corps and joining the SAS and becoming part of the Army instead. It was a strange turn of events but she was glad he had asked her for her opinion rather than just phoning her one day and telling her he was on SF training in Brunei or something equally as crazy as that.

John decided to offer a compromise, "listen hun if I fail selection I'll become an ML and serve my time in 45 in Scotland and you can relocate so we can be together."

Chapter 11

Selection

John arrived with the other 199 hopefuls at Hereford on Thursday 20th September 1990 to start their two days of lectures and tests prior to starting joint SF selection. The tests went quite smoothly and so on the Saturday 22nd they began their first stage of selection known simply as "Endurance". It didn't leave much to the imagination, this was SF selection and it took place in the Brecon Beacons so it wasn't about to be a stroll in the countryside. Anyone who thought differently was about to get a real big shock.

The troops had breakfast and then met on the parade ground awaiting instruction. The senior DS stood before them. Sgt Birch had been in the SAS for 18 years and didn't suffer fools. He took them for 45 minutes of PT before they were taken by truck to a point on the map and told where they were, the truck then dropped the first half of the course off with a member of the DS and he started them off at 15 minute intervals. Meanwhile the second half were dropped off some 5 miles further away and they were given grid references to reach within given timescales. Some of them would pass each other going in different directions but they were not allowed to communicate with each other for the whole exercise and they had no idea how long they would be out there. It could be a day or it could be for the full three weeks. They were carrying 50lbs in their Burgan and the SA80 rifle and the route covered every major peak in the Brecon Beacons.

Initially the 200 men didn't bother to get to know each other as they knew the numbers would be drastically reduced by the end of this first stage. It wasn't uncommon to lose a half by the end of stage one.

John was dropped with the second group at around 1100 hrs and he was 3rd out of the truck. Immediately orientated himself before setting off. This was John's world as far as he was concerned and there was no challenge too big for this pint sized man. He was 27 years old and an experienced combat soldier having fought in the Falkland Islands and NI and he wasn't about to let three weeks of tough physical endurance get in his way at this stage of his career.

John set off like a bat out of hell straight up the mountain side in front of him; he had no intention of missing any of the RV's. The only thing on his mind was check point one which sat some 3,000 feet above him in the clouds of the Welsh mountains. The weather was damp and chilly which he welcomed as it kept his body temperature down. He climbed the mountain side at a strong steady pace and his thighs felt like they were ready to burst under the pressure of the uphill slope, his lungs burned with every deep gasping breath he took but still he showed no sign of slowing down. As he came over the top of the mountain in under one hour, he stormed towards the first check point. He knew he was doing well as the DS (Directing Staff) were just arriving there to set up the check point. The trooper looked surprised which in turn surprised John. He slowed to a forced march as he approached the DS; the staff member spoke first which was a relief as John was struggling to get his breath at that moment. "Name?" came the abrupt tone from the trooper standing before him.

"Savage, staff," came the response and John immediately set about showing the DS where he was on the map with a piece of grass between his fingers. This was so if they were caught the oil's from their fingers wouldn't have left any finger prints or marks giving away places of interest on the map and the DS recorded John's time of arrival and gave him his next check point grid reference some 5 km away on top of the next mountain.

John set off without saying anything else; he began to run as soon as he was a few feet away from the DS. The DS was secretly quite impressed at the speed in which John had made it up the first mountain. However he knew that many people had started off too fast and ran out of steam as the days went on. They had no idea how many check points there would be, just like they had no idea how long this exercise would last before they'd be fed and watered.

John ran head first down the next steep slope struggling to maintain his balance and fell several times but he didn't care so long as he didn't get a stupid injury. He was at the bottom in 30 minutes and stopped for a moment to get his bearings again before heading up the next slope, a 1000 foot climb before reaching the flat section for the last 500 metres to the next check point.

The grass on this section was long and damp. It was hard going but he felt strong at this stage, but it was early days. He drank some of his water before starting off again; he knew he was making good time but didn't want to get too cocky in case he burned himself out.

He headed up the next slope at a steady pace which was relentless on his burning thighs and lungs, at some points it got so steep he had to use his hands to help him up the slope and as he reached the top of the slope he could see check point 2 in the distance, the day was clear and the temperature was climbing. Not that it mattered as he was burning up with the sheer level of exertion. As he was about 20 yards out he slowed to a forced march again to gain his composure and get his breath back.

"Get a fucking move on you lazy twat!" came the start of the barrage of abuse he was to become accustomed to over the coming months. You see in the marines they understood that their soldiers had it tough enough as to not have to scream at them for no reason where as in the Army it was common practice. Some men coming from none Army regiments sometimes found this verbal abuse as hard as the physical tests.

As John approached the DS he spoke, "Savage, staff."

"I don't give a fuck who you are arse jockey, drop and give me 50 for ambling into my fucking check point you lazy cunt," said the DS.

John immediately dropped and did 50 press ups with full kit on his back then stood up and grabbed a piece of grass to show the DS where he thought he was. The DS never actually told you if you were right. They simply gave you the next grid reference and let you go; you could have been going to the fucking Congo for all you knew. Your mind played all kinds of tricks on you when you started to run out of energy.

As John left the check point the DS shouted after him, "Water re-fill at next check point so get your water down you lad."

"Yes staff," he replied. He wasn't convinced of course and thought it could be a trick so he could run out of water too soon and end up dehydrated and fail through heat exhaustion. John carried on at his impressive pace and once again the DS had recorded his time of arrival and time of departure for the records. This would be used in decided a man's fate at the end of stage one.

Once again John dropped off yet another mountain and this time it took him along a valley before starting to climb again. Check point 3 wasn't at a major point on top of a mountain this time. It was situated at a small cairn around 100 metres away from the summit and was easily missed if your compass bearing was even the slightest bit out.

John was confident in his navigation skills and ploughed straight up a rocky cliff face which would shave off maybe 30 minutes if he could get up the top section which was more of a hard scramble or a moderate climb if you had the balls to go for it. Most didn't and thought the easier route would of course be the safest bet and still give them plenty of time to reach the check point. John on the other hand wasn't your usual soldier and never shied away from a challenge.

Even in the middle of the world's toughest selection programme. He charged up the cliff side on all fours, he could see in the distance another candidate just leaving check point 2 and suddenly felt the pressure mounting, for a second he actually wondered how fit these other guys were. The guy he saw was obviously not that far behind him but would he have the guile to follow John's direct route to save time, if it went wrong the candidate could end up in real trouble and have to drop down lower in order to regain another route up the mountain side.

John scrambled and climbed over the cliff face which was exposed and the wind was starting to pick up. He was thankful for the wind as he was roasting and still only stopped once on the climb for a small drink of water. As he emerged over the edge of the cliff the DS smiled at the ballsy attempt he had made and he had saved the 30 minutes he was hoping for. He ran into the RV before once again saying, "Savage, staff." John arrived as the man who had been set off first was leaving so he knew he'd overtaken one man and was hot on the heels of another.

"Well done lad, get your breath back and grab a pie while you show me where you are." This DS didn't see the need to resort to screaming at the soldier, he simply spoke to him with a sense of urgency and as John showed him the exact location he gave the 4th grid reference of the day and told him there would be water at the next station. He had guessed right and when the DS asked to see his water bottle he was glad to see that John had ignored the advice of the last DS. He handed John a mug of sweet tea to wash down the steak and onion pie before heading off again. As soon as he reached the summit he started running again and the DS was glad to see this as he would have been disappointed to see the recruit taking his time once he knew he'd saved a little. Once again the DS recorded every person's time of arrival and time of leaving.

The second man who John had seen coming down from check point 2 decided against the direct route, this gave John the great lead he had built up from the start. The weather can change quickly in the Welsh mountains. One minute it's like the Costa del Sol and the next it's pissing down with freezing rain and 30 mph winds.

As the day wore on light rain cooled the recruits down. It didn't matter how fast John got to each check point as it was the overall time that counted. Obviously overall it would count but he still had set times in which to reach the next check point and as the men were stripped of their watches they had no idea what time it was or how long they'd been going. This was a tough test on the mind as they never told you if you had succeeded in achieving the time allocated. They simply kept sending you onto the next one even if they knew you'd already failed. This in its self could cause a man to quit as he might think he'd failed when in fact he was doing quite well. Despite the relentless physical challenges of the SF it is said that the job is 70% mental and 30% physical. At this point in time I think John would have disagreed whole heartedly.

He came towards check point 4 when he noticed a second member of the DS standing some 400 metres to the left of his compass bearing. This put a slight doubt in his mind, but he knew to trust his navigation skills and so kept running towards the DS he thought was correct. "Savage, staff." And he set about showing the DS where he was. The DS then tried to confuse him by saying, "Are you sure about that sunshine?"

John immediately responded, "Yes staff," he was confident he was at the right point and he proceeded to show the DS on his map with the piece of grass. The DS gave him the next grid reference only this one was 10 km away across mountainous terrain, some of which doubled back on its self. This again added to the confusion and John thought about the best route to take.

"Drink your water here in front of me and then go to the next DS over there and re-fill your bottle to the brim, understood?"

"Yes staff," John polished his half a water bottle off before running over to the other DS situated 400 metres away to the left. He filled his bottle up and headed straight off without even speaking to the other DS. This time he opted for a flatter route as the distance was much greater and they hadn't mentioned that this couldn't or shouldn't be done at this stage in selection. It wasn't a tactical exercise so they should be allowed to cross roads etc.

John slowed down a little on the decent to avoid injuring himself as there was fog creeping in covering everything with a film of dampness. Treacherous conditions for running up and down mountain sides of scree. The slate gave way under his feet time and time again. He made it to the bottom of the valley and set off along a Bridal Way making good time. It was fairly flat for the first 3 km's and John had no intention of slowing down.

He hit a couple of steep inclines before heading back down to another Bridal path. He was now closing on 8 km's before he started to head back up the mountain side to get on the tops. He was going like a steam train as he had saved a lot of energy on the flat sections. He climbed hard and fast, as he reached the next summit he stopped to re-evaluate his position. He was about 400 metres away from the check point 5 so he set his compass bearing and ran over the crest of the summit to see the DS sitting just inside a half dome tent with a brew on the go waiting for his next victim.

John ran over to the DS, "Savage staff," and proceeded to show him where he thought he was. The DS spoke only to hand him a Mars Bar and give him the next grid reference to a point a further 6 km away over tough terrain. This time there was no way around it, he was given 3 points to reach along the way and he was to record what he found at each point before arriving at the check point 6. It was already dark as he set off again eating his Mars Bar as he went; it was amazing what you could do on the run when you had to.

The weather came in fast. Wind and rain lashed the men of the selection course and this was only day one. John wondered how many had already wrapped it in and was back at base getting a hot shower and getting ready for bed after a pint in the NAAFI. He quickly threw the idea out of his head as it was a sign of weakness to start thinking like that. It was the start of questioning why you were here and if you didn't already know that then you shouldn't have come in the first place.

He trudged on through the wind and the rain into the pitch black of the night until he eventually found all three targets and recorded what he hoped were the right items. He was glad of his sniping skills and his eye for detail as the first test of micro navigation lead him to a crisp packet. Inside it gave him a clue as to the next target which if found provided another item of food.

Target one, crisp packet and colour of rock of 2nd target. When he arrived 40 minutes later at the 2nd target it was a black volcanic rock that didn't belong in the Brecon beacons, under it was a bag. In it were 6 chicken and mushroom pies. No-one had actually said that you could only take one and as there were 200 men out there it was first come first served. He wondered if he should take more than one. But after 20 seconds thinking about it he thought better of it as he might get penalised for taking more than one and someone could be watching him.

Inside the bag was another clue telling them if they found it they would also find a drink of some kind. Target 3 was a gorse bush with an orienteering post under it and under the post was a number and that number was the final piece of the jigsaw. It gave the first letter of the place where you would be able to sleep. Plus it gave him info that 50 metres downhill from the target point was another buried bag which contained 10 bottles of Lucazade Sport orange drink, isotonic fluids which tasted like heaven.

John carried on until he reached check point 6, at this point the DS handed him a hot brew and another pie and gave him the last letter of the place where he could get his head down for the night. He had to be at check point 7 by 0600 hrs the next morning. Bearing in mind that he didn't have a watch he didn't know if this was a trick but he also knew that if it wasn't he would be able to grab some much needed sleep. It didn't look like this exercise was going to end any time soon. This time he was only given a four figure grid reference but he had the first and last letter of the building where a dry night awaited. He carried on again and figured he would evaluate his options once he got there.

He was soaking wet through when he arrived in the middle of the night to the place of rest and he was greeted by another member of the DS.

"Get your head down over there Savage and I'll wake you up in 2 hours," and he sat down in the corner next to a small stove where he cooked his rations. The smell was amazing but he knew he wasn't to ask for anything and if he was offered anything it had to be something everyone would be offered or it could be seen as a fail. John lay down in the corner as directed and grabbed some sleep, as it happened he didn't need to be woken up as John was used to grabbing power naps as a sniper and had a pretty good idea he must have only had about an hour. He lay there with his heavy smock clinging to his cold skin. His back was chafed and raw from the heavy burgen bouncing around.

He got up and drank some of his water before heading out of the door without speaking to the DS. The DS didn't speak or even look up at him. John was surprised that he was the only one who had made it there, this made him think that it might have been a trap but he had to carry on regardless and just focus on getting to the next point which was 2 km away and all uphill.

He made it to check point 7 before first light so he knew he was well within his time limit. Once again he showed the DS where he thought he was and once again there was another DS some 500 metres away on another summit which John believed was the false summit. He continued to trust his instincts as they had got him this far. As he left check point 7 he realised that he hadn't seen anyone since he was climbing towards check point 3. Surely someone would have past him coming this way by now. Just as he was thinking that up popped two men speed marching over the crest of the hill he was just about to start his decent on.

"Top of the morning to ya," called a cheery Irishman with a big smile across his face.

John responded with the same level of cheeriness, "Morning to you sir's, beautiful weather we're having for this time of the year," he carried on past them and started to run down the side of the hill in pursuit of his next check point.

Check point 8 was 2 km away but this time was in the middle of a wooded area and he was told it would be unmanned. He would have to find it to gain his next grid reference for check point 9. He made it to the edge of the wooded area in ten minutes and started to laugh to himself as he saw the wood before him. It was completely closed off to anyone; the coniferous trees were so close together it was impossible to walk through it. So instead he set off crawling under the branches of the conifers for the next 200 metres on his compass bearing until he found the box and opened it to find 10 Cadbury Whisper Bars inside.

He took one and the next grid reference which also told him that his time was recorded and he had 60 minutes to make it to check point 9 which was 6 km away across the mountains. He quickly ate the chocolate bar and carried on crawling for another 600 metres until he came to a clearing and off he went at a fast pace up the fire break in the woods. It was a long uphill section. The ground was caked in deep mud which covered his boots up to his ankles. He knew this was going to be a tough challenge and even though he had surpassed all expectations, he knew if he didn't make it within the given time it would be classed as a fail. He had been told that no-one ever makes it through stage one without failing at least 2 of the deadlines. He was determined to prove them wrong and went for it. He looked at his map one last time before continuing on his route up a gulley with a footpath along the side of it or he could go for a more direct route straight up the side of a steep waterfall.

"Fuck it," he said out loud as he ran towards the waterfall and started to climb the steep rock face. This was a dangerous tactic and if he fell he would be fucked or possibly worse, dead.

He made it up the waterfall without a hitch and ran towards the next check point gasping for air. He slowed to a speed march for the last 10 metres as he approached the DS and called out, "Savage staff," the same routine as always. Show them where you are and get the next check point.

Check point 10 was 3 km away in the bottom of a valley so off he went again. He was starting to slow by this stage and as he was only given 30 minutes to reach the next target he figured this must be the two check points that no-one ever passes. He didn't care, he went for it at full speed down the slope slipping and sliding as he went. He had stopped counting how many times he had fallen over in the last couple of days but his backside was telling him it had been a lot. He imagined his arse being black and blue from the trauma it had suffered.

He hit the road at the bottom of the slope and could see a truck some 500 metres away. He began to sprint for it as he knew he must be closing in on the given timescale. As he reached the truck its engines roared into action and the truck pulled away with a member of the DS in the back shouting, "come on, hurry up or it's a long way back to camp lad."

John knew this trick only too well but still kept on running, what he didn't expect was to have to keep on running for the next 60 minutes. The 4 tonner constantly pulled away up the road but again he knew he mustn't give up as this was what they wanted him to do. The truck was much more likely to win this challenge in the long haul but regardless John kept running and getting closer with each attempt. He could see several men in the back who were obviously from the selection too but he couldn't focus long enough to make out any of their faces. John kept running until eventually 8 km later the truck stopped and he made it to the back of the truck where he was told to get in before they left him again. The DS couldn't help himself, he was impressed with Sgt Savage of the Royal Marines and decided to make it known to the others.

"Now that's what you're supposed to fucking do coz believe me when your chopper is dipping into a hot LZ you better be fucking sure you make it to the back of it or your getting left behind to the rag heads so they can butt fuck you till you talk."

It was obvious that no-one in the back of the truck had put up the same gallant fight to catch the truck. When they arrived back at the barracks in Brecon they were shipped out and told to get a hot shower and some sleep. "Debrief is in 4 hours so I suggest you spend it in sick bay or in the sack. Unless anyone else wants to fucking wrap today? It's been a busy old day today for the quitters amongst you," said a Cpl on the directing staff.

The DS didn't care if you quit, they didn't want quitters by their side in a war. As the remaining men got their heads down in their bunks a few did as they were told and headed for the medical centre to have their broken bodies looked at. The medics in Hereford weren't there to dole out sympathy, they were there to assess if you were fit to continue. Five men went to the med centre, only three came back; all five were told they were fit to continue, but two of them wrapped. We found this out by the other three who returned to the bunks with only two hours to go until debrief.

As John got up out of bed and grabbed a quick shower he looked around the room and took a quick count of the men left. It was day three of stage one, "Endurance" and they were already down to 64 men out of the original 200. 136 men down after just three days and the fun had only just begun.

The next two weeks was a series of forced marches over the Brecon Beacons and Black Mountains which included river crossings, tactical navigation and the grand finale was Exercise Long Drag. This was probably the most famous exercise in the world. Known to have been with the SAS for years it had weeded some of the best soldiers out before they started the real SF training. Long Drag is a 40 km tactical forced march in the Black Mountains to be completed in less than 20 hours. It was said that another 10% of men fail at this early stage of selection.

The remainder of selection was a series of forced marches. It started with a 25 km march carrying 55 lbs and each day increased by 5 km's and the Burgan gained 5 lbs. The days were long and the recruits had plenty of time to dwell on their ailments during the long marches.

They set off at 0400 hrs on the Wednesday morning and so began Exercise Long Drag, this was no place for the weak minded or the physically weak. They set off from their start location at 15 minute intervals and as John's surname was Savage he was at the back of the group. This made him happy as he knew he was probably the fittest man on selection, injury free and motivated. He also knew that every time he caught someone up and overtook them it would be a mental victory for him and a possible fail for the person being over taken.

John made a good start, the weather was terrible. The rain was very heavy which meant the 55 lbs of weight they set off with was about to get a whole lot heavier if it wasn't water proofed properly. He was confident being a Royal Marines that he was prepared for any weather, especially weather like this. He was making good ground and within an hour he had caught up the man who left 15 minutes before him. He had spoken to him in the back of the truck as they approached the start line; his name was Sgt Jim "Jolly" Rodgers from the Royal Engineers. He was a big guy and as the name suggests was always jolly which was good in this kind of situation. As John ran past him he shouted some banter to wind him up, "Hey good golly Mr Jolly. You having a stroll are you?" and he ran past laughing at him.

"Fuck off Maureen." He shouted back laughing.

John continued to make good ground but he didn't pass anyone else for another two hours which meant one of two things. Someone was lost or wrapped. Either that or John was so far off track he was gonna be in the shit. He was convinced he was on the right track and knew exactly where he was, which was good as it was easy to get lost in this weather.

He continued to make his way along the route passing men one by one; he passed at least one person every hour and sometimes two if they were slowing down enough. The daylight came and went as the miles fell away. It had been a bright day despite the poor weather conditions. John kept putting one foot in front of the other and plodded forward almost in a daze by the time he reached the final RV which was only 4 km away from the finish line, a dirt track cross roads in the middle of the Welsh countryside.

It took 18 hours and 38 minutes for John to complete the dreaded 40 km TAB (tactical advance to battle), a TAB which had broken hundreds, maybe thousands of hopefuls before him. He had made it through Exercise Long Drag and as the remaining men met up at the finish they looked around and started laughing at each other.

They had made it to the end, not all of them made it in the 20 hour time limit but they made it to the end and they lived in hope that they had passed. No-one knew their times at that moment but there were only 23 men completed the exercise, another 41 had fallen by the way side, one through injury as he fell down a hillside breaking his leg, it was only by chance that a member of the DS came across him.

The other 40 men had wrapped or failed, the worst part was that one guy didn't realise he was only 1 km from the finish when he saw a member of the DS and wrapped his hand in. The DS didn't say anything, he just gestured for him to follow him with a twist of his head. So the man did, he followed the DS onto a road not more than 20 metres away and 1 km later he was at the truck. His heart sank and he broke down on the roadside. The DS put him in a land rover with the medics as they didn't want his state affecting the other men who had earned their right to ride in the back of the truck.

The following morning after a good night's sleep and a belly full of hot food the final 23 men of the original 200 stood to attention waiting for their results. It was an SAS Colour Sgt who read out the results and they went in the following order;

Savage	18 hrs 38 mins	Pass
Brotherton	19 hrs 18 mins	Pass
Stevens	19 hrs 29 mins	Pass
Cox	19 hrs 32 mins	Pass
Hands	19 hrs 39 mins	Pass
Burns	19 hrs 47 mins	Pass

The following made it in 19 hrs 50 mins   Pass

McKenzie
Grimes
Howard
French
Fox
Edgley
Saxson
Bree
Featherton
Patchly

Keen	19 hrs 59 mins	Pass
Lords	20 hrs	Pass

"The rest of you, there really is no point in reading out your names and wasting my fucking breath; you failed now piss off and don't darken our doors again until you grow a set of balls."

"Colour Sgt," called one of the men whose name hadn't been called out, "I think we deserve to know our times to see if we did fail."

"Oh you do, do ya? Well let me see," he decided to call out the remaining 5 men's times.

Ball	20 hrs 2 mins	Fail
Cowan	20 hrs 12 mins	Fail
Oxley	20 hrs 15 mins	Fail
Towers	20 hrs 29 mins	Fail
Gist	20 hrs 37 mins	Fail

"You fucking happy now sweetheart? Do you feel better knowing that you were 12 fucking minutes outside the time? Now get the fuck out of my regiment!"

Sgt Cowan of 2nd Battalion Parachute Regiment had been so sure that he'd made it through. He couldn't believe he was 12 minutes outside the time and he dreaded going back to the regiment having failed selection at such an early stage.

Colonel Bishop of the SBS arrived and spoke to everyone before they were dismissed; he was a cheerful fellow from an upper class family who spoke as if he had marbles in his mouth.

"First of all let me say well done to all who passed this time round and to those who failed, well it is better to have tried and failed than not to have tried at all. For anyone who cares to know the man who fell down the mountainside was Sgt Rodgers of the Royal Engineers. He has badly broken his leg and will be in hospital for some time. Get plenty of rest men and stay off the piss, next week is two week pre- jungle preparation. Fall out."

The men fell out and went back to writing letters, making phone calls, and carried on preparing their kit ready for stage 2. They would fly out to Belize the next morning and start getting acclimatised to the jungle climate in the safety of the jungle warfare training school while practicing weapons handling and patrolling techniques before going into the real thing. Six weeks of jungle training practicing navigation techniques, fighting skills, combat survival and more patrolling skills. It would be a very unique experience and this stage again was where many failed to come up to the standard. The jungle also had a habit of bringing on extreme cases of claustrophobia in men who had never suffered before.

John prepared his kit and wrote a letter home, it said that he was fit and well and would be heading off to warmer climates and by the time she received this he would be sunning himself half way across the world. Amy of course knew that this was his way of telling her in code that he had passed stage one and was heading to the jungle.

She was very happy to hear from him, she hadn't seen or heard a word since he left 4 weeks earlier and although that wasn't particularly strange if he was away on tour, she knew he was in this country training to become one of the world's most elite fighting soldiers and as if he wasn't already the most feared man on the battlefield he was about to increase that fear factor by 100% by becoming either an SAS or SBS operative. She had actually started to get excited for him but she did know that he had told her just how tough the jungle training was and that he wasn't due to go until the next 42 commando training camp in 1995 which seemed a long way away.

John did want to learn jungle warfare but didn't want to wait another 5 years before he could do it as a standard package, as he was an Arctic Warfare Specialist there wasn't much cause for jungle training an Arctic soldier at this time. He had missed out twice on this training in the last ten years, the first time in 81' he was on his Arctic Warfare Training Course and the second time in 89' when he was in NI. They just couldn't justify taking him out of either of those scenarios and nor would he have wanted to have been at the time, it was simply bad timing.

The jungle was no picnic and they wasted no time in getting to grips with their so called intro, by the end of week 2 they were fully trained in jungle patrolling techniques and were ready to put them to the test in the jungle now. They would go out a couple of days at a time initially each time getting slightly longer, each time slightly harder than the last. John came into his own on the observation tests as he was used to picking out detail as a sniper, there was only one other trained sniper on the course.

A small half cast guy called Private Bree, John had no idea where Bree's family originated and he didn't really care right now. He had slotted very nicely into the motion of not getting too friendly with anyone on the course as very few would pass and therefore they didn't really matter, especially as they were all from Army crap hat regiments none of which he considered anywhere near as good as his beloved Marine Corps.

Bree was a sniper in the Coldstream Guards; they were a lot tougher than anyone really knew. They were seen trooping the colour in front of Buckingham Palace and this lead other soldiers to believe they were soft blokes who dressed up in funny hats. Which was only partially true, yes they did dress up in funny hats but they were also one of the toughest infantry units in the British Army with many battle honours behind them.

John was lucky enough to be paired off with someone who had already done jungle training some 5 years earlier; he was Cpl Saxon from 1 Para. They put them together deliberately as they knew both units were arched rivals and usually hated each other's guts but this was different. Here they were no longer marine or paratrooper, they were on SF selection and they could end up serving together for the rest of their military lives.

Saxon had served with the Ghurkhas in Hong Kong and had the pleasure of training with them on jungle exercises on several occasions; he was an experienced soldier who had served for 14 years in the Paras.

He started out in 2 Para where he served in the Falkland Islands but after 5 years he had a fall out with his CO and thumped him breaking his jar so rather than lose a good soldier who had been provoked they transferred him to 1 Para as a punishment. As it happened he had never been happier, because the rest of the Para's tended to look down on 1 Para they worked even harder to prove everyone wrong. The only thing 1 Para did less of, was jumping out of aeroplanes which was fine by him, he didn't mind it of course, he wasn't adverse to jumping but in his 5 years he had jumped 259 times, which he recorded in a diary just out of curiosity at first but as time went on he started thinking it would make a good talking point in the pub when he was older if he could show how many jumps he had done in his career, even 1 Para had to do at least one jump per year but Saxon had managed to keep getting selected every time there was a jump and so to date he had actually completed 432 static line jumps and earned his free fall Para wings and was looking forward to taking his HALO (High Altitude Low Opening) wings with the SAS.

He had requested to join the Pathfinder Platoon three years earlier only to find the Captain he had chinned was now a Major with Pathfinder so needless to say his request was turned down. He didn't mind anymore as the only reason he was trying to join them was because he didn't think he was good enough to pass SAS selection but then he thought what the hell, what have I got to lose and here he was 11 weeks later in his final week of jungle warfare training with the SAS and he was doing really well after passing Exercise Long Drag with less than one minute to spare. But he made it and that's all that mattered and he was confident that he would make it the rest of the way. He was a hard man from Liverpool who didn't take any shit from anyone; he was a good bloke to have fighting on your side in a war.

The final exercise lasted 7 days and ended up with a full scale Jungle assault and a guerrilla warfare campaign against local militia who knew the land like their own back yard. It was a tough exercise with everything they had learned so far being tested. It was tougher than any of them thought it was going to be, even Saxon with all his experience said it was much harder than anything he had done previously.

Both John and Saxon received a pass for the jungle phase and as John had also had the highest pass mark in stage 1 he was doing incredibly well, but you could never take anything for granted in SF. One minute your doing great and the next minute you've got jungle rot in your feet and leeches on your balls like one poor bastard did on this course, the worst part of it was that he was a fellow marine. Marine Featherton from 45

Commando had made it through stages 1 and 2 only to let his personal hygiene slip long enough to catch jungle rot in both of his feet. Savage was furious with him and didn't hide it from him.

"What the fuck are you playing at Feathers? You're not some fucking crap hat playing at being a soldier, you're a fucking bootneck and you've let the side down with piss poor admin. I'm fucking shredders mate."

It didn't matter in the end did it, after all Featherton was heading back to 45 Cmdo having failed SF selection, he had dreamed his whole life of being in the SBS and this was how his journey ended. There were quite a few marines working in Brunei at the school, all of which had either been SF previous and now specialised in jungle warfare training or were still serving in the SBS and just honing their skills once a year by coming out to the jungle and doing a 3 month draft.

Brotherton and Stevens were both from Pathfinder Platoon, the Paras very own specialist recce troops, and they were classed as the closest thing to the SAS. Brotherton was a monster of a man with a lot of facial scars; his left arm had some serious burn scars too. He was a real Londoner with a strong cockney accent and had joined the Paras as a junior solider at the age of 16 and then progressed into adult Para training before serving with 3 Para for 6 years. He then joined Pathfinder Platoon and had served with them for another 6 years before applying for SAS selection. He was very efficient and you could tell he was an experienced combat soldier, he didn't say a lot really, he preferred to just get on with the job in hand and like John he excelled in the field. John was surprised he wasn't a sniper because he certainly had the skills to do it.

Stevens already knew Brotherton from Pathfinder but they were in different sections and although they had served in the same areas they had never actually spoken before the SF selection. Stevens had joined the Army a little later in life than most, he was 24 when he joined and went on to serve with 2 Para for 7 years before heading over to Pathfinder Platoon where he had served for the last 3 years. He was also very competent and equally tough; he was covered in tattoos and came from Glasgow only he was anything but quiet, he was a gob shite actually who rarely shut up, but he was very amusing so most didn't mind his relentless banter. John got on well with him but Brotherton was a hardened Para and didn't want to have anything to do with a bootneck.

They returned back to the UK on Thursday 6th December 1990 and had a long weekend off before starting their one week signals course. John went home on the Friday but returned on the Saturday as he had to do a bit of revision for his course. He was already signals trained so he didn't think he would have any problems but as always he wanted to be ahead of the game. Amy was glad to see him even if it was just for the day. He had driven up early on the Friday morning and got there by midday so he spent the day with Amy, they didn't tell the rest of the family he was coming home as they wanted to make the most of their time together.

He left at midday on the Saturday and Amy was sad to see him go, she didn't mention anything to him at the time but she was noticing some changes in him and she wasn't sure how to broach the subject. Obviously he was going through a tough time in selection and she knew that he was totally focussed as he always was in everything he did but there was something different about him and she couldn't quite put her finger on it. She was glad to hear the news that he would be home for Christmas and New Year this year. That would be the next time she saw him so this made it extra special to her and she planned to make his time at home very memorable.

The signals course was a breeze and the following week they had 'Special Weapons' training were they focussed on the weapons they would use in the SF. The Heckler & Koch MP5A3, Colt Commando, Barrett .50mm sniper rifle with an effective range of 2 km's, John enjoyed this week and felt like a kid in a candy shop. There was always fitness training, this didn't stop just because the endurance phase was over. It was relentless; they would get up every morning and do between 10-20 miles before breakfast and then in the afternoon they would hit the gym to do either circuit training or weight lifting and in the evening they would normally finish the day with the assault course in full kit with the added fun of a full sized telegraph post.

They got the go ahead for their Christmas leave and they went home on 21st December until the 5th January 91'. John had a great time back home and Amy had made a special effort and even planned a New Year's party with family and friends. It was good to see everyone, his old civi friends couldn't believe how much he had changed, they knew he had fought in the Falklands and had a rough time in NI so they no longer doubted his abilities to handle himself. There wasn't the usual abuse they had previously given him. In the past they still saw him as the soft lad form school but now he was a tough Royal Marine and no-one was going to mess with him. He had even managed to put a little weight on and was now weighing in at 10 stone of solid muscle; he was probably as fit as he had ever been in his life, he felt good and strong. He had no doubt that he would pass selection but he also knew that if he chose the SBS and failed the diving phase he would have to re-take the whole of selection again and that was something no-one wanted to do if they could help it. If you failed early on you knew what you had to do to prepare for it but to pass enough of the course to actually join the SAS and then fail the SBS boat & diving phase would have been devastating.

When John returned to Hereford after his leave he felt good, well rested but still fit as he had been training hard while up North. You never realise just how fit you are because the men you serve with are all very fit guys too, but when one of John's civi friends asked if he could join him for a run one morning John figured it would be fine as Mark was a club runner who regularly competed in half marathons and although he didn't know what kind of times he was putting in, he figured he must be fit so he agreed and they went for a 10 mile run one morning. Much to Mark's horror he was struggling to keep up with John and who didn't seem to be out of breath which really fucked with Mark's head. How could John have become this fit? He would never know, but it did make John realise that he must be pretty fit.

The next stage of training was the 'Combat Survival Instructors Course' which took place in the Outer Hebrides which as this time of year was terrible. It lasted two weeks and was followed by a two week demolitions course which seemed to go very fast and was a welcome treat after freezing your arse off on a survival ex. The course was down to 13 men now due to injury and failures on some of the assessments. The combat survival phase continued when they returned to Hereford unexpectedly. They were hunted down by the enemy played by the Paras and were all eventually captured, they were subject to rough handling and some fairly brutal interrogation techniques. It was the simple things that broke some men; the course lost 3 men in this phase as they just couldn't take the constant abuse they were subjected to. The exercise lasted 4 days so you didn't want to get caught on day one or you'd have three days of interrogation to suffer.

Once captured they were dragged around and constantly screamed at while wearing a hessian sack over their heads, this lead to confusion and when your cold, wet and hungry this can play havoc with the mind. They were thrown under a sheet of corrugated iron and the sheet was then beaten with heavy chains, as the noise can bring on the feeling of claustrophobia. They would be hung up by their hands on meat hooks in a cold warehouse as Land Rovers were driven at high speeds towards them, sometimes clipping them a little causing minor injury.

Cold water was thrown over their half naked bodies and over the hessian sacks so as they tried to take a breath it would suck the sack into their mouths and give the feeling of drowning. There was no two ways about it; this was definitely one of the hardest phases of selection and it seemed to last for an eternity.

John was dragged naked into an extremely warm room, no more than 8 feet by 6 feet, the heavy smell of cigarette smoke and the smell of strong hot coffee lingered. John looked down at the table, he had no ideas how long he had been subjected to this abuse and even he had started to doubt if this was part of selection or if they would actually kill him, the mind can't focus, he had no idea of day or time as he was questioned over and over again about the location he was found and what he was doing there. The interrogator started off gently;

"What's your name son?" asked the interrogator softly

"Savage, P049466Y, 3rd May 1963."

"What we're doing near that farm house?"

"I cannot answer that question"

"Why not son? Come on what possible harm can it do? If you weren't up to anything then you have nothing to worry about, what your first name Mr savages?" he continued with his friendly demeanour.

"I cannot answer that question," came the standard response.

The tone changed suddenly and his temper erupted, "Don't fucking play that game with me sunshine. I'll throw you in a cage with the fucking sodomites and they'll fucking rape the arse out of you! Is that what you want?"

"Savage, P049466Y, 3rd May 1963."

He launched across the table punching John full force in the left eye, bang! His eye felt like it exploded as he tumbled backwards off the chair. As he hit the deck the guard behind him stamped on his forehead while the interrogator tried kicking him in the balls. John curled up in a ball, hands tied behind his back pain flashing through his body. He had no idea what he was being hit with now but he was in serious pain. The next thing he knew he was sitting back up at the table and the interrogator was blowing cigarette smoke across it and into his face.

"I know your fucking name son. Your name is John Savage, isn't it?" his tone lowered again.

"Savage, P049466Y, 3rd May 1963."

"Is this how things are going to be John? You repeating that bullshit the British Army tell you to and me having to hurt you? I don't want to hurt you John but if I have to I will and you will tell me what I want to know son."

Just then the guard slammed a punch into John's kidneys winding him, he felt as though he would pass out any minute and just as he was thinking things couldn't get much worse he felt the hot coffee hit him in the face. He screamed with the pain and as he dropped his head to cover his face he hit his own chin on the table in front of him and felt a tooth smash under the force of the blow. All he could think of now was, "my tooth, my fucking tooth, I don't believe I just did that to myself."

He was being dragged out of the room by his feet along the floor, it was a cold stone floor in the corridor and he could feel the rough ground scraping across his naked body as it was dragged by two men. As they opened the door he quickly glanced around and saw another five men strung up on the meat hooks, they were being hosed with cold water. He knew it was cold by their gasps for air as they struggled to breath; he felt the boot land in his stomach as they saw him trying to look around and they quickly hung him up and sprayed him with the cold water. It seemed to go on forever but was probably only a couple of minutes.

He didn't know how long he'd been hanging there but he couldn't feel his hands anymore, he was on his tip toes as they had raised him a little higher so when the car hit him he would swing up into the air. It didn't hit him very hard, just hard enough to take his legs from under him. He rolled across the top of the car and fell off the other side. They took him down and forced him to run as they screamed and shouted in his ears at close range, he felt the heat again as they took him into a room.

This was different; he could here others in the room but couldn't see much through the hessian sack. The room was bigger and the walls were bright white, he was put into a stress position against the wall and told not to move, he could hear at least two or three people groaning with pain, then it began, the white noise was deafening and the pain was blinding.

His head felt like it would explode and this went on for some time. Time and time again he would be taken to the interrogation room and it would start again, the screaming and shouting, punches to the body and legs, dragged back into the white noise room and then back outside to be hung up and hosed down again and again.

John felt like he was dying, then everything fell silent and all he could hear was your own breath. It was eerily silent and this worried him even more than before, was anyone there? Was he about to be hit again just as he let his guard down? He had no idea, then the large corrugated doors to the warehouse opened and the rush of air came surging into the space they were hanging, he heard footsteps coming towards him and he flinched as he expected to be hit, but this time they cut him down and released his hands and removed his bag from his head.

There stood in front of him was Colonel Jeffrey, the CO for SAS selection alongside Colonel Bishop of the SBS. They were smiling and Bishop looked down at his left arm and was wearing a white arm band signifying it was all over, he then called out, "end ex!"

"Oh my God," he thought, John had never been so happy to hear two words in his entire life. He was a mess and as he looked down at his battered body he wondered how he had taken so much abuse, but he did and he'd made it. They were taken to the med centre and fixed up, given pain killers and had their cuts and abrasions taken care of. John had never felt so shit in all his life but man he felt good for surviving. The worst was surely over now, it had to be.

The following week they did OP Training and this was followed by two weeks of CQB (Close Quarter Battle) which was a welcome break to being beaten and abused. The DS's attitude changed towards them at this stage too, they had earned the respect of the DS and were close to the end. No-one knew if they had passed at this stage and suddenly they were told they were heading out on another E&E (escape and evasion) exercise in the Brecon Beacons. Everyone's heart sank as they heard the words but this was when you knew if you were made of the right stuff to be a SF soldier, someone who would never give in no matter what.

They gathered their kit and fell in outside. Colonel Bishop and Colonel Jeffrey were stood there; John couldn't believe it when he heard one of the guys break down in the barracks behind him. After everything he'd been through he just crumbled and was sobbing curled up on the ground. Once the remainder had fell in outside on parade for the exercise Jeffrey's spoke.

"Well done men, 12 of you have passed and earned the right to join the elite group of men we like to call the Special Forces. It really is a shame about Cpl Keen as he has just failed based on that little outburst but that's what being a member of this unit is all about. For those of you who are joining us here at Hereford I welcome you to the Special Air Service gentlemen, you are a rare breed of men who have proven yourselves beyond the mere mortal men who serve in all other British units or indeed any unit in the world. Next you will be attending the 8 week 'Individual Skills' stage before heading off to join your unit. You are joining the most feared unit in the world and we live and die by our motto, Who Dares Wins! Welcome to the SAS gents. I will now hand out the beige berets to the following men. But as there are two of you who will be continuing your training with the SBS I wish you the very best of luck."

22nd Regiment Special Air Service

Brotherton
Stevens
Cox
McKenzie
Grimes
Howard
Fox
Saxon
Bree
Lords

SBS Continuation Training

French
Savage

He handed out the beige berets while French and Savage were wishing this was the end of the line for them too. But they were Royal Marine Commandos and despite John's concerns about the diving phase he wanted to at least try to stay with his beloved Corps.

All 12 men were taken into an interview afterwards to discuss their futures and to be told which squadron they would be joining. Colonel Bishop took French and Savage in at the same time as they would be attending SBS training and weren't sure what was to happen next for them.

"Right men, first things first, well done. I'm very proud of you both and I'm especially proud of the fact that you want to stick with the Corps."

He started moving some paperwork around his desk as if disorganised but both of these men knew his reputation as a brilliant leader. He was a legend in the SBS and was their CO for 3 years but preferred to be operational as he loved to be in the shit. You shouldn't be fooled by his snooty accent and apparent lapse attitude; this was a hard military man with bags of combat experience leading some of the world's toughest men.

"Okay gents, here it is. You have given your three choices in their respective order of what individual skills you would like to attain. French your first choice was advanced medic which I am happy to inform you that you have got, so well done you'll be heading to HMS Raleigh to attend that with 4 serving SBS soldiers who are multi skilling and I think there will be a couple of Royal Navy Commandos on that too. That lasts for four weeks then you'll need to do your Para wings as you've never jumped before. Okay?"

"Yes sir, that's great news sir." Responded Cpl French

"Off you go then," he stood up accepted the salute from French and shook his hand.

"Okay Sgt Savage, what can I say apart from well done. You have received the highest pass on the course and for that reason you have been given a very special life line. You raised concerns prior to selection about the diving phase which of course is the main role of the SBS. Due to your results the SAS have decided to offer you an olive branch. If you fail the 'Boat & Diving' phase they will be happy to accept you into the SAS. How do you feel about that?"

"Wow sir, I'm flabbergasted. I wasn't expecting that at all but ideally I would love to pass the 'Boat & Diving' phase and be part of the SBS. After all sir I am a Royal Marine." He said with a smile across his face. He couldn't hide the fact that he was ecstatic about this news. This didn't mean he wouldn't try his best to pass SBS training, it simply meant that should the worst happen he had the option to transfer to the SAS. He was made up and couldn't wait to tell Amy the news.

"Okay Savage, but first things first, your being sent on your military freefall course which starts in a week's time so you've earned yourself a week's leave before that starts and then you'll be attending the language school in Poole. Looks like you'll be learning Arabic Sgt."

"Arabic sir?" John questioned

"Yes Sgt, Arabic. It looks like the Gulf is about to kick off and you may get pulled out of training before you actually qualify as a SC3 but then you won't be going in by sea so I don't think that will be a major problem for you."

John arrived home without telling Amy that he had managed to get a week off, so when he arrived she was sat watching TV. He peeked through the window to see his beautiful fiancé as she sat completely unaware. He watched her for around 30 seconds before knocking on the window and she jumped out of her skin.

"Oh my God, what are you doing here?" she screeched at him as she opened the door and threw her arms around him. He didn't get chance to respond before she was kissing him in the doorway.

"Come on let me in before the neighbours call the kissing Police," he said laughing. He had a huge smile across his face so she knew it was good news.

"Come in and I'll put the kettle on or do you want a glass of wine or a beer?"

"Wow, too much choice but seems that I'm a bit knackered I think I'll have a nice cuppa tea babe. You look amazing hun have you been training or dieting or something?" John said looking on at Amy as if he was ready to pounce on her.

"Hey down boy, I'm sure you can wait a little while longer." She went into the kitchen and put the kettle on. "So come on then tell me all about it, I assume you passed?"

"Well I have to say that I have just had the toughest few months of my life. I won't bore you with the details but let's just say I wouldn't want to re-live them any time soon that's for sure."

"What do you mean; I won't bore you with the detail? I wouldn't exactly call your life boring hun, anything but."

"Okay okay, I'll tell you some of it but just remember that I can't tell you everything."

John and Amy talked for hours about his experiences over the last few months, he gave some detail of the combat survival course but not the gory detail. He didn't see the point in upsetting her by telling her about the beatings he had taken and the level of abuse, he just told her it was rough and no wonder the British SF are the best in the world with what they go through.

They enjoyed their week together and talked about the wedding plans that Amy had been making in his absence. She was getting very excited and could hardly wait for the 14th July. John did have to pick a time before he went back to tell her that he might have to go the Iraq at some point this year.

At the end of the week he just couldn't do it, there was never a good time and he didn't want to upset her before he went back. It was too hard and didn't know for sure it would happen, so he decided not to tell her at all.

He arrived at RAF Brize Norton ready for his HALO training which he loved. It was the most enjoyable 4 weeks he had ever had in his military career. Freefall parachuting was great fun, but it took a serious tone when the HALO and HAHO phases kicked in, especially the night jumps. It was an amazing buzz and one he thoroughly enjoyed; he was responsible for his own fitness during this stage. He passed the course and then moved onto his linguistics course, it was an intensive Arabic course which was very important that he passed as it was likely that he would end up serving in many Arabic speaking countries in the coming years. He passed the course at a reasonable standard, he wasn't the best but a pass was a pass and that's all that counted at this stage in his career.

The UKSF were already in Iraq by the time John had finished his 'Individuals Skills' stage and as he suspected, the SBS were considering sending any marines who were on their SC3 course to war with their respected commando units. John was hoping and praying that he would either be sent in with the SF or be allowed to continue with his training but it wasn't meant to be. John and the other men attending the SC3 course were called into the lecture room in Poole to be given the news after only two weeks of training.

Major Abrahams gave the brief to the men. "Afternoon men."

"Afternoon sir," came the resounding response from the 8 men who had passed their SF selection over the last 12 months and were finally on their SC3 course. They were all gutted that after waiting such a long time they would potentially have to be pulled off their course.

John was incredibly lucky as he had only passed selection some 9 weeks earlier, where as some of these guys had been waiting for up to 10 months.

"Okay guys, I'm not going to beat around the bush. I have some bad news for you all; you are all to return to your units first thing tomorrow morning. Sadam Hussain has launched a full scale attack in the Gulf and war has broken out, now as the UKSF are already in place we have no choice but to delay the SC3 course for a further 6 months at which time you will all be invited back to complete and hopefully pass the course. Does anyone have any questions?"

No-one said anything; they just shook their heads, the look on their faces said it all and John was seriously pissed off by the whole thing. He started to question if the marines were the way to go after all and decided to put in a call to Hereford. He rang and spoke to a female Army officer, Lt Brook. He had met her while on selection as she was one of the women who were used to interrogate the men once they were cold, wet and as naked as the day they were born.

It was an old technique but an effective one, to have a woman taking the piss out of your manhood when you were at your lowest point was enough to make a lot of men snap.

He had also spoken to her when handing in his request papers to go to the SBS instead of the SAS. She said they would be disappointed to lose such a good soldier but at this point he still had loyalty to the marines and now look what they had done to him. He chatted with her and told her of his disappointment at the marine's decision to cancel the SC3 course and to RTU the men until a later date. What if the war raged on for more than 6 months, would all UKSF training be cancelled? She too couldn't believe the Royal Marines could be this short sighted so she said she would make some enquiries and get back to him ASAP.

He had just got on the train from Poole to Plymouth when she called him on his mobile phone.

"Hi Sgt Savage, its Lt Brook here."

"Hello maam, how are you?"

"I'm good thanks. I've spoken to the team here in Hereford and your right they have as a one off they've cancelled the SC3 course. It's never happened before and to be honest the Regiment can't believe they are not going to use you guys as part of the UKSF teams being sent in, especially as you have all passed SF training and it's just the 'Boat & Diving Skills' that you guys haven't done and let's face it you're not exactly going to be coming in from the ocean."

"Yeah well that's what I thought too maam but obviously not and if I can be frank with you maam," John said cautiously.

"Yes of course Sgt."

"Well, I'm considering transferring to the Regiment instead. It's not that I don't have the patience as I think I've proven that in the past and considering my original trade that shouldn't be in question. I just can't believe that I'm going to be sent back to 42 Recce......" he trailed off as more people entered the first class carriage he was sitting in. "I can't talk right now maam but I think you get the gist of what I'm saying."

"Yes Sgt I think I do, leave it with me and I'll get back to you ASAP. Take care." The young Lt ended the call and went straight into HQ and spoke with the CO. Colonel Jeffrey was very interested in what he was hearing; Colonel Bishop was not so happy as he stood by and listened to what was unfolding.

Colonel Bishop decided to step in, "Michael, if I may intervene?"

"Yes Roger, what is it?" responded Jeffrey's

"I have to say that I am less than happy about what I have just heard, the fact that Sgt Savage has taken it upon himself to contact Hereford because he's not happy with his course been cancelled is inexcusable."

"Shit Roger, come off it. You know as well as I do that he's not the type to go crying as soon as he hits a snag in his career. He's a top class soldier and already Special Forces Trained for Christ's sake. He wants to be in the thick of it, not leading men into the mountains to carry out blanket stacking operations."

"I guess so, but all the same he should have waited until he got back and raised the issue through the correct channels. Are you seriously thinking of pulling him back here and changing the paperwork to make it look like he selected the Regiment over the Corps?"

"Of course not my dear chap. You are going to say there was a mistake in his paperwork and that you had persuaded him to go the SBS and now in light of what has happened you think it would be only fair to give him the choice of what to do next." The Colonel smiled at his SBS counterpart and gestured him to follow the young Lieutenant back to the office.

"Okay bugger it, he's a bloody good soldier and I suppose he has earned the right to go where he wants. I'll sort it." He followed Lt Brook back to her office and made a phone call to 42 Commando's CO. He explained the circumstance and said it was only fair that he be offered the choice. Lt Colonel Garver wasn't happy about losing one of his Sgt's to the SF to start with but to be told that he was having his Sgt back for the Gulf campaign and now for this to happen. But he listened to what the Colonel had to say, as we said earlier, this guy was a legend in the SBS so was very well respected and connected.

John arrived back at Bickleigh Barracks in Plymouth late that evening, as he reported in at the guardroom he was told he had to report to the CO first thing the next morning in his Lovats.

John felt a little nervous, he knew it was a risk to contact the SAS directly and he also knew that Colonel Bishop would be aware of it and wouldn't be happy about his change of mind. John put it to the back of his mind and went to the Sgt's mess and grabbed a sandwich and a pint while he caught up with some of the other Senior NCO's who he hadn't seen for some time. They knew where he'd been. It wasn't as secretive as the paparazzi would make it out to be, the men you served alongside knew exactly who was applying and who made it or didn't. They had already heard that John had made it. News like that travelled fast and it had come from the guardroom as soon as Colonel Bishop had rung to speak to the CO they knew it could only be good news.

John decided not to call Amy that evening until he knew what was happening and so he fell asleep while thinking about his choices and was sure the CO was going to give him a bollocking and this could possibly ruin his career in the Corps going forward. If you pissed the top brass off they could make your life hell and they could also stop you from going anywhere else too.

John arrived outside the CO's office and knocked on the door, "come," was the curt response from Lt Colonel Garver who was sitting behind his huge oak desk sifting through a folder. John marched up to the desk, came to attention and saluted the CO.

"As you were Sgt, take a seat. So how was selection? Did you enjoy it?"

"Enjoy might be a bit strong boss but yes it was good. I feel like a new man after it," he said with a smile.

"That's because you are John. It's no mean feat to pass joint selection, some say it got tougher when it became a joint venture which has resulted in us losing more top quality Marines."

"Yes sir, it was certainly tough and I can honestly say that some of it was tougher than I expected and I expected the worst."

"Yes indeed, there is no way anyone can ever fully appreciate just how hard it is unless they give it a go and it is sometime the most unlikely people who end up passing and going on to become a member of the elite. Not that we're not already elite you understand," he laughed. "So how did you feel just two weeks into boat and diving phrase having the course pulled?"

"Can I be honest sir?"

"Please do John we're speaking frankly and I want you to relax and be straight with me. You wouldn't be you if you didn't."

"Well to be honest sir, I'm gutted to be back here at 42 and I don't mean that to be disrespectful. I have been through hell over the last 8 months and if I'm going to sent to war I think I deserve to go in with the SF."

"Okay John, I understand your frustration but that's just how things work out sometimes. Now the reason I've called you in here is because I've received a call from Colonel Bishop last night telling me of the situation and he informed me that you were already considering transferring to the SAS and that he had convinced you to stay with the Corps."

John was shocked and didn't know what to say, he just sat there waiting for the CO to ask him a direct question so he didn't have to lie to him, and he obviously hadn't been told about him contacting Hereford directly to request a transfer.

The CO continued; "So good old Colonel Bishop gave you the SBS are the best speech and you decided to stick it out with the Corps eh?"

"Yes sir I did. But I don't understand why you've called me in to see you?"

"Well needless to say Bishop has heard that we've cancelled the SC3 course and has decided it would be unfair to make you wait another 6 months for the next course. So he has decided to offer you the chance to reconsider your options. Of course I hope you stay here with us and come to Iraq with your own troops, lead your men into battle and then re-join SBS later in the year but the call is yours John."

"Sir I'd like nothing better than to stay with the Corps but it has become apparent to me that they would just as quickly cast me aside if they felt they had no need for my skills in the future and that has made me a little disillusioned about my future with the Corps."

"Oh, I'm sorry you feel that way John I truly am. You'll be a great loss to the Corps son but I wish you all the very best for the future and you never know, I might see you over there," he laughed before carrying on, "so John I need your answer."

"Sir it is with great regret that I accept the offer to transfer to the Army and joined the 22nd Regiment of the SAS. It has been a great pleasure to serve under you sir." John stood up and offered his hand to the CO; the CO stood up and shook his hand.

"Okay Sgt Savage, you are to report to Hereford by 1400 hrs tomorrow and they will take it from there. It's been a pleasure Sgt Savage, good luck."

John stood to attention and saluted the CO and the CO reciprocated. He about turned and marched out of the office and went back to the SNCO's barracks and got his kit together and went to collect his car which had been left there while he was on his linguistics course. He put in his hands free kit and started to drive to Hereford and decided to ring Amy while he drove.

Amy was in the kitchen just putting on a darks wash when the phone rang; she quickly walked into the living room and picked up the phone. She was hoping that it wouldn't be John but after seeing the news over the last couple of days she had a feeling it would be him on the other end of the phone.

"Hello"

"Hey babe's," John said, "How ya doing? What you up to?"

"Hey hun, I was doing the washing, nothing exciting. How are you? Well that's a stupid question really isn't it; your ringing me during the day which is never a good sign is it!" She could feel herself getting nervous as she waited for his response.

"Well babes they've cancelled my SC3 course because of the Gulf Conflict and they're sending the lads over there in the next few weeks."

Amy interrupted him, "so when do you go John?"

"That's not everything hun. I'm not going with 42 babes, because they've cancelled the course I've decided to leave the Corps and transfer to the Army. You know what that means don't you coz you know I can't say it over the phone?"

She sat in silence for a moment, "yeah John I know exactly what that means. So when do you go? I assume they will be going to Iraq?"

"I'm driving there right now, I have to report in tomorrow and then I'll find out what's going on and when I go. I'll let you know as soon as I know anything hun I promise."

"No John, you won't because if they tell you you're leaving tomorrow night then you'll drop everything and just go won't you?"

"Amy please, I need you to be with me on this. I'll let you know ASAP babe I promise, okay?"

"Okay sweetie, listen I better get back to that washing. It won't do itself now will it, we'll speak soon hun," she said struggling to hold back the tears.

"Amy," he said softly.

"Yeah."

"I love you."

"I love you too babe, I have to go now." She put the phone down and started to cry; she curled up on the chair and sobbed into her hands. She couldn't believe that he was changing everything just so he could be in the Special Forces. She was devastated he would be going to war, but to be going as part of the SAS terrified her more than ever before and she wondered if she'd ever see him again and if the wedding would happen.

John had to stay at Hereford for the next 4 weeks while he honed his CQB skills, he also took an advanced course with the Army sniper school on some of the different weapons that he may come across such as the Dragnov Snipers Rifle, H & K PSG1 and the AK family of weapons, he also did a lot more pistol handling and some advanced driving skills. All of this was crammed into a four week period.

Operation Desert Storm was about to go live and the war was in full swing by the time he was flown in with G Squadron.

Each Squadron was split into four units, Mountain, Air, Mobility and Boat Troop. John was posted to the SAS mountain troops and as he was a highly trained sniper they thought he would make a great addition to their team. It was kind of good that the option was taken away from John as he wasn't sure which squadron he wanted to join as he hadn't planned on staying with them after selection and he didn't see the point of joining their Boat Troop or he may as well of stayed with the Corps.

It was the hardest phone call John had ever had to make in his life; he picked up the receiver and dialled the number.

"Hello," answered Amy.

"Hey babes," John waited for Amy to respond but she fell silent, "are you there babe?"

"Yes, I'm here John," her heart was thumping in her chest as she sat only a few feet away from her mother and Rebecca. She didn't know what to say as they all sat there planning the fine details of the wedding that was due to take place in just four weeks time.

"Okay babe, are you alone?"

"No hun, my and your mum is here too."

"Oh okay, well listen I don't have much time as I'm flying out in the next couple of hours so I'm really sorry to have to do this babe but we're going to have to re-schedule the wedding." He could feel his own emotion welling up inside and his eyes filled with tears at the thought of what he was doing to his fiancé.

She started to cry and couldn't speak for a minute while John sat on the other end of the phone waiting for her to respond. His CO knew he had to break the bad news to her and so let him use his office to make the call. Rebecca took the phone out of Amy's hand as her mother tried to comfort her.

"Hello John," came his mother's voice.

"Hi mam, is she okay?"

"I don't know John, what the hell is going on?"

"I leave in the next couple of hours for Iraq; the wedding is going to have to be postponed mum. Listen; put her back on the phone. I need to speak to her before I go and I really don't have much time."

She handed the phone back to Amy, "he wants to talk to you hun."

Amy took the phone and tried to gather herself before speaking, "How long you going for babe?"

"I don't know sweetie, I'll let you know as soon as I know anything."

"But you must have a fixed draft, so how long do these guys go places for? I'm only asking coz the second you land back in this country Mr John Savage we're getting married whether you bloody like it or not," she gave a little giggle as she tried to put on a brave face and voice as she knew this could actually be the last time she ever heard his voice.

"It doesn't quite work like that anymore babe, I go where I'm told, when I'm told and no-one really knows for how long. But the CO knows our situation so he's doing his best to get things organised for me and I'll be happy to marry you the second I get back babe. You just try and stop me."

"Okay then babe, you take care of yourself and come back to me in one piece you hear me? I want the whole package and I want you fit and well, you tell your bloody CO that from me mate," she was trying her very best to hold it together and although she didn't want him to put the phone down she couldn't wait to break down as soon as he was gone.

"I'll be sure to do that babe, now hun I'm really sorry but I got to go. I'll see you soon, say hi to everyone back home for me," he was just about to put the phone down when she spoke.

"I love you John, please come back to me."

"I will babe and I love you too. Bye!"

She completely broke down once the phone had gone down and her mother and Rebecca tried their best to comfort her. Rebecca didn't understand why he couldn't give her a timescale but of course Amy knew she couldn't discuss it with anyone else. He was in the Special Forces which meant so was she; she had been made to sign the 'Official Secrets Act' as part of the package when he joined selection so even though she knew very little she wasn't allowed to discuss anything with members of the public or the press or she could face criminal charges.

John's time in Iraq would be a turning point in his life, it was a time when much like Cpl Saxon who counted how many jumps he had made, John decided to count how many kills he notched up. Slightly sick he knew, but he didn't give a fuck what anyone else thought. Who would know, it would be his little secret, something he would write in code in his diary. He put up a header of C and R and left it to people's imagination what they stood for. It stood for confirmed and real number.

John headed off to the G Sqn hanger where he was met by Trooper Saxon and the rest of the team, all new troopers were stripped of their former ranks but obviously as they progressed within the Regiment they didn't have to go through the JNCO and SNCO courses again. Unless of course they hadn't taken it already.

"Hey what the fuck do ya know guys, it's fucking Maureen," he laughed loudly. The nick name given to a marine if they transferred to the Army. The name didn't stick, by the time they arrived back from the Gulf some 8 months later he was titled 'Royal', a name that stuck with him for the rest of his career.

"Hey big man, how's my shower buddy doing? You miss me?" John was joining in with the team immediately and they instantly liked him, they'd already heard about the bootneck who stormed through selection as if he owned it. Saxon knew a few of the guys from days gone by, three of the guys in G Sqn were from 1 Para and another two from his time with 2 Para. The amazing thing was, as John looked across the team of 30 men he recognised one of them. It was a not so young looking Cpl who he'd met while in the Falklands Campaign; his name back then was Cpl Jack Finnegan from 45 Commando. It had been 9 years since he had last seen him and his face looked tough and weathered and he was wearing Sgt stripes and had the respect of the men stood by his side.

"Holy shit is that you Finn?" John called out across the hanger; Sgt 'Finn' Finnegan turned and looked at the man he owed his life to. Finn was one of the men of 45 Commando who was pinned down by sniper fire when Savage came sauntering along and stuck his head over a wall in plain view of the enemy so he could get a better look at where the enemy sniper was situated. He then dropped back behind the wall, crawled 30 feet along the base of the dry stone wall and popped a lose rock out of it before taking aim and dropping the sniper. This was another unconfirmed kill as the SBS came along behind this position some 5 minutes later and threw in a few grenades which they claim took the life of the sniper. John knew and so did Finn. Finn got up from his Bergen and walked towards John with open arms.

"Holy fucking shit man, how the fuck are you?" The average build Scotsman threw his arms around John and gave him a hug. "Guys I want you to meet Mr John fucking Savage of 42 Commando and now part of G Squadron 22 Reg," he laughed and they all cheered like a bunch of drunken kids following the leader of the pack. "This mother fucker saved my arse back in the Malvinas boys. He was one crazy fucking sniper back in the day and I'm glad to have you aboard."

"Good to see you Sgt Finnegan," John joked with him knowing that no-one really pulled rank in the SAS unless they were on parade which was rare in the regiment. It wasn't that kind of Regiment, they knew what they could do and they didn't care much for the pomp and circumstance of the Guards or any of that fancy bullshit. They were SAS troopers, an elite band of fighting men who existed only to fight and win wars. They called each other by their first or by nick name and it was a very relaxed atmosphere.

They packed their gear and climbed aboard the C130 Hercules and begin their trip to Iraq, they landed on the airstrip several hours later and de-bussed. They grabbed a crappy hanger in the back of the base only 200 metres from the fence. There was a lot of strange looks on the faces of the soldiers in camp as they saw this motley crew of 30 men with huge bergen's and kit bags, then the Land Rover dragged two huge crates into the same crappy hanger. The other regiments on the base included the Coldstream Guards, the Light Infantry and 1 Para who had shared the flight in with G Sqn.

They had been in camp two days when they started to run their desert patrols in the dead of the night, John was in 1 section with his old buddy Saxon and this was lead by Cpl 'Chip' Charlton originally from the Black Watch Infantry and who had been with the Regiment for the last 6 years. He'd seen action all over the world and was part of the team that took out the IRA suspects in Gibraltar some years earlier.

They went out into the desert around midnight, they had been travelling for around 90 minutes when they reached a wadi that provided good cover. They had heard that Scud Missiles were being transported across this part of the desert and they were sent out to find them and gather as much Intel as possible and if an opportunity presented itself then they were to take it out.

They climbed into the wadi and started to monkey run along it, a monkey run is a run in a crouched position where you can use one hand to balance yourself on the ground while the other hand carries your weapon poised and ready for any contact that may come. They crept up to the edge of the wadi and could hear movement up ahead; they used only hand signals at this point and Chip lead the section along the ridge of the wadi which was roughly 20 feet high.

He popped his head up for a second to see what was going on and as bad luck would have it walking straight for them were two enemy soldiers carrying AK47's. Fortunately due to the level of experience in the 4 man team three of them spoke Arabic and heard one guy saying that he was bursting for a piss so it was pretty obvious what he was going to do. They all lay still as he approached the edge but as Chip dropped back down he slipped causing loose stones and sand to fall away beneath his feet, the guards ran towards the edge of the wadi shouting back to their colleagues. As the first enemy soldier's head came within sight John raised his H & K MP5SD silenced sub machine gun and put two rounds through his face, the sound of a puff of air could be heard as the silenced rifle did its job, the second man came 2 seconds behind him and he didn't have time to stop when John caught sight of the top of his head and shot him through the eye with another double tap.

He fell backwards onto the cold desert floor and Saxon jumped up and let rip with the Jimpy (GPMG) and started tearing up the enemy troops as they ran towards them, the night erupted into a frenzy of tracer and gun shots, grenades were been thrown at the enemy as they retreated back to the cover of their vehicles.

John ran over the top of the wadi to a mound of rocks some 15 feet away and let rip with everything he had, he pulled his M16 assault rifle from behind his back fitted with M203 grenade launcher and started popping grenades into the two 7.5 tonne military trucks parked some 30 metres away. The fire fight lasted over an hour before finally there was no more enemy to kill, 15 enemy surrendered and 25 lay dead on the ground around them.

None of the team were injured apart from Chip suffering with a badly sprained right ankle as he had to throw himself out of the way of an enemy grenade before blowing the officers head off at close range with a Spas Franchi semi-automatic shotgun, it made quite a mess of him and the 3 men stood directly behind him who tried to surrender just as Chip shot the second man in the face at no more than three feet away.

They weren't equipped to take prisoners back and as the night wore on they knew it would put the team at risk if they hung around much longer.

Chip radioed back to camp to see if they could get a squad of men out quickly or else they'd have to let them go in the hope that the patrol would get away before they got picked up by their mates and put in a chase.

The message came back; a Chinook would be inbound and should arrive in 20 minutes, could they hold them until then. Chip looked at his men and knew they could but he knew it would put them at risk. He told the camp they would hold them here but they should get their arses moving or this would be one hot LZ. Six minutes had gone by when the enemy radio burst into life and the voice on the other end said in Arabic, "Troop leader, this is National Guard Leader Captain Hussein do you copy; we were expecting to see you on the horizon by now. We are heading your way, copy." End of transmission.

Saxon was up on an embankment north of the ambush site, the smoke and flames could clearly be seen in the distance and they knew they would be in the shit if the unit didn't show up soon to collect the prisoners. Saxon shouted down to Chip, "enemy spotted at 1 click (km) and moving fast, we've got to get the fuck out of dodge." He stayed in position so he could keep watch while Chip thought about his next move. Chip wasn't happy and wished he'd never put the call in now, if he'd never put the call in they could have shot the lot and moved on as if they'd died in the contact, it was too late and he had no choice but to hold the position until back up arrived.

Chip grabbed the radio and spoke to camp again, "you better move your asses boys coz we're about to be hit by a huge shit sandwich and we're gonna be taking a huge bite out of it in about 2 minutes time, copy."

The officer on the other end of the radio was not impressed and started to tell Chip off when it all kicked off, the radio was dropped and the speaker was held in the open position so everyone back at base could hear everything that happened. Saxon started to put down grenades from his M203 and Trooper Andrew 'Guv' Kettlewell ran up to the embankment with a Charlie G (Carl Gustav Anti Tank Weapon) and launched a missile straight at the convoy heading for us. They could see 6 personnel trucks and two light armoured vehicles (LAV) as the missile made contact with the lead vehicle, one of the LAV's exploded in a ball of flames and the convoy skirted around the debris and carried on moving towards their position. At this point John thought about what was happening and wondered if this was it, his first time out with an SAS patrol and it would all be over for them, they wouldn't be hailed as hero's, most would never know they existed or what they had done on this day.

The Chinook full of troops from the newly arrived 1 Para would see the destruction in the distance and knew they were heading into a shit storm, a full blown battle that was being held up by four men. John had secured the prisoners with a length of rope so they didn't have to think about them for a little while and took up his position with his L96A1 snipers rifle which he had ran back to the Land Rover to collect it.

Once in position he proceeded to take shots aiming mainly at the drivers who were now swerving their vehicles in a desperate attempt to avoid being hit after they saw him put a stop to the first two trucks and as soon as the driver's position was taken over by a second man he took out the replacements too.

One of the trucks had made it through though and got within 400 metres, they all de-bussed and around 20 men armed to the teeth were heading straight for them. John continued to put down sniper fire but came under mortar attack within a couple of minutes of the truck unloading so he had to pull back as did Saxon and Guv.

Chip had noticed the prisoners were attempting to get away as a group, so dropped two of them, one at each end with head shots with his Browning 9mm pistol.

The enemy got within 100 metres and the four men dug in behind some rocks and continued to defend their position for what seemed like hours, the sun was rising as the Chinook came swooping in behind the enemy troops and opened up with .50 cal tearing up the desert floor around them and killing dozens immediately, the Paras came storming out and took up the fire fight while Chip got his section back down into the wadi and headed back to the Land Rover which amazingly hadn't been spotted. They jumped in and stared to drive around the wadi; to the enemy this must have looked as if they were running away as it did to the prisoners who tried to get loose to join their comrades but Chip drove around the wadi so they could join into the fire fight armed with the .50 cal machine gun which Guv opened up with as he seen the prisoners start to break loose.

The fire fight lasted another 80 minutes before the Paras accepted the surrender of the remaining 35 Iraqi soldiers. The four man SAS patrol rounded up the remaining prisoners from the original contact. It was 0700 hrs by the time it was all over and the patrol had been in action for almost 5 hours, they walked over to the Chinook with their 11 remaining survivors. The Paras took off some 20 minutes later, around 5 minutes after the SAS team headed back to camp. They were supposed to be out and back within 4 hours with Intel and here they were driving back through the gates at 0900 hrs some 9 hours later.

They walked back to their hanger and dumped their gear before heading off to the showers without saying much, the camp CO wanted a de-brief with the team at 1100 hrs so they quickly showered and ate some of their personal stash of food they brought with them. John grabbed a silver packet out of his rations, Meatballs and pasta it said on the side of the packet. He tore it open and ate the contents cold and boy did that food taste good. As they were getting into clean fatigues Fenn popped his head in the room and said, "Saxon, Royal, welcome to the Reg," he laughed and walked away smiling.

As the four men walked to the de-brief block Chip turned and looked at his men, "what a fucking day eh?" he laughed, it was pretty obvious that the SAS was going to be similar to the marines for their warped sense of humour and John felt happy to be there having survived his first contact with the Reg.

The de-brief went well and the boss was happy with the prisoners, they seemed to be getting some pretty good info out of them.   The next 8 months was a series of desert recce's and contacts all of which were pretty full on and resulted in John reverting back to his sniping days on many occasions, which he didn't mind. It was what he did and who he was, a sniper first of all and then a foot soldier in his eyes.   He got very well acquainted with the Barrett .50mm Sniper Rifle too, several of his shots were taken at over 2000 metres and his reputation as a top sniper in the SAS was growing fast.

John and Amy's wedding plans changed drastically due to his change in career direction and she was extremely pleased to be welcomed to Hereford for his return from Iraq. He arrived back on camp with most of the guys he went out with, there were around 60 men in G Squadron 22nd SAS and these were split into 4 teams of 16 men in each of the troops, Air troop, Boat Troop, Mountain Troop and Mobility Troop.   Mountain, Mobility and Air Troop had shared the same hanger and been involved in numerous cross functional op's out in Iraq and John had enjoyed seeing what each troop did, especially in war time, you could train your whole life for something but you only truly know if it works when it's been put to the test. In Iraq they were tested.

Only 57 men returned, when they got back their families got together in the mess to celebrate the lives of those who had fallen while in combat. Amy found the whole experience fantastic, she loved being part of something after all this time, John had been a Royal Marine for 11 years and Amy had never felt like she was welcomed into the ranks or into the family circles of other marines partners or wives, but this was different, he had only seen active duty for 1 year and already she felt welcome. She did of course realise that these women did have one very big thing in common, their husbands would always be at war, always be at the front line of whatever conflict or disaster was happening around the globe and each time they said goodbye it could be the last time. But they accepted this as part of life and supported their partners no matter what, Amy felt honoured to be part of this and she was extremely surprised and excited when the CO's wife came in and started talking to her about the wedding.

They got married in Hereford at a small chapel some 5 minutes away from the regiment HQ, it was a small affair with John's new found military friends and Rebecca, Amy's parents and her brothers and their partners. It came as quite a shock when they arrived in Hereford to see John for the first time in his SAS dress uniform.

Rebecca didn't understand what had happened to her son and his life in the Royal Marines but she could see he was happy and Amy wanted to move to Hereford to be with her husband and the other wives. They decided to rent out their home in the North East and buy a small place in a neighbouring village to Hereford, Amy had never been so happy; she had managed to get a relocation package with her job as a pharmacist and so they would now live together more often than they had before. The wedding took place in the September 1992.

Life in the regiment wasn't all fighting and adventure, although the training never seemed to stop. Somewhere in the world there is always war and so they would always have to be ready no matter what the situation was, he spent the next 6 months with Mobility Troop in the UK learning new skills and advancing in others.

John could now speak fluent Arabic and was doing pretty good at Spanish and French, he also did advanced signals, advanced driving, motorbike and his heavy goods licence (HGV1) so he could drive pretty much anything.

Although he didn't want to get drafted into Mobility Troop he did enjoy learning the new skills and over time he would no doubt transfer to other troops throughout his career, of that he was sure. One of the greatest skills he was to master was CQB and FIBUA (Fighting in built up areas) which would serve him well for his future as it was common for the SAS to be brought in for such duties as Embassy Sieges after their great public debut in 1980 with the Iranian Embassy Siege in London.

In Feb 1993 John was part of the SAS team sent to America to advice the FBI on the Waco Siege when a group of religious extremists decided they would show the world their views. A siege which ended terribly as the FBI floundered in some of their decision making, insisting that the SAS were simply there to advice and would not be sent in to deal with the actual siege. Maybe if they had it might not have resulted in 76 people being wounded and killed, 24 of which were British nationals. John spent several months working in America in 93' and 94' working with the American Green Berets, Army Rangers, and the US Marine Corps (USMC).

In 94' and 95' he served extensively in Bosnia, Kosovo and Sierra Leone, it was in Maglai, Bosnia when John was faced with one of the most horrifying things he had to deal with. The section had been out on a recce patrol during the night when his team came across a small village with some British vehicles in the centre, it was a clearing no more than 50 x 50 ft squared. John and his team could hear a British officer ordering his men to gather all the people of the village and separate them into three groups, men, women and children. There was a lot of commotion and they witnessed the men of the REME (Royal Electrical Mechanical Engineers) shoot and injure two of the men who were deemed influential. One was shot in his left foot, they laughed as he danced around writhing in agony. The second was shot in his right shoulder, he hit the deck screaming. This infuriated John and his team but they were told not to make contact unless absolutely necessary. What happened next sent a shiver down John's spine and it changed everything for him.

John noticed a Sgt lead five men into a building which for some reason hadn't been cleared, once inside they heard the screams of a female coming from inside, by now the noise outside was quite loud so John slipped over to take a look through the window, as he looked through the broken pane of glass he saw the men holding down a young girl, she looked about 14 years old and was being held down by four of the men while another kept watch as the Sgt took great pleasure in molesting her before getting out his penis and raping her, once he was done the other five men took it in turns to rape the young teenage girl.

John didn't stay to see what was happening as he was told by the section commander that it wasn't their battle and that they should keep moving. John and the others were not happy but as John had the least experience, when they got around 1 km away Chip said to him, "John boy you got to learn that in this game we see a lot of things that we can't act upon. When we're given an order we carry it out and if they tell us that we can make our own decisions on a target of opportunity then we'll deal with that too, but what we don't fucking do is get involved with British wanker Sgt's like him raping young girls. So unless you know a way to drop him from a distance without it leading back us then let it go. Okay?"

"Okay mate, but she's a fucking kid. It doesn't sit well with me!" said John angrily.

They carried on for another 2 hours before heading back again. At the abandoned village that they decided to turn back from John made a startling discovery. Hidden amongst the rubble was a Dragnov Snipers Rifle, just sitting there, waiting to be found and as John always carried 7.62 rounds he was good to go. As they came past the village in Maglai again they noticed the villagers had now been released and they were going about their business as usual.

They continued until they were 800 metres past the village when John stopped and said, "Chip, you and the guys go on and I'll catch you up in a few minutes."

"Fuck me Royal, what you doing man?"

"I'm gonna make them wish they never fucking raped that little girl. You said if there was a way and now we have a way so fuck em!"

The three men looked at John as if he had a screw loose but they all agreed with him, so they decided to set up a four way observation circle to cover all directions in case anyone approached, plus the Dragnov didn't come with a silencer so once the shot was fired the whole REME company would begin to let rip. John lay in position and tried zeroing the rifle without firing a shot. Normally at 800 metres he would go for a head shot but as he couldn't zero it properly he decided it was a safer bet to aim for the heart.

John lay still, regulating his breathing while watching the cross hairs rise and fall over the Sgt's torso. He saw one of the young men who had assisted him step directly behind the Sgt and the sniper motto of 'one shot, one kill' suddenly had new meaning. John quickly decided to go for a head shot, he took two breaths and on the third held it at the half way mark and squeezed the trigger. The shot rang out loud against the night; it hit the Sgt in the back of his head which sent his head hurtling forward smashing into the face of the Private standing behind him. The night erupted into an explosion of gun fire in every direction, they had no idea where the shot had come from but it was pretty obvious that it came from a sniper. Once the dust settled the soldiers and officer secured their perimeter and the SAS team had long gone.

At first the soldiers thought the private had been head butted with such force it had broken his nose and knocked him unconscious but once the pulled the Sgt up they could see the exit wound where his nose had once been and the round had gone into the forehead of the Private killing him at the same time. One shot, two kills!

Things were pretty quiet for the team in Bosnia for a few weeks but then suddenly every night they would get into a contact, it was a tough tour with plenty of action and a lot of contacts and calling in air strikes in Sarajevo, luckily for the British these guys were on their side, most of the time. The SAS regularly ran what is called 'Black Ops' where they are told to carry out an operation in a place where they shouldn't be or the British Government will deny they were ever there.

In 97' John transferred from the Mountain Troop to Air Troop known as the sunglasses and ice-cream troop for two years were he did more HALO and HAHO parachuting which he loved, he felt like he was on a holiday and once again found himself constantly in training, until he was called into Lima in Peru when the Japanese Embassy came under siege. The 16 man team flew out to Peru and set up an OP to gather intelligence when they noticed the hostage takers getting very agitated, so they decided to take action and end the siege by force. John was in the 4 man section on front door duty, once the word in the ear piece shouted "Go!" John's team stormed the front door as the explosives went off at the back of the building; men went in from the roof, side window and front door with a 4 man back up team.

Saxon hit the door with the door hammer, a huge heavy weight bar with two handles used by the Police for forced entries when they carry out raids. John was first through the door and he quickly threw in a flash bang (white phosphorus grenade) to blind and disorientate the terrorists, as he ran in he saw a man turning with a rifle in his hands, TAP, TAP, a double tap to the head and he was down. The four men ran through each room on the ground floor at great speed, speed and aggression is

306

the regiment's way. They took out eight terrorists but after John's first contact the 2nd and 3rd weren't as lucky as to get a quick double tap to the head.

Once the siege was over and the dust settled it was noted that some of the terrorists who were killed had up to 60 rounds in them and others had two. John had taken out 3 of the eight on his floor and another in the cellar, as he kicked the cellar door open the man jumped at John knocking his rifle down and a round shot the terrorist in the left thigh, but as he did this John grabbed his knife from its holster and stabbed it upwards so it went under the man's rib cage splitting his lungs inside, blood gushed over John and he quickly threw then man to the floor and grabbed his rifle again and quickly searched the room for more of the bad guys.

Within two hours of the siege being over all 16 men were on a plane heading to Gibraltar, where they were to spend the next 3 months based with the Royal Marines. It was a great surprise for John when he got there to see it was 42 Commando, he would have known if he had really thought about it as he normally knew what he would be doing for the next 3 – 5 years in advance in the Corps but he'd been so busy in the regiment that every week, month, even year was becoming a blur.

Most of 98' was spent in Iraq again and John was quite the desert warfare expert now as well as mountain and arctic warfare specialist. In 99' he spent 3 months working with the Canadian Special Forces which was a great experience that he would always remember. He thought it was the easiest and most fun he'd ever had on a draft to another country, he skied, ice climbed, rock climbed and played in the snow for two of the three months and had a great time. He then went on to serve in Kosovo which again was a tough tour when he was involved in numerous contacts and was once again called upon to use his sniper skills to their fullest.

He stayed in Kosovo for three months before coming back to Hereford. Amy was so glad to see him, she knew he was going to Canada and while there she was getting regular phone calls and letters from him so she felt like she was involved and part of it, then the letters stopped and she got one phone call in three months so she was upset about that. When John got home she had the dining room table laid out beautifully with flowers and candles, she had cooked a lovely meal for him to welcome him back.

"Right Mr Savage, for a starter we have mussels done in a white wine sauce served with some crusty white bread. For your main course we have a fillet steak cooked medium rare with steamed vegetables and finally for first of your deserts we have Carte D'or ice cream."

"And what's my second desert?" asked John

"Me," she said with a smile on her face.

"Ah my favourite," he returned the smile. "I have to say that I'm a little confused though sweetie."

"Why's that then darling?"

"Well you seem to have set the table for three places. Or are we expecting company and you just haven't told me yet?"

"Oh sorry hun that was very rude of me wasn't it. Yes we are expecting company but not for a while yet."

"Really, so who is it?" John asked looking confused.

"Oh well that would be your son or daughter, but like I said it will be a while yet seems that I'm only 6 months pregnant." She said with a huge grin on her face. She watched as John sat there speechless, she had never known him be lost for words.

"Oh my God, six months. But you're hardly showing, bloody hell that's fantastic babe."

John got up and grabbed her giving Amy a huge hug and kiss; he was totally made up about it and couldn't wait to tell everyone back on base the next day. They ate their three course meal and Amy showed him how she had covered it up and how she couldn't believe that with all of his training he didn't notice any change in her.

"I can't believe you didn't notice how much weight I've put on. I've put like 20 lbs on."

"Well actually I did notice hun but I didn't want you to think the first thing that I thought was 'bloody hell she's getting fat now' did I?"

"I suppose so, but that is what you thought then," she said laughing

"Yeah exactly," after they had a catch up they went to bed and started chatting about baby names and Amy remembered thinking how normal all of this felt and yet she knew that there was nothing normal about this child's dad or what he did. His job was to take peoples fathers away from them, killing people was a huge part of his job and he was good at it, it was difficult to imagine him doing anything else other than be a soldier, it was all he knew.

John couldn't believe that Amy had kept the fact she was pregnant a secret since finding out 3 months earlier, she found out just one day after he last spoke to her from Canada but she knew he was heading somewhere else that he wouldn't have regular contact with her so she figured it must be a rough place or operation and that it was better if he didn't know in case it affected how he performed while away. She knew he was one of the world's elite fighting soldiers but she didn't want to be responsible for him being distracted. He took risks that were part of his job. If he suddenly started being more careful maybe that would put him or his oppo's at risk and she didn't want that.

John spent the rest of 99' and the first six months of 2000 in the UK as a member of the directing staff (DS) in Hereford, it was a 9 month secondment to give him a rest from operational duties. It felt as if he'd been at war constantly as he was called up over and over again to take part in Op's around the world. But John had a motto that he had learned from the men he served with and he believed in it whole heartedly, 'Si vis pacem, para belum' which translated from Latin means, 'If you wish for peace, prepare for war!'

Chapter 12

<u>2000 – 2009 The end of the road</u>

Amy gave birth to their first child February 3rd 2000; their first son David John Savage weighed 8 lbs. They were ecstatic about it and they doted on him every minute they had together, John made an effort to get home at a reasonable time whenever possible but couldn't help volunteering to take part in the exercises in SAS selection and training, that was the bit he loved the most and he was a tough instructor to please. He was firm but fair but he knew what he had been put through had served him well during his life with the regiment.

Later in 2000 John was sent to Sierra Leone again to take part in Black Op's and he aided 1 Para in a rescue mission from the rebel group known as 'The West Side Boys' a few days before he headed back to the UK. He was only back 3 days when he got a call to go to Macedonia with the Pathfinder Platoon; little did he know this would be the start of the Balkans Conflict that would rage for most of 2001. John ended up staying there for 9 months and saw some serious action. An eight man SAS team were holding the line at a small village which the opposition desperately wanted to take control of the whole of the West side of Macedonia. The enemy came in company strength throwing everything they had at the village; the villagers also took up defensive positions in a gallant attempt to support the British troops.

John was on the GPMG with Saxon and they were coming under mortar attack for most of the day but they were dug in well with good overhead cover to protect them from any shrapnel, of course it wouldn't have mattered much if a mortar landed on top of them. It would have been game over for the two of them and they wouldn't have been able to do a damn thing about it. They had been holding the village line for 4 days under constant attack and it was on this 4th night when they thought for sure their number was up. It had just turned 0100 hrs when the shamooli flare went up over the edge of the village as the enemy troops tried to spot the SAS positions, the 12 men on duty at this time held their fire waiting for the flare to go down but before it was half way down they saw the terrifying sight of some 60 + enemy troops come over the crest of a ditch complex that ran around the village to the North & West.

John let rip with the GPMG while Saxon took up position with his AK74 and started to drop the enemy, "Fire front!" screamed John as he witnessed the rush of men coming towards them at a distance of no more than 400 metres. He ran a thousand round belt of ammo without stopping to take a breath, his heart thumped in his chest as he thought they would over run the position any minute. He could hear the 4 man team from the centre of the village putting down mortar rounds along the crest in an attempt to force the enemy to retreat but they kept coming, John could hear the other trenches to his left and his right shouting to each other and letting rip with everything they had, then he heard the first of many screams.

A shout came from the trench to the right of him, "man down, I need fucking ammo now. Last box of Jimpy!"

He could hear the urgency in the man's voice, the man in question was 'Big Vic' a monster of a man who had been sharing a trench with 'Mouse' another ex marine. Saxon kept laying down fire as the enemy grew closer; they were 200 metres now and trying to stay low to avoid having their heads blown off.

John grabbed a box of 7.62 ammo and jumped up out of his trench running to Vic's trench and literally throwing the box at him, as he ran he was still firing his M16A2 assault rifle at the enemy. He looked into the trench at Vic's face, he was focussed, "cheers Royal, I'll see you in hell mate." And he let out a laugh of a mad man, he looked down and saw Mouse had took a round in the face taking the back of his head off.

As John turned to run back, he was knocked off his feet and feeling winded, he thought he must have tripped and hit the ground hard and so jumped back up and carried on running back to his trench when he saw the trench to the left explode under a mortar, John turned and could see a man no more than 6 feet away running at him screaming his war cry, "Raaaaawwwwwww!!!!"

John turned and used his rifle to knock the enemy's rifle away from him and struck his under his nose with the palm of his right hand which took the guys head back with enough force to splat his nose across his face, John grabbed his knife and started stabbing the guy in the chest, he could hear the gasps for breath as he took his life, John looked up as another lunged at him with fixed bayonet, he felt the flesh in his right shoulder tear under the pressure of the full weight of a man plunging his bayonet into him. He fell back, but the pain was so blinding that his brain didn't know what was happening to him but he knew Saxon was about to be overrun by the enemy and that mattered more than his own injuries. He stabbed at the man's throat as he fell towards him and felt the arterial spray from his neck cover his face.

He climbed back to his feet and pulled the bayonet out of his shoulder, as he looked down he could see blood to his left side and wondered what that was from but again he ran towards the trench as he saw Saxon let rip with the final belt of ammo on the GPMG, he heard Vic behind him as he jumped out of his trench and started running towards the enemy. Saxon saw this and also jumped out of his trench and as John turned he noticed the remaining men of his 16 man SAS unit all grab their gear and start to run at the enemy positions.

"Fuck it!" he screamed as he ran to the trench and grabbed an LMG (Light Machine Gun) and last 50 round magazine of 5.56 ammo. He turned and started to run towards the enemy, the enemy stopped in their tracks and didn't know what to do, they seemed shocked and panicked by the move and started to retreat but it was too late the men of G Sqn 22 SAS were ready to die and all John could think was "Fuck it!" He was going to die with glory and the enemy would know that they had faced the devil himself.

The advance lasted around 15 minutes before the enemy decided to cut and run, they had been beaten into retreat but at a huge cost as another two SAS men fell under the attack. The villagers seeing this gallant display of bravery took up positions and started to drop the enemy soldiers as they ran away. When they stopped and began their retreat John was feeling very light headed and Saxon came running alongside him laughing, they were all laughing and John joined them and started laughing but he felt like shit inside and was losing a lot of blood.

"Fuck Royal, your hit man," called Saxon looking at his friend

"Huh, am I? I got stabbed in the fucking shoulder mate, it hurts like a mother fucker," he responded not sure what else Saxon could be talking about. He fell to the ground and lost consciousness, when he woke up he was lying in a hospital bed with white walls around him, at first he thought he might be dead and this was heaven. He looked around the room and heard English voices and wondered if he was back in the UK.

"Maam," he struggled to speak as his voice was croaky and he felt very light headed as he tried raising his head to speak to the nurse.

"Hey hey look who decided to join us," the nurse smiled at him with beautiful teeth and full lips, he noticed how pretty she was.

"Where am I?" asked John

"You're in a field hospital; don't worry you're not alone. We have a couple of your friends in here with you. Well, they didn't want you getting all the attention did they," she smiled as she helped him sit up.

As John sat up he felt the sharp pain in both his right shoulder and his left side and wondered how badly he was hurt.

"So am I okay? I mean what's up with me nurse?"

"Well let me see, you have a serious tear in your right shoulder from a stab wound from a bayonet which is fine, it will be okay in a few weeks and you were shot in the left side but luckily the bullet went straight through, clean as a whistle. You'll be leaving in a couple of days and heading back to the UK."

"How long have I been here?"

"You've been out for three days honey, now relax and stop talking. You still need your rest, I'll have the kitchen rustle you some food up and I'll let your mates know you're awake."

He gathered his strength back and surely enough he was sent back to the UK 3 days later. They had lost eight men in total during the battle but they found 74 enemy dead lying around the village, once again the SAS had lived up to their motto of 'Who Dares Wins' and they had scared the crap out of the enemy who never did take that village and never forgot the crazy brave soldiers of the SAS and how they gave their lives to protect a bunch of people they never really knew. It was the way of the warrior and the way these men fought in every conflict.

John came home to Hereford and Amy was a nervous wreck, she had been notified that there was to be a big doo to commemorate the dead and she panicked not knowing if her husband would be one of them. When she saw him, she broke down in tears and ran up to him and threw her arms around him. She was so relieved to see him but could see he was badly injured, when she asked him what had happened he said he didn't want to talk about it, so she respected his wishes as she knew he had witnessed terrible things and that some things were better left unsaid.

John stayed in Hereford for the next six months and Amy fell pregnant again which they were both very happy about. He continued working in Hereford as part of the DS while he recovered and the US had sent over some men and women from the CIA to work with the SAS and complete certain parts of selection so they could see for themselves why the British SAS were in fact the best in the world.

He enjoyed training people but was missing the action; it was a strange feeling to want to be in the thick of the action. John continued to improve his language skills, continuing with his French and Spanish but also started learning Russian as this would have served him well when serving in certain countries. He was also looking to get a draft working with the Russian FSB Special Operations Service in the next six months while he was healing.

Strange turn of events lead the SAS to send a group of men back to their original units for a 6 month draft as part of cross functional working. John had mixed feelings about this and was sent back to 42 Commando as they were about to leave for a six month tour of NI. He joined the Recce Troop as he had before and they were glad to see him, there was a lot of catching up to do, John realised that he missed the guys he had once served with.

His time in NI was fairly dull in comparison to his previous few years with the regiment and while there he bumped into Fenn again and they had a catch up. The SAS had sent Air Troop in for 3 months before they handed over to Boat Troop who were expected to serve for 12 months in NI. John didn't fancy being stuck in NI for 12 months and was glad he wasn't part of Boat Troop even though they constantly asked him if he'd like to transfer over with him being an ex marine. He said if he was going to do that then he might as well go back to the Corps and join the SBS.

John went back to Hereford and became part of the DS and was promoted back to his original rank of Sgt which was great and he was put in charge of joint selection for SFUK. He got to work with several Royal Marines again which he really enjoyed and putting people through selection was a great job, very fulfilling to see the men grow and turn into elite fighting men, men who would serve alongside him in the future.

Amy gave birth to their second child on 1st September 2002, a baby girl named Bethany Rebecca; she was 8 lb 2 oz and looked so much like Amy. The birth of a little girl made John think long and hard about what his next career move should be.

In 2003 John was sent back to Iraq where he stayed without any leave for 12 months, this was a tough time in his marriage as Amy was left in Hereford raising two small children and being so far from home she was starting to struggle and wanted him to re-consider his career. Maybe he could return to unit with 42 Commando and see out the rest of his years with them in a safer environment. This didn't appeal to John at all and especially after a year in Iraq kicking ass out of the Iraqi hard liners.

In 2004 John bumped into the CO from Poole who headed up the SBS and they got talking about his situation with Amy. The CO seemed very interested in having John back in the Corps and informed him that there would be a 'Boat & Diving' phase running in 4 months time if he was interested.

He thought long and hard about it and decided it was worth giving it a go. Unfortunately Amy wasn't happy about this move from one SF to another.

"How the hell does you transferring from the SAS to the SBS make our life any easier John?" she shouted

"I thought you wanted me to go back to the Corps?"

"Yes John, as part of a normal commando unit. Not the special forces again! How am I supposed to think that this is going to be any different to what we have now? If anything you could end up doing more Op's only more secretive than before. I just don't think I can do this anymore babe."

Those words hit John like a sledge hammer and he wasn't sure how to react. She regretted saying the words as soon as she finished but it was too late now, she could see the look on his face and his silence said it all. She had truly hurt him.

"What are you saying Amy? That I have to choose between being part of SF or you?"

"No babe, I'm sorry I didn't mean what I just said. I just.......I just find it hard now with the kids and everything. Maybe I should have stayed up North then at least I would have had some help, that's all I'm saying."

The conversation went on into the night and John felt very confused about what to do, the reason Amy was so upset was that she was once again pregnant and wasn't sure if she could handle brining up three kids on her own. They even spoke about the possibility of abortion but John couldn't let her do that, he wanted his children and decided that he would have a vasectomy to prevent any further pregnancies.

Nathan was born 3rd May 2004 and weighed 9 lbs; they were happy with their family now and didn't want anymore. John accepted the offer to return to the Corps and take SBS training much to the disappointment of the regiment and his oppo's. They felt he was making a mistake and that the SBS wouldn't provide the same level of action he would enjoy in the regiment.

It was September 2004 when John joined the selection course for his SC3 course and because it had been a long time since he had done selection they made him take part in Exercise Long Drag with a selection course two weeks before he went to Poole. He walked it of course as he was still monstrously fit for his age. He was at a peak in his life as far as he was concerned but at 41 years old others had their doubts.

He took the combat fitness test which he breezed through and came in with the second highest score, only just beaten by a 25 year old marine called Cpl 'Buck' Rogers. He was a cocky young fella who didn't know who John was as none of the others on the course were told that he was returning from 12 years active service with the SAS.

John asked himself on occasion what the hell he was doing there, what was he trying to prove? He had no idea; all he knew is that it seemed like a good idea at the time. John had just completed 25 years in the military when they offered to extend it another 5 years and he was glad for this, it would have been a waste of time and money if he'd just gone through all the SBS training just to leave a few months later. He did find it amusing that he had served for the length of this guy's life; it made him smile when the younger guys on the course called him granddad.

The swimming test wasn't as hard as John had anticipated but maybe it was just all the years of serving with the SF he had just become immune to the hardship of training exercises. The swim test was 600 metres in 15 mins which he did comfortably; this was followed by 50 metres fully clothed and with weapon and webbing and then followed by 25 metres under water. There were several long marches in line with much of what he had done with the regiment but there was an interesting 5 km forced march carrying a 50 lb Bergen and half of the canoe, this was done in pairs and the whole canoe weighed 180 lb so his half was 90 lbs on top of his other kit so needless to say this was a tough march but as usual he completed it without too much trouble. The test he found quite tough was the 30 km canoe in the sea as the weather was a little rough and his pair made it in with only 3 minutes to spare, John wasn't used to struggling with things but enjoyed the challenge and he felt young again and fitter than ever. It was different and new and so he was happy.

They then moved onto skills such as underwater navigation, underwater demolitions, negotiating surf zones, infiltration via submarine, lots of diving practice and the final exercise consisted of a 55 km canoe navigating to set check points in the middle of the ocean with no land marks. They would be greeted by divers who had left a submarine in order to pass on Intel to the trainees and this would end up on land with the swimmer canoeists (SC) setting up demolition on a telecommunications tower and some escape and evasion practice.

John was glad to get to the end of training and be awarded his SC3 badge and was welcomed to the team in Poole.

His next draft was back to the jungles of Malaysia with the UKSF team to update his jungle warfare skills. It was good to be back in the jungle again and he realised how long it had been since his last visit and how rusty his skills had become. He joined M Sqn who specialised in Maritime Counter-Terrorism which included working on ferries, cruise ships, hovercraft, oil tankers and oil rigs so was completely different to anything he had done with the regiment and he embraced the challenge.

Amy had decided to move back to the North East and moved into their original home in Washington. It was tough decision but she didn't like the sound of moving to Poole as she had never felt welcome by the marines in the same way the SAS had welcomed her into their circle of friends and she was missing the life they had at Hereford.

John saw active service with the SBS in Iraq, Afghanistan and Somalia over the next 18 months and he was rarely at home. He was glad when he was told he had to attend the SC2 course which put him back in the UK for most of the next 12 months, with a little 8 week stint in the Arctic topping up his skills.

Then came the news that once he passed this qualification they would be sending him to Arbroath to serve alongside 45 Commando's Commachio Group who specialised in much of the Maritime Counter-Terrorism skills he had recently learned, obviously they weren't trained to the same level he was but at least he was going to be closer to Amy and the kids. He would try to get home every weekend when he was on base which he did quite regularly and it wasn't long before he was back in Poole taking is SC1 course at the same time he was promoted to Colour Sgt in 2007 with only two years left to serve, the Corps had made it perfectly clear that he would no longer be allowed to take part in active duty. He suddenly realised the reason for pushing him through the SC2 and SC1 courses. Amy liked the fact he was much closer when serving with 45 in Scotland and it meant the kids formed a better bond with their dad as sometimes they wouldn't go to him as they hadn't seen him for so long.

John spent the remaining two years of his career working 30% of the time in a strategic role up in Scotland and the other 70% delivering amphibious training to men on the SC3 and SC2 courses as well as working with the Royal Marines Raiding Sqn working with small boat units in Poole.

John loved to train people but he also knew he was coming to the end of a long and satisfying career. In 2009 he had given 30 years to the British military, the last 19 of which were with the Special Forces.

He had seen the world with a rifle aimed at him but he had experienced a life like no other, more than he could have ever imagined. He was 47 years old and as he left the Corps he was awarded his 'Long Service Medal'.

He stood on parade for the last time in front of his CO in Poole and amongst the men he had served with he wore upon his chest medals, from Northern Ireland, Kosovo, Bosnia, Iraq, Afghanistan, Sierra Leone, Macedonia and those were just the countries the government was willing to admit he had been to, he'd taken part in Black Op's around the world and had 76 confirmed kills to his name but by his count is was 240 who had died by his hands, his sniping ability, his battles when he had charged at the enemy, stabbed men with bayonets in CQB, killed men with his bare hands and with a dagger. His life was splattered with blood from the enemy, men who had threatened the lives of people he didn't even know but yet he stood up and protected.

He left the Corp with a full war pension and boy had he seen war; he also received an additional SF pension which meant he was still getting paid around £30,000 per annum without having to work again.

John went back to Washington where he got a job teaching French and Spanish to beginners at the local college in the evenings. How long would this last, nobody knew but Amy was living with the constant knowledge that men he had served with in the past rang him regularly and she would hear him say, no thanks mate. But she always suspected that he wouldn't be able to maintain this sedentary life style for too long.

Chapter 13

The retirement fund

John had been retired from the forces for 15 months and Amy was getting increasingly worried about him. He would wake up during the night with a start, he would be sweating and on occasion she would find him slipping out of the bed and crawling across the floor as if he was on operation, this scared her as she wasn't sure what he would do if he was startled. Every time she tried to talk to him about it he just snapped at her.

He'd started drinking too, every night he would down a bottle of red wine and he still trained almost every day as if he was getting prepared for something, even at almost 49 years old he was fitter than most athletic young men. You can't do what he did for 30 years without taking something away from it but his injuries were also starting to take their toll. His knees and back were starting to give him some grief and he was so bored that he took up free fall parachuting again and would go to the hanger twice a week just to get away from things.

He would pop into the Royal Marine Reserves (RMR) for a drink about once a month to catch up with an old friend who was now the RSM at RMR Tyne.

It was obvious that John was missing the action he had once craved and it was starting to affect his moods. He was too stubborn to get help. The doctor's said they wanted to assess him for PTSD (Post Traumatic Stress Disorder), a common condition for soldiers who had seen war and John was a prime candidate for this condition.

It was 2011 and they had just celebrated Nathans 7th birthday when John started to act very strange, he would walk outside to take calls on his mobile phone and Amy started to worry that he was having an affair. One night when he went in the bath she checked his phone but John was far too clever for that and there were very few messages and the call records were always deleted so she decided enough was enough and confronted him.

"We need to talk John. I'm not very happy at the moment and I can see you're not either so I want to talk about some concerns I have."

"If this is about me going to the doctor again you can forget it, I don't need a fucking quack to tell me I have PTSD okay. I'll be fine."

"It's not about that babe," She said sharply.

John's heart skipped a beat as he thought the worst and was now worried that she might be going to tell him she was in fact having an affair or was going to leave him unless he got help. His voice softened like a nervous school child waiting to be told off.

"What is it babe? You know I love you hun," he said trying to cushion the blow he was expecting to follow.

"John, please just let me speak."

"Okay" he responded waiting for the heart breaking blow.

"I have noticed you taking call's away from me and I'm just gonna come out and ask you straight. Are you having an affair?" Amy's eyes filled up while she waited for the answer she dreaded but as she looked at him his face lit up and he smiled at her with the look that always melted her heart for the last 30 + years.

"Ya daft bugger, I thought you were about to tell me that you were having an affair. Oh my God darling, No definitely not."

She was so relieved and she totally believed him, "so who have you been talking to John?"

"Okay babe I've been talking to some of the guys I used to serve with. They've been offering me jobs, just a few months away for some big money."

"What!" she interrupted him sharply, "are you fucking kidding me? Are you seriously thinking of becoming a mercenary John?" She was angry at the thought of this and the fact that he was thinking of doing it at all.

"It's just 3 months security work hun for £100K; I mean how can I turn that kind of opportunity down?"

"Easy, you just say no John. I mean what the fuck kind of job pays £100,000 for three months work?"

"You know I can't tell you that darling, but I'll be going next week for three months."

Silence hit the room as she stood in complete shock, not just at the fact that he was telling her he was considering such a plan but he had already made arrangements to leave her and the kids in a week's time. She was furious and threw a complete temper tantrum lashing out at him punching and kicking him as hard as she could but John just tripped her and threw her to the ground pinning her down. She kept fighting and struggling with him but he just pushed his head on hers and forced a kiss on her and whispered in her ear, "I love you babe but you know I can't live like this anymore."

Amy cried and kissed him back, they made passionate love on the floor of the living room before she got up and stormed off walking to the bathroom to get cleaned up. John sat there on the floor not knowing what to say.

John left the following week for 12 weeks work in Iraq protecting a high powered American business man. It went without any problems but he did enjoy being back in the world of danger where at any moment it could all go tits up. He was only home for a couple of months when he started to disappear for an odd week here and there. He even missed his own 50th birthday as he was had a job to assassinate a Columbian drug lord, this contract was set up by the British Government and he wasn't stupid, he knew how this type of Black Op worked, he goes in and kills the drug lord and an SAS team are waiting to kill him so the bill never gets paid.

He was of course one step ahead of them and he took out the target at a distance of 1200 metres and returned home safely with another big lump sum going into his bank account is Zurich.

Amy knew he had an offshore account but didn't have any of the details and had no idea how much he had in it. She knew they never wanted for anything and they decided to start to enjoy life together, John was happier now he was back in a world of danger and Amy quit her job to spend more time with him when he was home. He spent roughly 5 months of the year away again, a trait she was used to having followed his career for 30 years.

In 2016 John received a job from an American billionaire, who wanted a crooked business man in Chile taken care of. His business interests in Chile were coming under constant threat from a local bully who thought he was the Mafia. This was a big job worth a lot of money and John was thinking that if he pulled this one off he could settle down and retire. He wasn't feeling so good lately and wasn't sure what was happening to him. He felt tired a lot and got confused occasionally but yet when he was in action there seemed to be an instinct that kicked in as if that was his natural behaviour, a feral instinct.

He accepted the job and took two others with him, it involved doing some reconnaissance work for a couple of weeks then they would arrive as if they were part of the business working with the management team. When the criminal sent in his boys they would track them back to his location and take care of the culprit and make it look like a local dispute as he had many enemies.

The men he took with him were none other than his old friend Saxon who had survived countless conflicts with John and a new comer to the mercenary world. Bill Sparkes was 40 years old, a Scouse who had just done 22 years in the Paras and severed the last 12 with Pathfinder Platoon. They had watched the plantation for 10 days and the men came on three occasions but it wasn't until the third occasion they were able to get a good tail on them and found the location of the head guy.

It was a plush house with high walls, security cameras and a couple of armed guards so it wasn't going to be easy to get in undetected, plus they had heard that he was paying the local Police protection money. John noticed that the Police were carrying a SIG SG Assault Rifles which was good as he knew he could get three of those without too much trouble and make it look like the Police had decided to get a little heavy handed.

They turned up at the plant the following day and prepared the management for what was going to happen next time they turned up. The managers were clearly scared in case it went wrong and their families would become a target

It was 1800 hrs and the majority of the plant workers were leaving as the big 4 wheel drive vehicle pulled up outside the office with its blacked out windows, the two guys who stepped out of the back of the vehicle were huge. Both over 6 feet tall and easily 20 stone, they looked mean and were armed with side arms in a holster. The two in the front seats didn't get out until they noticed the three unfamiliar faces in the office area. They decided it was better to be mob handed as they were not used to seeing Westerners and even the American owner very rarely came to this place.

The men walked into the office and spoke in Spanish to the two managers present, unaware that John and Bill both spoke fluent Spanish but they acted as if they didn't understand. Only one of the visitors seemed to speak English and he was the driver, he looked like a Vietnamese Pimp in his shiny green suit. He spoke in broken English and aimed his question at John who was the smallest of the men weighing only 12 stone.

"So who da fuck you are gringo?"

John smiled as he answered, "I'm a business associate of Mr Dillon and I'm here to speak to your boss on his behalf."

"No-one speak to da boss, you tell miser Dildo to fuck himself and you pay big time if not careful."

"I'm sorry you feel that way, I'd like you to take a message back to your boss if you don't mind?" John was steady as a rock as he spoke and never broke eye contact with the enormous man, something he was not used to, especially from such a small man like John.

"What is message gringo? I see if I like first then tell you if I tell boss or tell you fuck you," he said getting aggressive and feeling uncomfortable about the three men who had appeared from nowhere.

"You tell your boss that he will stop bothering Mr Dillon's business and he will no longer receive any money for protection or for any other reason. Failure to comply will result in his family being killed in front of him before he has his own balls rammed down his throat," John still spoke gently as to not arouse the suspicion of the three other men who clearly didn't speak a word of English.

As the man began to speak in Spanish John launched into action striking him in the throat with his fist dropping him to the ground, as he did this Bill and Saxon both pulled out 9mm hand guns and shot two of the men in their faces, bang, bang, double tap to both men's heads.

John took out a machete and spoke in Spanish to the third man who was now on his knees begging for his life as Bill and Saxon had him in their sights.

John repeated the message in Spanish to the third man and as he did this he grabbed the 1st man dragging him to his knees as he still held his throat, John took the chete and slit his throat from right to left so it would look like a left handed person had committed the crime. They put the three dead men in the back of the 4 wheel drive and sent the man away to deliver the message to his boss. They immediately followed at a distance and prepared to take out the boss when he was least expecting it. John knew he would react badly and let his emotion take over and this would be the perfect time for them to strike while everyone was rallying around ready to make a full assault on the plantation.

As soon as the vehicle was inside the grounds they cut the power to the cameras and moved in behind the vehicle through the front gate armed with SIG SG Assault Rifles and 9mm Beretta hand guns and took up their positions ready to make their assault. The driver ran in screaming that they were ambushed by American military Special Forces, possibly US Navy Seals and they had killed the other three men and let him live to deliver the message.

The boss spoke slowly but aggressively, "What was the message you fucking imbecile?"

He repeated the threat and the conditions of which he was to abide by before the boss went absolutely bezerk. He was shouting and calling his guards to get armed with machine guns and they were going to go to the plantation and show those bastards who was in charge in this country.

As soon as the 4 guards went for the rifle cabinet Saxon burst in and opened up with a full 30 round magazine, John jumped out in front of the boss and put 4 rounds down, a round through each elbow and knee and as he squirmed on the deck screaming his family were dragged out of the living quarters by Bill. There was his wife and three children, twin girls who looked to be around 16 years old and a son who was around 9 years old. The man they allowed to live was standing there by the side of his boss not sure what to do as John raised his rifle and put 3 rounds through his chest.

Bill brought the screaming family down stairs and stood them in front of their husband and father as John spoke again in Spanish.

"Unfortunately we knew that would be your reaction and as I am a father I couldn't take the lives of your children but of course they will talk and we can't allow that either so I give you the choice. You can watch as my friend here shoots your children one at a time or I can give your wife and children a pill to take."

The boss looked up at him with hatred in his eyes, at that point John turned and shot his wife in the face with a single round from his hand gun, as she hit the deck the children went crazy, screaming and he screamed and begged for their lives to be speared. Before John could even speak again Bill turned his rifle and blazed a full 30 round magazine into the children, spraying their heads and upper torso, the blood splattered across the white walls and the boss screamed and then begged for

.n. John looked the man in his yellow eyes and put e end of his pistol to his forehead and squeezed the trigger, the back of his head exploded, half of it was missing as brain was strewn across the floor. He didn't want to have to kill the family and if they could have been kept in the living quarter they could have been saved, John wasn't happy with Bill's decision to bring them down.

"What the fuck did you bring them down for? They didn't have to fucking die!" he shouted

"We were given an order and that order was to deliver the message and in that fucking message was the threat that he would watch his family die before we ended his life," he responded so matter of fact, he showed no remorse.

"Let's get the fuck out of here and collect our money. This is it for me lad's, I'm done." John was disgusted at what had just happened and wanted to get as far away as possible as fast as possible. Saxon had already poured fuel around the building and as they left via the front gate he threw down a packet of matches and the place went up like the 4th of July.

Saxon didn't say anything about the family being killed, he just did what he was asked to do and he was glad it was over, he didn't say it but he too wanted this to be his last job, just as they were about to get into their car Bill dipped his head to get in the front, Saxon was approximately 5 feet away from the back of the car when he saw the flash come from inside the car and heard the two shots ring out. John raised his 9mm and shot Bill in the face, double tap through the nose area of his face and Bill's body fell backwards as John leapt out of the car. Saxon didn't have time to react even if he'd wanted to, he was in shock and thought John was going to kill him too.

"Grab his feet and we'll throw him in the building with the rest of the fucking scum." John ordered.

Saxon grabbed Bills body and threw him over his shoulder and quickly ran back to the house and put Bill face down at the start of the fire and planted a hand grenade under his neck with the pin removed. This would remove his face and any dental records as well as the corrupt Police who would surely be on their way by now, he ran back to the car and John already had the engine running and sped away for a few miles before slowing down so as not to attract any unwanted attention. Two hours later they were checking in at the airport and heading to the States to meet with the Mr Dillon.

They arrived in New York 20 hours later after numerous changes along the way, another part of John's comprehensive planning to ensure they wouldn't be caught. Mr Dillon wanted to meet the men who had delivered the fatal blow in person, this wasn't the way John usually did business but this was his last job and he figured it was worth the risk for the amount of money they were talking about. They arrived at his office and in the foyer with the receptionist, a pretty young maybe 20 years old with a lovely welcoming personality, a perfect choice for such a job they thought. She looked on at the two rugged men dressed in their expensive suits and thought they looked quite handsome for their age, they were obviously very influential business men for Mr Dillon to insist on dealing with them himself. He also had his accountant in his office so she knew this was big business but she never questioned anything. She enjoyed her job and was paid well and hoped she would become a manager in the business one day.

Mr Dillon buzzed reception and asked her to send the gentlemen in, which she did. They followed her to the office door and she put her hand over a scanner to gain access, this was state of the art security technology. They entered the room and Mr Dillon was on his feet with a huge welcoming smile across his face and John reciprocated this gesture as if they were old buddies from high school, Saxon smiled and offered his hand. He shook their hands and introduced the accountant.

"Gents this is my accountant Michael Finnigan, he takes care of my offshore investments if you know what I mean."

"Nice to meet you Michael, now Mr Dillon if we could cut to the chase and get right down to business my colleague and I have another plane to catch in just a few hours," John said in a very firm business manner which Mr Dillon liked.

"You're not the run of the mill rouge mercenaries are you fella's? I love it, a keen business head on his shoulders," as he gestured towards the accountant

"No we're not sir, not in the slightest," said John.

"Call me Cas, my name is Castor Dillon but I have to tell you I was expecting 3 men today." He mentioned curiously.

"He didn't make it Mr......I mean Castor, he didn't make it," said Saxon cautiously.

"Oh I am sorry to hear that, well let's be getting on with the job in hand and get you gentlemen paid. So I will transfer 1 million American dollars to the accounts given to me," John cut in and stopped him in his tracks.

"I don't think so Castor. That's not the deal and you know it and trust me when I say, we're not the kind of men you want to short change," he said with a firm tone and a wry smile on his face.

"I'm sorry what do you think the deal is then Mr Smith?" John had given him a typically amusing name which everyone knew was of course fake.

"The deal was 3 million English pounds for the job and we did the job so therefore we're going to need that money sharing between the two accounts and you can forget about the third account number ending with 66214."

Oh I see, I was under the understanding that it was dollars. That changes things slightly gents as I had only authorised the afore mentioned amounts and to change that would take a further 24 hours. You could stay in a nice hotel for the night while we make the necessary arrangements?"

John thought for a moment and knew this put them at risk of being set up and Saxon was clearly getting nervous about the situation now as he had started to sweat.

"Would you like the air con turning on Mr Brown? We're so used to the temperatures over here we don't notice it like you guys."

"No I'm fine Castor, but thank you," Saxon responded

John decided to make the decision and to push his luck with Mr Dillon knowing full well that this billionaire could easily transfer other currencies.

"You will transfer the full amount in American dollars right now Mr Dillon if you don't mind. If it's a problem to transfer the dollars then you can send the rest in Euros as there are no limits on transferring that particular currency," he smiled with the knowledge that he knew Mr Dillon would already know that would be an option.

"Ha ha ha," laughed Mr Dillon, "yes indeed we can can't we. Michael sort the figures out now while I pour our astute business friend a drink,"

"Certainly sir," and Michael set about calculating the figures and started the process of the transfer up to the point when he needed the password to the accounts. "Mr Brown if I could have your password please?"

"Certainly, it's Castor Sugar, capital C capital S," he said with a smile and castor laughed out loud at the simplicity of it all.

Michael continued and showed Saxon that the transfer was now complete, "Mr Smith if I could have your password now please?"

"Nightmare 666," and he too smiled as Michael started to look uncomfortable, he did the transfer and showed John the transfer had been completed successfully.

"Thank you Mr Dillon, it's been a pleasure and if you'll excuse us we have a plane to catch."

They said their goodbyes and shook hands again, as John and Saxon left the building a huge feeling of relief came over them. John rang Amy from the airport to tell her he'd be home in the next 48 hours and to book them a few days away somewhere in the UK. They flew back separately, John from JFK and Saxon from Newark Airport. It was the last time they saw each other and they had finally come to the end of their colourful careers together. They had seen and done things that would terrify most of society and they felt no shame for the majority of it, John felt some guilt over a woman in Mogadishu who had come at him with a machete and he had stabbed her in the stomach with his bayonet not realising that she was pregnant, once he realised he finished her off by repeatedly stabbing her in the chest and stomach area. The nightmare never left him and he often thought about the lives he had taken. He figured the total was somewhere in the region of 250 and he sat on the long flight home wondering how he would be judged in his final days.

Chapter 14

The final curtain

In 2017 while John and Amy were in the Lake District with the kids taking a short break they came across an old vicarage for sale. The estate agent said it would make a beautiful B & B but they weren't interested in a business proposition, they wanted a home with some land and this little beauty had no less than eight acres of well looked after grounds to it. They viewed it while they were there and fell in love with it, the estate agent asked how they would be paying for it and John responded saying he was a cash buyer. Amy just looked at him and smiled as she knew he had earned a lot of money by doing what he had done, mostly which since he had left the forces.

By the end of 2017 they were living in the property and the kids had changed schools. They had always gone to private school so it was an easy transfer for them, they loved their new life in the countryside with plenty of mountains to climb, and they took after their father for his zest for life and need for action.

In 2020 John was diagnosed with Gulf War Syndrome along with PTSD but as this was more psychological Amy and John knew there was something more physical wrong with him for him to be feeling so ill all the time and he had lost so much weight. He was down to 10 stone when the news came, John was diagnosed with terminal cancer of the bowels and kidneys and it was too late to do anything about it. The doctors talked about chemotherapy and pain relief but John made a final brave decision to face the cancer head on. He decided that he would die in his own home at the pace of which the disease would travel.

Over the next couple of years John's health rapidly deteriorated. Amy stayed at home and took care of him, it was terrible to see the man who had fought countless conflicts around the world and was once one of the world's most elite soldiers having served with the Royal Marines Commandos, the SAS and the SBS in a career spanning three decades. He put up another gallant fight and every time they thought he was getting worse he would bounce back and surprise the doctors and his family with his grit and determination.

It was a beautiful autumn day with the sun shining and a crisp frost on the ground when John opened his eyes and looked around the room to see his beautiful wife and three children sitting by his bed. It was at this point that his youngest son Nathan leans forward to speak to his father and repeated the words that were previously muffled. "Dad, if you had your life over what would you do differently?"

He spoke softly and struggled to catch his breath every couple of words but he made one final effort to answer this question.

"Not a thing son, not one thing. I have lived a life beyond limits and found the love of a woman that knows no boundaries. You must always believe in yourselves, you can achieve anything you want if you want it enough." He held his son's hand and smiled as his son Nathan leaned over with tears in his eyes and kissed his father on the forehead.

"You've been a great dad to us and a good man, I love you so much and I will miss you every day." Nathan moved aside to let David in, he also kissed his father and said his goodbye, then came Bethany who looked a double of her mother Amy when John had first met her.

"You look just like your mother," John whispered struggling for breath, "you are an angel sent from heaven and I am so proud to have had three wonderful children with a fantastic wife. I love you all so much." John's voice began to break and he could feel himself filling up with emotion.

Finally his wife Amy sat by his side and the children left the room, she looked on at her husband. They had been together for 46 years and they had been happy for most of it, life had thrown its challenges at them but they had always come through stronger than ever. She loved this man with all that she was and didn't feel sadness as he looked up at her, she felt happy to have spent her whole life with a dedicated husband and father who had loved her like no other ever would or could have.

John slipped away peacefully while looking up at his wife with a smile on his face, she was watching him as he simply stopped breathing, his eyes were still open and the blue in them had never looked so bright. He was happy and content and his final words from his mouth were simply, "I'll miss you."

He had lived his life on an ocean wave with pride and valour and without regrets, his will left his family without financial worries and his wife who never married again lived to the age of 80 before she passed away peacefully in the same room as her husband some twenty years earlier.

Acknowledgements

My wife Monica for her constant love and support, my children Abbey and Dylan for believing in their Dad, my stepson Aaron for accepting me into his life, my parents Thomas and Doreen for more than I can ever say, my many friends but I must give a special mention to my close friend Wendy for keeping me sane (well, kind of) and last but not least the talented Christian Turford for the professional help and support with my book cover.

Printed in Great Britain
by Amazon.co.uk, Ltd.,
Marston Gate.